REDLINED

TuTunics

REDLINED

Final Editor: J. Flowers-Olnowich.

Dear Darren

Those that are brown know you only shot him down because he was Brown.
Were he peach you would have been impeached on the stand and not have
claimed fear and hear
the grand jury say no true bill
and they Bobbed and nodded along as he tried, and lied, and legally justified a
moral injustice
and told us that night not to display our anger but go home keep calm and keep
cool heads
while we always said
that your implicit biases were allowing for your exoneration for yet another
generation of subtle systemic genocide by unjustifiable homicide
the modern day burning of crosses means the constant losses of teenaged brown
bodies in our front lawns
they lie untended for hours while brown crowds came to see
and acknowledge the humanity
that you dehumanized and victimized
in another young king
we sing
the songs of our ancestors that we shall overcome and shall not rest
were he a white mother's son he'd be here and bullet free
but since he
was ours there's no outrage by yours or those
trying to deceive us with discussion of cigarellos
and boys in blue
who knew
what's true,
that you only shot him down because he was brown.

-A poem by Dontay Lands

1

brothers' keepers

In what would turn out to be our very last night in the small, dilapidated townhouse we had known most of our lives, I found myself in an all too familiar predicament—deciding whether I would let my brothers talk me into doing something stupid or doing what I knew I should. Unfortunately for me, I chose the former.

Not even the roaring thunder and heavy rain, or even the bangs and screams from the argument in the apartment next door kept me from dozing off after an evening of staying up late to play Fortnite with friends. Growing up in small spaces with four brothers had trained me to do nearly everything in the midst of chaos. Around midnight, my dozing was interrupted with a call from my sixteen-year-old brother Daveon, who wasn't supposed to be out.

"Bro, you gotta come get us before K get home," Daveon said.

"Day, what you mean, bro?" I asked as I squinted and pulled my cell phone down from my ear to look at the time.

"We kinda lit. Just grab K's spare keys again. You can't use my car—it needs oil, and my tire needs some air," he said.

"Day, I'm sleep!" I mumbled with dryness in the sides of my mouth.

2

"It'll be quick! Just hurry so we can get back before they do. The last time I snuck out and didn't come home 'til the next morning that nigga tried to end my life. And he gon' lose it if he find out I let Clay smoke en' drink wit' me," he said. I wasn't sure why it required the threat of our oldest brother going off for him to understand that our thirteen-year-old youngest brother shouldn't be out smoking and drinking with him and his friends.

"Aight. Gimme a couple minutes," I said with a stab of annoyance before ending the call. I stared at the ceiling after lowering the phone back down to my side, trying to decide if I should call him back and tell him I wasn't coming.

I reluctantly slid my feet over the edge of the bed and down until my toes touched the cold wooden panels on the floor, gradually standing to groggily pace the room and rummage for a hoodie and socks to pair with the shorts I was wearing.

Within minutes I was down the road from our apartment complex, watching impatiently as Daveon and Clay stumbled out the front door of an apartment building and down the walkway towards the passenger side of our oldest brother Kemis' truck. My patience thinned further as Daveon fumbled with the doorknob in an unsuccessful attempt to open the passenger door, while Clay lurked over to my side and climbed into the backseat.

"Bro, hurry up!" I urged while reaching over to manually pull the interior handle and help Daveon inside.

"I gotchu!" He climbed in and reclined his seat back, holding his head with his free hand. "Love you bro. You know you my dude," he said with his speech sounding even more slurred than it had over the phone.

I could smell exactly what they had been doing once the doors were closed, and I knew they would have to dump their clothes somewhere to mask the odor of blaze and booze that followed them inside the truck.

"Yeah, whatever. If we get home and K there, you better love me enough to tell him the truth!"

3

"You know I gotchu baby," he said.

Fortunately, there was no sign of Kemis or Kory, his fiancé, when we returned, as Kory's car was still missing from the parking lot. I was relieved we had beat them home, but still anxious to get inside before their arrival. I hurriedly parked the truck in the exact same spot and ran over to the passenger side to open the door and help Daveon get out. He reached his arm around my shoulder as I helped him hobble across the lot and up the walkway to the porch.

"Yo' parking is trash, bro," Clay noted once we reached the door.

I frowned upon seeing the truck parked a few too many inches and maybe feet away from the curb, unlike the way it was before I had tampered with it.

"Make sure y'all take y'all clothes off and spray! I'ma fix this real quick," I said before crossing back through the lot in order to attempt a second round of parallel parking.

I climbed in and reversed the car just enough to pull forward and inch closer to the curb. Satisfied with my work, I hopped out failing to notice a pair of headlights that was creeping closer, the headlights belonging to Kory's car.

While my limbs froze, my heart raced as I watched the car jerk from the way Kemis suddenly braked. He shot out of the driver's seat and jumped out screaming at me from the middle of the lot, while I considered ways to avert an impending crisis.

"Really Tay? This what we doing? We sneaking out now too? In addition to everything else you been doing, you wanna sneak out the house and drive without a damn license!" he yelled as he stormed in my direction, snatched his keys from my hand, and smacked my arm with a punch so hard it threw my body into his truck.

"Wait, K, chill. It ain't what it look like!" I said after I grasped my arm to rub out the pain.

I closed the driver's side door and inched backwards away from him and toward the rear of the vehicle, but he quickly followed. While I had no intentions of snitching on Daveon and Clay, I struggled to come up with a good enough lie to account for what he had just seen.

He clearly had no interest in my attempts to explain it away. My feet suddenly left the ground when his hands gripped my hoodie to lift me up and slam my back against the rear of his truck.

"Ah, K! Chill!"

"Naw, bro, it's exactly what it looks like! It looks like you need yo' ass whooped for taking my car! And you think it's cool to be out in this neighborhood at this time of night!" he exclaimed.

Before I could contemplate my next move, he was swinging a belt he had already folded in half in my direction.

"Bro! Wait! Ah! C'mon K, hold up!"

Instead of responding to my pleading, he violently swung while I scrambled around to the opposite end of his truck, but he had always been faster and stronger. I dreaded the thought of him grabbing onto me and did my best to keep ahead of him.

"Bro, you done straight up lost it out here. Get over here!" he yelled.

"C'mon bro!" I yelled in between trying to block and dodge successive hits. "I was just getting something out the car!"

I ran behind Kory, who had jumped out of her car, and hoped she would talk to Kemis and calm him down.

"Naw, don't try to hide behind Ko! She ain't take the car!" he yelled.

"Kemis, just listen to him!" Kory shrieked with her palms reached out facing Kemis as he approached. "Maybe he has a reasonable explanation!"

"For being fourteen and driving my car in the middle of the damn night in this neighborhood? Unless one of my brothers is at the hospital or the apartment burned down, which it looks like it hasn't, ain't no explanation! He started high school and started acting a plum fool. Come 'ere!"

I did the opposite of what he said, shuffling away until he caught up to me and struck me so hard I yelped before begging him to stop. I tugged away, hoping I hadn't been loud enough to cause any of the neighbors to start peering at us through their apartment windows and add to my humiliation. I dove toward the ground, managing to break free of him and nearly tripped over my own feet when I started my dash across the parking lot, through the wet grass, and into the apartment.

Flinging open the front door, I flew up the dark steps, but Kemis trailed close behind me. He cornered me in the bedroom, where I had tried to run in and lock the door, but he forced his way through before I could get it shut. He nearly knocked me to the ground with the impact of his body thrusting against the door from outside the room.

The scowl on his face stood out from the rest of his tall form, which told me he was ready to break me in half with his bare hands. He was followed by Kory, who repeatedly and unsuccessfully pleaded with him to calm down. I was hoping one of my brothers would quickly sober up enough to rescue me from the wrath that I was taking for them, but they both slept soundly through the clunks and clashes I made in attempts to dodge blows from my brother.

In one motion I catapulted over my bed and snatched my blanket down to shield myself.

"Kemis, wait! Calm down!" Kory yelled and grabbed his arm. "You've hit him enough!"

"Have I? Enough for him to know he better not ever do something crazy like that again?" he yelled back. He turned back to me, looking as though he wasn't done. "Where you been, Tay?"

I shook my head and tried to catch my breath, terrified that I would say something that would prompt him to continue hitting me. "I ain't go nowhere!" I told him as I knelt against the wall and clutched the blanket across my torso.

My answer only infuriated him even more, and he yanked at my protective covering in order to continue hitting me. I clung to it with all my strength while trying to maintain my stance and keep my feet from sliding out from underneath me. I used every joint and muscle to inch away and pull on the blanket, but I was no match for the strength of my brother, a consistent personal trainer, martial artist, and weightlifter who towered over me.

"You gon' stop lying to me, I promise," he said through gritted teeth, and successfully snatched the blanket completely off of me, threw it onto the floor, and started going at me again.

"Kemis, stop! He's not gonna talk if you keep hitting him," Kory told him, forcing her body in between mine and his.

"Damn, K. Chill!" Clay mumbled. He had finally popped his head up from the bed, sounding like he was only halfway alert and lacking in understanding as to why our brother had been trying to end me.

"Cuss at me again and I'm coming for you next!" Kemis threatened.

"Whatever dude! Save yo' energy for some real shit for once!" Clay said.

"BRO I JUST SAID—"

"Kemis! Clay, you know you shouldn't be talking like that! Kemis, let's go," Kory said sharply as she grabbed his wrist. She looked disturbed at what she saw, and I knew if she hadn't been there, I would have still been getting my flesh pounded, and Clay probably would have been dead.

I watched his chest and shoulders rise and fall with each heavy breath as he stood still, unsure of whether he should listen to Kory or the rage he battled within.

"Take your ass to bed, Tay. And don't think we done talkin' about this!" he barked before turning to walk out of the room, with Kory right behind him.

Clay exhaled when Kemis was finally out of the room, while I was on my back pondering the fact that nearly every beatdown I had ever taken was for one of my brothers. From the times in elementary school when I tried to help my brothers hide notes from the teachers to the times I had lied and said they were in one place, knowing they were in another.

The last time Kemis had hit me was when Clay had snuck out to a late-night house party with his friends, and I lied and told Kemis that Clay was in our bedroom sleeping, knowing he was out getting lit with a bunch of seventh graders in the middle of the night.

My brothers had hardly ever been in trouble for covering for me, but I had never snuck out the house like all of them had before. I had never asked them to answer the phone and pretend to be our older brother or uncle, as they had done for each other on multiple occasions to keep Granny or Kemis from talking to teachers at school. I had never snuck a girl into my room in the middle of the night like Jason and Daveon had. I had never missed my curfew or completely failed to come home like they all had. Still, our nearly lifelong no-snitch pact, which primarily benefit them, prohibited me from ever telling the truth about any of their dealings, no matter how mischievous.

"That nigga need help," Clay said while readjusting his blanket and plunging back down onto his pillow.

I didn't feel like talking to him, but felt like I should respond. "He irks. And he prolly gon' snitch me out to Unc," I said as I sat up to take off my hoodie and throw it on the floor. "Cut off the light, bro."

I pulled back my blanket and sunk my head into the pillow, wanting only to sleep and not think about the fact that I was about to be on punishment, or about what Uncle D would say when he found out what I did. I reflected on Kemis' explosiveness, my brothers' near-constant dumb choices, and my own stupidity for always covering for them.

I closed my eyes, ruminating over my frustrations about my brothers' behaviors, doubtful that I would get any decent sleep. Little did I know, it would be the last night we slept in our beds ever again.

2

eight months prior

"Sup bro? How'd your entrance exam go?" my brother Jason asked as I got into his car from the sidewalk.

Kemis had asked Jason, who was eighteen, to pick me up after a test I wanted nothing to do with. I had been standing in isolation while groups of other incoming freshman stood nearby talking amongst themselves.

"Some of it was easy and some was hard, but I think I did okay."

"You don't seem too excited about it," he said as he looked over at me out of the corner of his eye. Jason could read me well enough that I rarely needed words for him to know I wasn't content.

"I know this is like the best private school in the area and all, but I'm not trying to be at this school. I wanna be at school with Day. He'll be able to drive us to school, I can see my friends, and it's closer to home. I don't want to come all the way out here to go to school with all these rich white kids!"

"K crazy if he wants you coming all the way out here!" Daveon chimed in from the backseat.

"Tay, you gotta chill," Jason said. "You not even in the school yet. This school costs hella money that we don't have. You smart, so I'm sure they'll want you in. A couple of the guys from my old AAU team went here. One of them got a family with money, but the other one was just like us. I wouldn't get too amped about it yet. I'll talk to K, aight? He said it's a couple of other schools he likes besides this one."

Jason usually had a way of calming me down and giving me a different perspective. He was nothing like Daveon or Clay, who hardly ever took a calm or reasonable approach to anything.

"But you not gon' be here the whole summer, and then you moving out for good in August," I reminded him, thinking about how my time with him was limited.

The thought of my second oldest brother leaving the house to go to college was bittersweet. I was happy that he was going to a division one school on a full scholarship, and enjoyed the idea that we would be watching him play basketball on national television. But his more tranquil personality provided a necessary balance in the house that countered the explosiveness of our other brothers.

"With schools like this, you'll know before summer if you're getting in. But you should at least wait until you go on the tour before you decide you don't like it. We played them in basketball, and their gym and locker room is bussin' for real! They got a new library; they have new everything, and they give all of their students a laptop *and* an iPad to keep. Either way, we'll get it worked out."

I knew he meant it. He was our advocate when it came to talking to Kemis. He had miraculously convinced Kemis to let Daveon take his driver's test that day to celebrate his birthday.

Historically, Daveon hadn't chosen the most law-abiding group of friends to hang around. Some of his friends had gotten locked up in juvenile detention multiple times, and some were still posting pictures on social media with wads of cash and guns in their hands, similar to Clay's old friends. His history of bad choices made Kemis hesitant when it came to Daveon's milestone birthday.

"Enough about my test. Day, you pass yo' driver's test?" I inquired of Daveon, who was lounging in the backseat. He only offered a scoff in response to my inquiry, and I glanced over at Jason for an explanation.

"He passed, but he pissed that K and Unc making him go to the youth retreat tonight...he back on punishment," Jason said.

"All 'cause I missed curfew by a little last night, bro! They lame!" Daveon added.

"Actually bro, you missed curfew by a lot, and you came in smelling like weed!" Jason reminded him.

"On my daggone birthday weekend!" Daveon said.

"I told you that you was gon' end up on punishment on yo' birthday!" I laughed.

"Only 'cause K and Unc lame as hell, bro!" Daveon said, still reeling from the fact that his plans for a second night of partying had been ruined.

We were stopped at an intersection, and Jason briefly looked back at Daveon with a frown. "Bro, you was lit lit last night anyway. What else is there even to do?"

"More of the same, bro. Besides, today is my actual birthday, and Candace got more grown man shit for me that y'all too young to know about," Daveon said, while Jason and I chuckled.

"Bro, I'm older than you, and I'm telling Unc on you dude," Jason said.

"Man, don't play. Ay, stop at the store real quick bro, I need to get some stuff for this stupid retreat," Daveon said.

Jason looked down to the center console and tapped his phone to see the time. "Bro, aight but we gotta hurry up! Unc meeting y'all at the house and want y'all to be done packing soon!" Jason said.

"Bump him dude! I hope we leave late!" Daveon said.

"He gon' know you did it on purpose. You might as well suck it up and try to have a good time!"

"Says the nigga that ain't been forced to go!" Daveon said.

"I'm eighteen! Besides, I got business of my own tonight!" Jason said.

"What's her name?" I asked, causing him and Daveon to laugh.

"Now I'm telling Unc," Daveon joked.

"Ay bro, I told you about that time we were in Texas on that unofficial visit," Jason said.

"Talking 'bout that school that won one year?" Daveon asked.

"Yeah!"

"You ain't tell me!" I said to Jason.

"Bro, I went to a party with these guys on the basketball team. The party was at this frat house, but I told Unc it was on campus. I messed around and left my location on, and basically, I wasn't where I told him I would be!" Jason said.

"What Unc say?" I asked.

"He embarrassed the *hell* outta me," Jason laughed. "He busted in the room I was in and found me with this girl I had met, yanked my ass outta bed, hit me, and told the girl I was a high school virgin and he was calling the police! Then he dragged me out the frat house in front of the whole team. I saw hella people pointing and laughing. I knew then I couldn't go to that school! Plus, there was that one youth retreat he caught me sneaking off. Just remember my stories if you get tempted to sneak off to the girls' cabin tonight, 'cause Unc don't even play," Jason said.

"Wait, girls gon' be there?" Daveon asked, voicing a newly-heightened interest in the retreat.

"Yeah, bro! I almost went 'cause one of the chaperones is this fine chick in college!" Jason noted as he pulled up to the store.

"I'ma have to get a couple more supplies then," Daveon said with a devious grin as he got out of the car.

There weren't too many supplies we ended up needing that night, as the site for the retreat was a campground that was located in a remote area with no Wi-Fi. Uncle D seemed to enjoy the looks and the sounds of everyone griping upon finding out there was no Wi-Fi when the bus pulled into the campsite. It forced us to interact and stay partially engaged with the speakers who presented. We all dined in what was called a "mess hall," and Clay, Daveon, and I consulted one another after we had each scoped out all the girls and decided which one would be our individual target for the night.

Daveon didn't quite take Jason's advice, as he organized a massive sneak-out after lights-out and arranged for a bunch of campers to meet in an abandoned cabin in the woods for a candlelit truth or dare game. I hadn't been there to witness it myself, but Daveon told me the next day how he was in hot water with Uncle D, who had stumbled across the secret rendezvous, and watched firsthand as Daveon tongued a girl to fulfill a dare. Clay was also in trouble since he had joined in on the melee and used profanity in front of Uncle D once they all got caught. It wasn't until the bus pulled back into the church parking lot after the retreat was over that Uncle D returned the cell phones of everyone who had been caught sneaking out.

"Daveon Kahari Lands, I see I'ma have to knock you out when we get home!" Uncle D said when he drove the three of us home afterwards.

"Unc, you on me 'cause I *kissed* a girl?" Daveon asked, sounding annoyed.

"Daveon, I talked to nearly ten kids that were at your little party, and pretty much all of them said you were the organizer. You used your influence for bad. And I heard you were doing a lot more than kissing! Someone told me you snuck off with another girl, and that you even brought alcohol with you!"

"Unc, I ain't twenty-one. How would I even get some daggone alcohol?" Daveon asked, knowing his age had never stopped him before.

"So you not denying sneaking off with Pastor James' daughter? And they said you were the one that offered a cash prize for the best twerk! A twerking contest at a retreat where we're supposed to be focusing on God!"

I tried to stifle my snicker but couldn't, placing myself in the line of fire.

"Do you think the Lord is laughing or pleased at that sort of behavior, Dontay?" Uncle D asked. He rarely used my full first name, which I knew meant he was unhappy with my reaction. I hung my head and did a better job of controlling my laughter to get him off my back.

Daveon sighed. "Y'all the ones made me go to a stupid church retreat on my birthday weekend!" Daveon said.

"Sounds like you were right where you needed to be. But don't worry, we're having a long talk tonight!"

Dwayne Farmer was not our uncle by blood. The only uncles we knew of, the brothers of our biological mother, were incarcerated. But we were much closer to Uncle D than any of them or any other adults in our life besides Kemis. Our relationship with him started when Granny forced us all to attend the church where Uncle D was the youth pastor. Realizing the serious financial and other struggles our family was facing, he started regularly coming over to check on us or call us. Sometimes he would pick us up for the weekend and take us to his home or on a short trip, or school shopping, or invite us over to have dinner at his home. Other times he or his family would bring dinner to us and sit and dine with us while we talked. He often stopped by just to bring money or food, or to talk to Daveon or Clay, both of whom had lengthy histories of finding trouble.

He had taken Jason on recruitment visits to college and helped him pick a school. Clay had spent days and weeks at Uncle D's home when he was suspended from school. Over the years we had gotten so close to him and his family, we went from calling him Pastor D to Uncle D. He had become a constant presence in our lives—too constant, according to Daveon, especially after Granny died.

Kory had come by the house to prepare dinner and cake for Daveon, which we were about to eat after Daveon received his lecture from Uncle D and Clay and I finished our homework. We were joined by Auntie Robin, Uncle D's wife, along with their children, Caleb, who was nine, and Sophie, aged seven, who wanted to bring Daveon gifts and share his cake.

"Tay, I forgot to ask you how'd your test go?" Uncle D asked after I sat down at the table to eat.

"I hope I failed it."

I thought I said it low enough where Kemis wouldn't hear, but apparently that wasn't the case, and he jumped into the conversation.

"Tay, seriously? This school is one of the top-ranked high schools in the whole country! Do you know how good it would look on your college and scholarship applications? Bro, all your teachers and your counselor said you need a more challenging curriculum. I even spoke to the gifted coordinator at the high school and she agreed that you should go to a different school if we can get you in. This school would allow you to take college-level math and science, and other college courses as a freshman," Kemis said.

I didn't hide my eye roll. It was clear that his mind was made up that I was going to the school. Mine was made up that I wanted no parts of it.

Uncle D chimed in, "Tay, there's a couple kids from the youth group that go there—Paris, and her sister Gia is at the middle school. There may be another young man too. They seem to like it."

"Ok Unc, but hardly anyone else at that school looked like me. They all rich, and their parents drive these expensive cars. I don't want to be the broke black kid that's there to help them reach some quota," I said.

"Tay, you know my sister went to that school and had a pretty good experience," Kory piped up after popping back into the room. "Plus, I think they still have a chess team, and a club for black students. I think you should give it a chance!"

"And sometimes God takes us out of our comfort zone to take us to the next level," Uncle D said. He knew he was telling me things I didn't want to hear. "I would encourage you to talk to God about it. But in the meantime, try not to worry about it. School's not even out yet, and we have a ways until it starts back."

"I hear y'all, but I feel like this is gonna create a huge conflict 'cause that dude over there don't listen to nobody!" I leaned my head and shifted my eyes towards Kemis as I spoke.

"Conflicts are a part of life. I'm sure he'll listen to what you have to say if you approach him respectfully," Uncle D said.

It had been a bumpy transition when Kemis went from being just our oldest brother to also our legal guardian after Granny's death, and my brothers had all tested his authority at one point or another, but none probably more than Daveon. He didn't really challenge Kemis with his words as much as with his behavior. He always knew what time his curfew was, and where he was supposed to be, but had seasons when he didn't care. He had gotten out of hand the summer after Granny died, and Kemis hardly ever knew where he was. Daveon would skip out on summer school classes and other activities, and go out with his friends to smoke, drink, steal, and get into everything bad into late hours of the night.

All of Daveon's drama caught up with him one night when the police brought him home after he had snuck out to hang with his friends. Daveon and his best friend Tray, along with some other kids, had stolen a car, and were riding in it when the owner of the car fired shots at them, hitting the car but none of the occupants. When police pursued, Tray crashed the car. Fortunately, everyone survived with mostly minor injuries, but Daveon almost did not survive once Kemis and Uncle D came face to face with the police officers that escorted Daveon home.

Jason only had a few moments when he challenged Kemis, but since he was the next oldest, Kemis treated him differently than the rest of us. They only clashed over curfews, girls, and drinking. Otherwise, Jason didn't get into much trouble, and didn't really disrespect Kemis intentionally; the only one who did that was Clay.

Clay's disrespect was not limited to Kemis; he challenged anyone, adult or not, who would trigger him and his quick temper. Those triggers could come at school, home, church, or the grocery store, and he had cussed out fully grown people in all of those places and many others. The only people I hadn't seen him cuss out was Granny, when she was alive, and Uncle D. Otherwise, Clay's mouth kept him in near-constant trouble and fueled many of his suspensions and detentions the past few school years; his mouth, his fighting, smoking weed, and "insubordination," as the principal called it, created a lot of his problems with Kemis. He had only recently gotten off punishment after being arrested when the police discovered that he and his other seventh-grade friends were running an entire crime ring. He told me that Kemis tried to kill him after the police released him, and that Kemis only stopped because Uncle D intervened.

I usually approached Kemis differently from Clay and Daveon, who were a lot more animated, impulsive, and sometimes explosive, which was not always well-received by Kemis, a reformed hothead himself.

"I see y'all just gon' talk about me like I ain't here! But y'all be acting like I don't include y'all in decisions!" Kemis said.

"You don't!" Jason, Daveon, Clay, and me all shouted in unison.

"That's cap, but okay! Tay, we got plenty of schools to look at— this ain't the only one, so your opinion is gonna be the main thing I'm trying to hear when we decide," Kemis explained.

"I'll believe it when I see it," Daveon said. He had taken the words right out of my brain.

3

all the wrong moves

I tried to spend the summer proving to my brother that I didn't need some swanky private school to get a good education. I joined the Young King's summer book club at the library, a program for teenage boys that was run by the library director, who was also Jason and Daveon's boss since they worked there part-time. The club met weekly to discuss African American literature, and Mr. Blackshear, the director, would give me additional recommendations of other books to read that I would discuss with him when he had free time. The readings kept me busy throughout the summer, in addition to an African American studies class, an advanced coding class, and photography and videography classes that I was able to take for free at the YMCA. My brothers would often tease me for "wasting my summer away" in books and in online teen tech groups.

Kemis and I had been back and forth about the school I would attend in the fall and hadn't reached an agreement at all. He finally called a family meeting, stating that we had to discuss school and a few other matters.

"What's this about, K? Did you get a call from school? I swear I been good all week!" Clay said. He and Daveon had both been playing on basketball teams all summer, in addition to attending summer school.

They both had to right some wrongs on their report cards, as Kemis described it.

"Actually, not this time! But look, there's a couple of things going on. For one, you know I graduate in a few months, and I'll be able to take this job that Deacon Waddell is saving for me at his company. But, until then, we gotta get Jay off to school, which Ma and Pops already said they gon' take him to get the rest of his things moved in."

Kemis had been calling Auntie Robin "Ma" and Uncle D "Pops" for quite some time, stating that he had become more like a father to him over the years he had known him. On the one hand, we celebrated the fact that the two of them were so close, as sometimes it seemed like Uncle D was the only one who could talk sense into Kemis. On the other hand, Kemis called Uncle D nearly every time one of us had gotten into something, which usually meant we would end up getting lectured twice for the same thing.

"With Jason leaving soon, Day, you know I'ma need you to step yo' game up. Some days Ma and Pops are gonna help pick Tay up from school, but when basketball season ain't in, I'ma need you to help too. Plus, you can—"

"Wait, wait. Why he gotta pick me up from school? You told me you would think about letting me go to high school with Day." I was confused and needed clarification.

"Well, that's the thing. I been thinking, and I don't think it's wise to keep you in school out here since y'all all probably gon' have to change schools in the near future anyway. See, things have been pretty serious with Kory, and I want to ask her to marry me."

"Whoa!" Daveon said, expressing the disbelief we all felt. For years we had watched Kemis balance multiple girlfriends at a time. It seemed to stop suddenly, and we didn't see him with anyone else until he dated Kory.

"By us getting married, we're inviting in another official family member. Kinda like Pops. I mean, we're not blood-related to him, but that's our family. And Kory would be big sis, which means she would help me take care of y'all, but y'all would also take care of her, respect her, and listen when she tells you to do something. She has already helped us out financially, and she's willing to continue to do so while I'm finishing school," said Kemis.

Kory was a new attorney at a large firm and earned a lot more money than Kemis. He never asked her to, but once she saw that we had been struggling with having clothes and school supplies, she pitched in money to help us out, along with Uncle D and other church members.

"Y'all would have to treat her like an older sister. If I'm working late or out of town and she's the only one home, what she says goes. Then, you know one day, she'll probably want to have y'all some nephews."

Kemis had always lectured that unprotected sex led to us giving him nephews and had made it abundantly clear that it wasn't acceptable.

"I thought the rule was that we couldn't have no nephews," Daveon joked.

Kemis shook his head. "No nephews for y'all. That didn't mean no nephews once you get married and are ready for them. For now, none of us are ready, but one day we will be. But Kory makes pretty good money, and with this job, I'll be doing better—much better than we have been doing. And neither of us are really a fan of this neighborhood. I know this is mostly all y'all have known, and we're used to it, but I've been wanting to get y'all out of here, and she doesn't want to live here. So we'll probably move right before the wedding. We have already been looking at properties near Pops' house.

"That night when Clay snuck out to his boy's house and Kyle and I were driving around looking for him, it made me realize that this area isn't what it used to be. We hearing more gunfire at night. I mean, Jay and Clay were at the gas station when it got shot up…all these fights around the corner. So, since y'all would have to change schools anyway, and Loyola Institute gave you a scholarship, Tay, I figured we might as well go ahead and move your school now."

Up until that moment, I had really liked Kory, and had their plans for marriage not been intertwined with my schooling, I would have likely given my wholehearted support. But since I knew he was using it as the justification for me leaving all the friends and school district I had known, I hated everything about their wedding day. Not wanting to tell the truth about my objections to their nuptials, I threw in a completely different wrench.

"So, I'm just curious," I said, "what about Ma?"

We hadn't seen or heard from our mother in nearly one year. We were used to her coming and going our entire lives, but she had stayed with us on the couch for a pretty lengthy stretch before the latest departure. At first Kemis had given her a room, but when her coming and going became more and more fickle, he took the room back and told her she could sleep downstairs. We never really knew where she was going when she would leave, or how long she would be gone. She didn't offer that information, and none of us asked.

She never tried to actually parent since Granny had always raised us, with the help of Kemis. She never talked or ate with us, and she was more like a mysterious stranger than a family member. Jason said she sometimes talked to Kemis, but it was usually to ask for money. The last time she left, she took a lot more of her things than normal, and added in items that were not hers, such as money from Daveon's room. None of us besides Kemis had many memories of her, but we could all name a time when we caught her taking money from us, even if it was just pennies from a jar of change.

"I don't know, Tay. I tried her phone the other day and it's cut off again. And she hasn't tried to call me either. Her cousins haven't seen her. Auntie hasn't heard from her. Uncle Vel or none of them have heard from her. I thought about it, and I can't put my life on hold for her anymore. The four of you are my top priority, and Kory.

"So, I need to know how y'all feel…about all of it—Kory, changing schools, moving. But the most important thing is that y'all know I love y'all and I got your back forever."

Daveon spoke up. "I don't really want to change schools before my senior year. But at the same time, sometimes I wish we had a better neighborhood and a bigger house too. As far as Kory goes, I think it's dope. But Unc a hater, and I ain't trying to be his next-door neighbor."

Clay said he didn't want someone else in the house he had to listen to. He also was not happy with the idea of changing schools, but Kemis said changes wouldn't happen overnight, and we'd have time to prepare. I was definitely not happy about changing schools, but my concerns about school seemed to be the least of his worries. It was an issue I wasn't going to let him ignore.

4

an unfresh start

The day we all dreaded, maybe all except Kemis and Jason, came towards the end of summer, when Jason packed and Uncle D drove him to Lexington, Kentucky to get the rest of his things moved into his dorm before his fall semester started. I didn't think I would cry when I watched Uncle D's van pull out of the parking lot with Jason and his belongings inside, but it was hard knowing my primary confidant and advisor in the house would be hundreds of miles away instead of a few feet down the hall from me. Even up until the night before he left, he tried to convince Kemis to let me pick my own high school while we were packing his clothing away, and Kemis sought to reassure us that the new school was exactly what I needed.

After school started for the rest of us, it didn't take long for me to find additional reasons why I wanted to transfer back to my old school district. For one, it was my first time without having my brothers or any neighborhood friends at school, and I wasn't used to not knowing who to sit with or socialize with outside of class time. There were a couple kids from church who took pity on me and invited me to sit with them and their friends at lunch.

While I was grateful to avoid the dread of sitting alone in a large, fancy cafeteria, I quickly realized that it wasn't just the white kids I didn't fit in with. Many of the black students were kids of doctors and lawyers, lived in two-parent homes, and had never even driven through a neighborhood like mine. Even though they were cool enough to talk to and didn't seem to judge me, I still declined when they would offer to drive me across town after school to get home. I didn't want them to know where I lived after hearing about and seeing the types of homes they lived in, which was the other thing I noticed.

It seemed like everyone around me was rich and always wore the most expensive clothes, shoes, backpacks, watches, headbands, even socks—any way to wear their wealth they would do it. I had no wealth to wear, other than the hand-me-downs I got from Daveon and the occasional new outfit Kemis bought with money given to him from Uncle D, but those clothes were rarely name-brand.

The biggest issues started one day during a Civics and Government class. The teacher always facilitated discussions on current events and politics before each lesson. I liked that she never took a side, but with many divisive, controversial events going on in the country, I felt there were kids who spoke boldly on issues they knew nothing about.

One day in class, another freshman named Mark Paul spoke in a manner that made me tense up. He sat in the back of the room, surrounded by his friends, while my seat was second from the front, to the far right of the room. He was emboldened in a way that was bothersome to me, particularly on issues that involved people of color, and I pondered whether our physical distance, as well as the nearby location of his friends, contributed to his boldness.

"The Black Lives Matter movement was started by a bunch of ignorant, uneducated black thugs. It's a terrorist organization that just wants police to let black criminals go free," he said boldly in response to a question posed to the group.

An uncomfortable silence fell over the room after he spoke. I couldn't believe he had said it out loud, and I raised my hand ready to respond and fill the silence that had taken over. It was a discussion I had inadvertently prepared for the entire summer, especially after a few book discussions with Mr. Blackshear at the library. I hadn't known that the information I had learned would become so relevant.

"These privileged white boys with a silver spoon in their mouth aren't expected to understand the meaning behind this movement," I said. "They criticized Dr. King even though he took a non-violent approach to civil rights. Then they killed him. In the sixties and seventies, people criticized the black panther movement that was trying to empower those that were underserved. Those same groups are still underserved in this country today. We still get profiled in stores and by police when we're driving. We're more likely to be suspended from school and murdered by the police than our white counterparts that do the same things."

"That's because you all are the ones committing all the crimes!" Mark Paul blurted out.

I was certain that a vein was protruding out of my neck at hearing him say "you all." I thought about how Kemis had discussed trying to get Daveon and Clay into the same school as me. With discussions like this, they would have already been kicked out for bashing this kid's head in.

"Really? 'Cause y'all the main ones shooting up these churches and schools and movie theatres but ain't no police stopping you! Contrary to what your Klan parents are telling you, not all black people are criminals. But that doesn't stop y'all from calling the police on us when we're driving through your neighborhoods," I said so loudly that my classmates that had dozed off were likely wide awake.

"You people don't have houses in our neighborhoods, and you shouldn't be there anyway."

"We're there because your sisters and mamas invite us," I said while looking directly at him.

The class was oohing and hissing by that point, causing Mrs. Drake, the teacher, to interrupt.

"Okay, okay, boys, let's stop there. I like that we are discussing these matters, but I think we're heading in the wrong direction. Dontay, I am impressed with how well-spoken you are. Maybe you can focus your project this semester on comparing the similarities between the Black Panther Party and the Black Lives Matter movement," she said.

She tried to steer us in a different direction before diving into the day's lesson, but my brain never left the initial discussion. As the bell rang, she yelled out some instructions regarding our homework, but I was too fired up to hear them as I stormed out of the classroom and stewed over that fact that she had called me "well-spoken" as if she was surprised I could speak intelligently.

I thought the incident was over, but Mark Paul visited me after lunch that day when I was getting books out of my locker. The visit quickly went south.

"You should probably shut your fucking mouth in a class where you're outnumbered. You're in Trump country now; not that piece of trash hood school you came from," he said.

I turned to find his face within a foot of mine, and he was surrounded by the same friends he sat near in class. They all glared as though they were awaiting my response. I felt caged in and slightly anxious since I wasn't sure what his next move was. I had never faced such a predicament without my brothers, particularly Clay or Daveon, who seemed to thrive when faced with potentially violent encounters.

"Yo, you better back up before your teeth get knocked straight into your fuckin' throat!" I barked.

When I inched toward his face he backed up, looking surprised that I had spoken up. Had I been at my old school, I would have already clipped him in the jaw, but he didn't seem to understand that getting in my face was the equivalent to requesting a fight.

"Mr. Lands," my math teacher shrieked while jumping in between us. "That type of language is not permitted in this school!"

"Right," Mark Paul added, "and neither is bullying!" he said with a smile on his face.

I shot a look at him when he said the word "bullying," and then looked around to see the reactions of the students who stood nearby. Not one of them spoke up or said anything in my defense. They looked at me as though I had started the entire encounter and was getting what I deserved.

"Dude, you're full of shit; ain't nobody bullying you!" I said while attempting to work my way around the teacher and get back into his face.

"That's enough, Dontay. You're going to have to go to the office now. Let them know I'll be sending an email shortly," she said.

I glared at her while I decided whether I should tell her how I really felt or keep quiet. I turned my attention to Mark Paul, and considered if it would be worth the suspension and a punishment at home to pound his face in. I snatched my things from my locker and stormed toward the principal's office, making sure I gave Mark Paul a firm shoulder check on my way.

5

checking in

It was Daveon's day to pick me up after school, and he texted to tell me that he would be late. I figured he was either with Tray or sneaking around with his girlfriend Candace, and I stayed in the library after school to complete my homework and think about what I would tell Kemis about the detention I had gotten.

I went outside after Daveon texted me that he was parked alongside the curb.

"What up, man?" he greeted me smiling after turning down the music he was loudly bumping through the parking lot.

"Hey," was all I could manage.

"Damn, what happened to you?"

I let out a sigh and told him everything that had happened from the classroom to the incident in the hallway to sitting in front of the assistant principal, who didn't seem to believe a word I said.

"Yo, I'm coming up there tomorrow to kick lil' dude's ass!" he yelled.

"No, Day! That's why I ain't wanna tell you. I just gotta figure out what to tell K. He gon' be hot I was cussing in front of a teacher."

Daveon's phone rang as I spoke, and I looked down to see that Jason was calling. Day put the phone on speaker mode and placed it back down on top of the center console to drive.

"Big brooooo!" Daveon yelled.

We were always happy to hear Jason's voice. It didn't replace his presence, but it was still good to hear from him.

"What up bro, what you into?" Jason asked.

"Nothing, just picked up Tay from school. I'm proud of the lil' homie today!"

"Tay, what's up! What you do that Day so proud of?" Jason asked.

I looked over at Daveon, not really wanting Jason to know I had gotten detention.

"He up in here telling these lil' niggas how to be woke! And got his first detention in the process!" Daveon said while chuckling.

I wasn't nearly as amused as he was, and I knew Jason wouldn't be either. Jason and I had nowhere near the amount of detentions and suspensions Daveon and Clay had on their academic resumés.

"Wait, what? Tay, you got detention?" Jason asked.

I was hesitant to admit without telling him the full story, but I didn't feel like repeating it.

"Yeah, Jay. It's a long story," I said.

"Ay, I told Clay I would come down there on the Greyhound to kick his ass if he kept acting up. I ain't know I needed to tell you too. Don't make me buy a bus ticket bro!"

I had no doubt that if Kemis told Jason that we were running wild, Jason would find the next bus home and make good on his promises.

"Jay, on me, it's not even like that. I did get detention, but this dude was all up in my face talking about I'm in Trump country!"

"You ain't hit 'im, did you?" Jason asked, sounding concerned.

"No, I just told him to back up...but I cussed and the teacher heard me and wrote me up even though he cussed too when he got up in my face! Junk pisses me off and K gon' be pissed!"

"Just don't lie to K about it, and tell him as soon as you get home. Y'all don't give him enough credit—he actually pretty cool about stuff if you just talk to him. Look, I just got to the gym. I'ma call y'all back. Check in with me later after you talk to K. And don't let this dude bother you!" Jason said.

"Aight, Jay. I'll call you later," I said, wondering if later I would still have a phone to actually do so.

6

nope, naw, no thank you!

Since Kemis was on the phone at his desk working when Daveon and I got home, I took Clay up on his offer to join him at the basketball court. I was happy to vent to him during our walk to the court, making me miss our bus rides home in middle school where we could both talk about our school day.

Clay threatened to sneak up to the school to beat up Mark Paul, and I had to take the time to talk him out of it, knowing he would do it if he secured the transportation.

"Yo, K would kill you if you snuck up to my school. Plus, I can fight on my own. I just want outta there," I said as we arrived at the basketball court.

"Just gotta tell K you ready to go! The school year still early enough. Ain't no reason he can't let you come back and roll to school with Day."

"I've already asked him a bunch of times to let me come back, and you know what he's on."

"That's what you get for being so smart…getting labeled gifted and all that shit. If you got bad report cards and phone calls home like me, he would never put you in no lame-ass private school," Clay said.

"I actually like keeping my phone after report cards come out, bro. And I kinda need good grades if I'm going to Howard Law one day," I reminded him, knowing he wouldn't be swayed.

Playing ball for a couple of hours allowed me to blow off steam from the day's events, and we probably would have stayed longer were it not for a fight that broke out. A man we didn't recognize arrived at the basketball court with a group of guys to confront, someone from the neighborhood everyone called T-Dub. What started as a heated discussion ended with them threatening to fight, and a friend of T-Dub's saying he was about to "drop bodies." The altercation made me check my phone and tell Clay we should go after seeing the time.

"I like when you play mad, bro! You had buckets! Out there cookin' them niggas! We the new splash brothas!" Clay said as he bounced the ball on the sidewalk toward home.

"Get on, dude. You crazy."

We walked in the door at home and found Kemis seated on the steps, knees to elbows, talking on his cell phone with his forehead resting in the palm of his free hand. He stood up and frowned in our direction after Clay and I walked in.

"He's here now, I'll call you back, Pops."

Both of us froze wondering who the "he" was that he had been waiting for, and it dawned on me that I didn't follow Jason's advice and tell Kemis right away what happened at school.

"Clay, did you run off to the basketball court without finishing your homework?" Kemis asked, glaring at Clay.

I exhaled in relief upon finding out it was just Clay's typical trouble of going out without his homework being done.

Clay started protesting, knowing he was wrong. He usually came up with the dumbest excuses, and this time was no improvement.

"I mean, it was math, and I do better with math when it's dark outside. I did some of it though."

"How many times have I told you doing some of it doesn't make it done? Bro, I'm having this conversation with you too many times." He snatched the basketball out of Clay's hands. "Grab a plate and go finish your work. I promise you that you better not get into anything else without your work being done first!"

Clay started grumbling about how the homework rules were dumb as he headed toward the kitchen table. Kemis glared and raised his finger and pointed at Clay, but then shook his head with a sigh and turned toward me.

"Yo, we need to talk too!"

By his tone, I knew he must have found out about school. I slowly shuffled behind him onto the couch and braced myself for a tongue lashing.

"Bro, when was you gonna tell me you got detention?" He reached for a piece of paper on the table and started reading from it. "They said you got in another student's face and yelled at him in a profanity-laden rant. That student has accused you of bullying!"

I rolled my eyes in silence, my anger brewing up all over again. I couldn't believe they just accepted the word of this kid and the teacher and gave no deference to my side of the story. The fact that all of those other kids saw the entire exchange and didn't speak up on my behalf upset me even more. All of that coupled with the fact that I already felt as though I didn't belong made me desire even more to return to where I fit in.

"Two cuss words ain't no daggone profanity-laden rant! K, I don't want to be at this uppity-ass school," I said, ignoring his inquiry about what happened. I was hesitant to tell him at the risk of him not believing my version of events either. Even worse, I didn't want some stupid talk about being the bigger person and walking away or turning the other cheek.

"Tay, I had to put a deposit down for the semester, for the costs that your scholarship didn't cover. We're paying less than a fraction of what most of these families pay, but it's money I can't afford to throw away. You know we don't have money like that! We've talked about this!"

"No, *you've* talked about it! And I told you I don't want to be at this stupid-ass school and to keep your money. You so busy wanting me to be like these white kids that you not listening to me! We could be saving this money for more important stuff!"

"First of all, you need to calm down, Tay. I ain't one of your little friends at school," he said with a hint of impatience.

"I don't have no little friends at school! You took that shit away!" I said, watching as his patience grew even thinner.

He briefly paused before continuing. "Secondly, this is an amazing opportunity for you. You'll be able to go to any school in the country after this. Do you know what I would have given for this quality of education?"

His words made me angrier, as it seemed he was trying to make me live the life he wanted for himself.

"This is what *you* wanted. *You* wanted this type of education. *I* can get an education from *my* school, and I can read books like I do already. I can listen to Ted Talks or watch YouTube. There's nothing special at this school. It's filled with a bunch of fucking snotty rich white kids who've been in private, overpriced schools their whole lives, and they don't want people like me there! Why I gotta go to school somewhere where I can't even be myself?"

He spoke calmly. "I told you to watch your tone and watch your mouth. I'm not taking you out. You need to tell me what's going on so we can figure out how to handle it."

"If I gotta stay at that school, then I don't got nothing to say."

He looked shocked that I said it, which kinda made me nervous, but I knew I couldn't back down. In my brain, the discussion was over. It was another way I differed from my brothers—everyone knew exactly what they were thinking because they usually said it before they thought it. I wasn't into sharing my thoughts with someone I didn't feel worthy of them, and I didn't deem him worthy since he was discounting my ideas about my own education.

"If you don't wanna talk to me about this, that's cool, but that just means I base your punishment off of what's in this write-up, and I don't get your side of the story."

I had no intentions of telling him anything. While part of me longed to pour my heart out, I was too angry, and I had looped him in with Mark Paul, the principal, the teacher, and everyone else who I considered the enemy in that moment. Tears of anger and defeat were trying to form in my eyes, and I wanted out before I was tempted to cry and talk. I reached and pulled my phone out my pocket.

"Take this shit then," I said in a low voice and hurled my cell phone all the way across the couch and hurtled out of the room.

He called after me, "Tay, get back here bro! Yo, I said get back here!"

I furiously scaled the steps to my room and slammed the door, unaware that he was just as upset as I was, running up behind me to bulldoze his way into my room, not realizing I had already locked him out. He banged on the door like the police in hot pursuit of a fugitive.

"Tay, open this door, bro! I promise you I'll knock it down!"

I searched for my headphones, hoping to drown out the noise of him kicking down my door. I knew I had made the situation worse, but I wasn't about to open the door after hearing the way he screamed. I heard Daveon rush up the steps soon after the banging started.

"K, chill man. You can't kick in the door! They said they gon' kick us out if anything else gets messed up!" Daveon said in the hallway. He and Jason had once fought so hard that they left behind a tennis ball-sized hole in the drywall and an inoperable bathroom sink. That was only one of many times we pissed off the property manager with costly damage to an already run-down unit.

"Bro, he is hella disrespectful right now. He just threw his phone at me and walked out when I was still talking. We not doing this tonight or ever! I SAID OPEN THIS DOOR, TAY!"

He pounded the door so hard it looked as though it would rattle off the hinges with any more impact.

"K, c'mon bro. Just let me holler at him," Daveon said.

Kemis' voice calmed slightly. "I'm going out right quick. When I get back, his ass better be downstairs."

With Kemis gone, Daveon lightly tapped on the door.

"Tay. C'mon bro, open the door."

I reluctantly got up and let him in, frustrated that nothing had gone the way I had wanted.

Daveon closed the door behind him and locked it back, joining me on the bed.

"What the hell you do man? He usually only mad like that because of me or Clay."

I told him about the phone-flinging, and he took a deep sigh.

"Bro, why didn't you just tell him what happened at school like Jay said?" he asked.

Daveon's phone rang, and I could sense the frustration in his voice when he answered. "Hey Unc...He's right here. Okay." He took the phone down from his ear and put it on mute. "Yo, he on the way over but he wanna talk to you real quick."

I grabbed the phone. "Hey, Unc," I said.

"Tay, how you doing?" he asked.

"Aight."

"Listen, I'm about ten minutes away. I want to come talk to you. Is your homework done?"

"Yes."

"Okay, good. I tell you what—put some clothes on. When I pull up you come on out to the car okay? We'll go grab dinner."

"Okay."

I scoffed and rolled my eyes as I handed the phone back to Daveon and quickly folded out of bed to get ready.

Daveon turned to me after ending the call with Uncle D. "Bro, you know you can't be talking crazy to K. I be telling y'all he crazy and he got temper issues," Daveon said.

"Day, I hear you, but he irks!" I said as we both left the room and headed down the steps.

"Bro, you know K told you to do your homework after you ate! Turn the tv off and go do your damn homework!" Daveon ordered Clay as we reached the bottom of the steps by the door. Clay had to be reminded to do homework multiple times each night.

"Fuck you!" Clay said, without breaking eye contact with the television.

Daveon started walking over to him and Clay hopped to the other end of the couch and ran toward the steps, knowing he was about to get stomped. I shook my head at them and their shenanigans, accustomed to the near-daily minor spat that went on between them. They both had the worst mouths and the worst tempers in the house, and Jason and I had always joked that they deserved each other. At the same time, I had always been grateful they were my brothers and not my enemies. They could kill each other, but kill over each other or the rest of us much more easily.

"Take yo' little bad ass upstairs and do your homework!" Daveon yelled after him. Chances were much higher that Clay would sneak off somewhere or play video games than actually get his homework done, but he moped upstairs at least pretending like he was about to give it an effort.

Daveon and I talked in the front room until we heard Uncle's D's van pull up.

"I'm gone man," I told Daveon, as we gave each other deuces and I left him to deal with Clay's drama.

"Good luck with yo' lecture, bro," he said with a chuckle.

7

more problems, no solutions

Kemis was waiting for me on the couch when I returned from a nice dinner, accompanied by a tedious lecture, with Uncle D. During dinner, Uncle D at least let me talk and explain my point of view before lecturing me about being disrespectful when I got upset, but also made it clear that I owed Kemis an apology for my behavior.

"Fellas, I want the two of you to talk with cool heads and respectful tones," Uncle D said as he looked at me while Kemis and I awkwardly stood in front of the couch. "If there's anyone in this house that can accomplish this, it's actually only the two of you. Let me say a prayer before I go."

My thoughts danced around in my head while he prayed, and I wondered if Kemis would resume screaming at me after Uncle D left. But he stayed behind for a few minutes to check on my brothers and then to remind me to apologize to Kemis.

It was dark by the time Uncle D left, and Kemis walked him outside to his car. It was something he did with everyone who came by since we knew a lot of people were getting robbed in our apartment complex lot when they were getting in and out of their cars. Uncle D always told

Kemis that he could handle his own, but Kemis insisted on accompanying him.

Kemis hoisted the top of the folding chair underneath the doorknob and up against the door when he returned, and then joined me on the opposite end of the couch with his hands folded against his chest.

"Tay, I don't appreciate the way you were talking to me earlier."

I could tell he had calmed down some but not completely. I looked down and briefly gathered my thoughts, knowing what Uncle D would expect me to do. "Sorry."

"I accept your apology, but why did I have to hear the story of what happened today from Day? Why couldn't you just tell me that?"

"It's not like it would've changed your mind about school," I said. I was only slightly annoyed with Daveon, but knew he was probably trying to keep me out of trouble.

"Maybe not, but at least I could've had your back a little bit and talked to the principal. You just let me believe that you were in school acting a fool for no reason! Bro, just tell me in your own words what happened. But real talk, I'm not sure one incident is going to persuade me to take you out."

After I told him everything that had happened, he vowed to go to the school the next day despite me begging him not to. He also said he still felt I needed a punishment but would decide what it would be after he spoke with the principal. I was upset as I walked upstairs but felt better that I had gotten everything off my chest, and even better when I arrived in my room and found my phone waiting for me on my pillow.

Clay greeted me by offering a new solution to persuade Kemis to send me to school with Daveon. "Dude, I know exactly what I would do."

"Yeah, what?"

"Get kicked out of school!" He was being earnest and considered it a reasonable option.

"Bro, are you serious? First off, I don't need that on my record. And secondly, did you forget Kemis and Jason would prolly kick my tail?"

"It'd be worth it though. Just don't do something so bad where the police have to get involved—the police-involvement whoopins be the worst."

I shook my head in disbelief. He and Daveon were the only two of us that had ever been in police custody, even though Jason had told me Kemis once got brought home by the police when he was a teenager as well, but the rest of us were too little to remember. Jason had never been in custody but said he and his friends would get stopped by police all the time when they were driving. There were a couple of times when he and Daveon got stopped and the police ordered them both out of the car at gunpoint for no reason at all.

Police involvement or not, I had no plans of listening to Clay and his outlandish ideas for changing schools. He continued on anyway, thinking he had it all figured out.

"I'm sure if you get suspended enough for little things, they'd eventually kick you out! Just skip a bunch of classes or get a bunch of detentions or something. Or you could just have one good fight where you break a nose...cuss out a few teachers and a principal..."

"So, you want me to be like you and get my ass whooped multiple times for multiple suspensions at school, and go without a phone for five months?"

"But you'd be out though! And I ain't even get my ass whooped for every single one—only some of 'em! And it was only two months with no phone!"

"Bro, K had to pay money for me to be at this school. And Unc probably helped him!"

"Yeah, they were dumb for that," he said nonchalantly while sliding on his shorts. I was silly for thinking the money part would have persuaded him.

I had no doubt he was serious, and were he in my predicament, he would not stop getting into trouble until he got his way, no matter the cost. He was what Granny had always called "hard-headed." I was pretty sure she had whooped him every day during certain elementary grades, since that was how often his teachers sent him home with a bad behavior report. I couldn't imagine parenting a kid like him. It was hard enough being his older brother and trying to keep him out of trouble.

"Clay, you got issues, dude," I said as I plopped down onto the bed and unlocked my phone.

"Yeah aight. Keep trying things the goodie two-shoe way and you'll be there 'til you graduate," he said.

Kemis insisted on speaking with the principal the next day, who made a promise to talk to Mark Paul about my allegations. Mark Paul made it clear to me that he wasn't happy about having an encounter with the principal. He stared me down in the hallway every time he walked past my locker and even bumped shoulders with me once when walking by. I wanted to sock him out right in the back of the head, but I knew I would be labeled the aggressor. I prayed I could catch him off school grounds one day so I could send the message I needed without a suspension.

It was frustrating enough watching him walk by and glare at me nearly every day after class, but my frustrations heightened when his behavior became even more shocking. The week after I had detention, I got to my locker after school and discovered there was a picture of a noose taped to my locker, with a note at the bottom that read "Go back to the hood. This school is not for dumb niggers." While I had no proof, and doubted any witnesses would come forward, I knew Mark Paul was behind it since our discussions in class had become even more contentious. I hurriedly snatched the note down and crumpled it into my pocket, but not before snapping a picture of it on my phone.

I hadn't planned on telling my brothers what happened, afraid that Daveon or Clay would behave irrationally. But after stewing over it all day I could no longer hold it inside. They all reacted the way I thought, with Daveon and Clay making secret plans to come to the school. Kemis called the school the following Monday, and the principal insisted there would be a thorough investigation.

At the beginning of each class the day after, each of the teachers read a statement about being sensitive to students of other races, and how bullying a student based upon his or her race would not be tolerated. Trying to remain still and stare straight ahead while the statements were read didn't help the humiliation, considering I was the only black kid in most of my classes. Not that I was surprised, but even after all of the announcements and threats, nothing ever came of the investigation.

With no consequences to face for his actions, Mark Paul's bigoted banter continued. We had a discussion in Civics and Government class about white people's usage of the "N word," and Mark Paul spoke up.

"I think it's stupid for entertainers to use a word in their songs but then say only black people are allowed to say it," Mark Paul stated.

"I think other races have used that word towards us for long enough," I responded. "When you continue using it, it's a continuation of the oppression that white people have done to black people for hundreds of years!"

"Nobody has oppressed black people but themselves. If y'all would get jobs and stop stealing and killing each other everyone would leave you alone."

I looked up at the ceiling as though I'd find something there to calm me down. When it didn't work, I spoke up but tried not to say anything that would get me into trouble. "You're delusional. You need to stay out them Klan meetings and read some books."

"I got clips saved on my computer of a bunch of black people stealing from stores during the riots. If they can steal and get away with it, I have a right to use whatever words I want. Free country!"

"There were white people stealing too. And I'll definitely show you a clip when I clip yo' fucking jaw if I hear you use the N word around me! We'll see how free you are to speak when yo' mouth gets wired shut!"

"Mr. Lands!" Mrs. Drake shouted. "Profanity and threatening language are not allowed in this space! You can go to the principal's office, young man!"

I felt like I deserved a reward instead of a write-up, considering that I only used one cuss word during my threat when there were at least one thousand other ones that I held in. The sounds of me gathering my belongings were the only noises in the room, as everyone else looked too uncomfortable to speak; everyone except Mark Paul, who glared at me and smiled victoriously, gloating that he had secured my departure from the discussion.

8

where's clay?

Kemis had word of my write up by the time I made it home that day, and it didn't help my cause that Clay came home with a detention slip from his school the same exact day. He lied and told Kemis he walked out of class because his teacher wouldn't let him go to the bathroom. The truth was that he didn't ask to go to the bathroom until he saw Lakisha, a girl he really liked, in the hallway. When his teacher told him he couldn't go, he left anyway and skipped class to roam the halls with Lakisha for the rest of the period.

"Baby bro, you ain't learn nothing that last time you walked out your class and got suspended from school?" Daveon asked while we all sat in his room talking.

"I didn't walk out of class that time. I just got there late so I could watch a fight, and the principal said one more write-up and I'd be suspended, and that lame-ass teacher wrote me up!" Clay responded.

"Either way, you got suspended for like the umpteenth time and K kicked yo' ass, and you said you weren't getting in trouble no more," Daveon said with a laugh.

I laughed along with Daveon, knowing that Clay always said he was going to be good after getting in trouble, but usually returned back to his craziness within a few weeks.

"I ain't sweatin' dude. Teachers shouldn't question kids that say they gotta pee," Clay said.

"Bro, they will if it's you," I said, glad that I was no longer tasked with keeping track of his daily troubles. Since I no longer rode the bus home with him, I was no longer asked to give an explanation about his whereabouts when he refused to come straight home like he was supposed to.

"Whatever, I'm 'bout to go to the court," Clay said, walking toward the door.

"No you not!" Daveon shrieked. "K told you you're on punishment, and your homework ain't done!"

Clay had other ideas. "Man, I got too much homework tonight. By the time I finish it my boys will be gone already. I'ma do it when I get back. You ain't gotta be extra."

Daveon and I looked at each other in disbelief as Clay left the house and headed down to the basketball court. I decided to head to my room and get my own work done so at least when we were all getting yelled at later, I could look like I had done at least one thing right.

When Kemis came into our room later to talk, he was surprised to see that Clay wasn't there. "Where's Clay?" he asked.

I hated when it happened. I couldn't lie to Kemis, but I couldn't rat Clay out either. Jason, Daveon, Clay, and I had a no-snitch policy for as long as I could remember, and never told on each other, no matter what it would cost us. I just looked at him and shrugged my shoulders, hoping he didn't ask any follow-up questions.

He looked in the closet to see if Clay's basketball shoes were there. "I know he didn't go to that damn basketball court after I told him he on punishment!"

He stormed downstairs to put on his shoes and rushed outside to his truck. I was selfishly hoping Clay's stunt would keep the attention off me for the night. I picked up my phone to call him and tell him to run home from the basketball court, but he didn't answer. Right when I put the phone down, Uncle D called me, so I knew that he and Kemis had talked. I ignored his call, which I almost never did, but I knew he would have words for me after hearing about my latest write-up.

Daveon came into my room after a few minutes, followed by Clay, who stomped into the room and threw his shoes in the closet and hauled his homework out of his backpack.

Kemis stormed into the room behind him, still fussing at him. "You better not leave this room until every drop of that homework is done, bro! You don't just roll out to the basketball court after I told you that you're on punishment. You think you just gon' act crazy at school and then come home and do whatever you want?"

"Recreation and socialization are an important part of academic success!" Clay said.

Day and I looked at each other in disbelief, one that he always had something to say, but secondly at his word choices.

"Clay, if that were true, your grades wouldn't be a dumpster fire right now. You get all the recreation and still have shitty grades! Your life is about to have neither one those if you don't figure some shit out." Kemis looked over at Daveon and me. "Did y'all know he was going to the basketball court?"

I definitely wasn't about to tell the truth with the way he glared at us. Fortunately, Daveon lied for both of us. "Naw, we was doing homework!"

"Tay, is your work done?" Kemis asked.

"Almost."

"Well, get it done. Pops is on the way, and he wants to talk to y'all. I gotta go meet this wedding vendor with Kory. I don't want to get back and y'all still don't have your homework done, especially you, Clay. And give me your phone."

"You taking my phone for walking out one dumb-ass class?" Clay shrieked. His loud tone and the way he stood with his arms partially raised told me he was irate and about to do something stupid.

"You walked out of class and then you walked out this house after I told you that you're on punishment, so give me your phone!" Kemis inched closer like he was about to throw just as much as Clay was.

Clay mumbled profanities as he grabbed his phone off the dresser to hand it over to Kemis.

"Here. You on that bullshit though," Clay said.

"Baby bro, you got one more time to cuss at me!" Kemis barked.

"Why? You gon' whoop my ass for saying the same shit you do?" Clay asked as he took his seat on his bed.

"Clay, say sorry man," Daveon said.

Clay pulled another folder out of his backpack and threw it on his bed.

"I ain't never apologized for the truth. Fuck that," Clay said.

Daveon put his head in his hands, while I looked around for my headphones, assuming the room was about to get a lot louder. Kemis stormed out the room as he pointed at Clay saying he would be right back, and Clay subsequently jolted to the closet to grab his shoes and quickly ran out of the room and down the steps.

"Bro, I promise you! YOU BETTER NOT RUN OUT THIS HOUSE!" Kemis yelled from downstairs, followed by the sound of the front door opening.

Daveon and I ran toward the top of the steps and watched Clay fly out of the house while Kemis hurled a flip flop that crashed into the screen door, narrowly missing Clay's head. Kemis bolted out behind him, and Daveon ran out and called after them both. I retreated to my bedroom, not wanting any parts of whatever drama would unfold on the sidewalk and tried to focus on my homework.

Within a few minutes, Clay walked back in the bedroom, followed by Uncle D, who had driven up in time to interrupt Clay's fast break toward the basketball court and had ordered Clay back into his room.

"Fellas…you two—Daveon, where you going?"

Uncle D's attempt at a speech was interrupted when he saw Daveon headed toward the steps.

"I'm about to go out front with my friend for a few minutes, but I'ma finish my work right after that, I promise," Daveon said, eager to meet Candace outside on the porch.

"Just make sure your friend stays *out*side. And don't go anywhere, I wanna talk to you."

"Aight Unc." Daveon shook his head and walked out.

Meanwhile, Uncle D came in and sat down on Clay's bed and immediately pounced on me. "First of all is your phone broke? Because I don't know a teenager on the planet whose phone isn't glued to their hand."

I wasn't going to lie to him about how I had ignored his call earlier. I sighed and waited for him to finish.

"Kemis told me you're probably getting another detention, Tay. It sounds like you're not censoring your tongue when you get upset. When something is angering you at school, I would encourage you to take a break and say a prayer somewhere. Talk to God quietly. He will help you if you let him. And I know this sounds cliché, but if you try it, you'll find out it's true."

I didn't want to talk to God about it and then face the same situation. I wanted God to make some bodies drop. I wanted God to make some more brown faces appear at my school. I wanted God to tell my brother to quit being extra and let me attend the school of my choice, but I knew that wasn't going to happen, so I didn't understand the point.

"So tell me something honestly. How many times have you prayed about your school situation?" he asked.

I looked around as I thought about it. I didn't want to tell him the truth, but I always felt bad about lying to Uncle D. He always was completely real with me, even when I asked hard questions. Plus, since he was the youth pastor, it felt slightly extra sinful to lie to a church man.

"None I guess," I said.

"You guess? Or none?" He looked at me intently.

I turned my head away from him in shame. "None."

"Thank you for your honesty," he said before turning to Clay. "Clay, you told me this would be your school year to turn your behavior around. And what I tell you about talking to your brother like that?"

"Unc he took my phone over one stupid detention though!" Clay said.

"Over one detention? You were on punishment and still went down to the basketball court! I'll tell you this: after all that trouble you got into this past spring, were you my child you *still* wouldn't have a phone *or* a behind, so count your blessings. Your brother does way too much for you to be disrespecting him, because last I checked you haven't paid one bill in this house. He is grown, and you are not. You need to rethink how you speak to adults. Next time you do it I'm coming to pick you up for the week.

"I understand we all get frustrated sometimes, and when those times come, it's time to talk to God about it before you do something that's not wise. He really does want to hear from you, even if it's that your brother or your teacher or your classmate is getting on your nerves. Little things and big things—but you're both going to have to make better choices. Every choice you make will have a consequence, whether it's good or bad. Let me pray for both of you. Is there anything else I can pray for either of you right now? Anything on your heart?" he asked as he looked back and forth at Clay and me.

I wanted Jason back home, and my Granny back alive, and my mother off drugs, or whatever she had going on, and my father out of prison, and a million dollars could probably help too. I also wanted a telescope and piano lessons, and a larger, nicer house, friends at school, and maybe a girlfriend, but all that sounded silly, and God wouldn't do it anyway.

We both shook our heads in response to his question. He looked at us both for a moment, and then closed his eyes and began to pray. Clay's fidgeting and annoyed looks that he was giving seemed to stop after prayer, but his calm demeanor was short-lived.

"I got something for you both," Uncle D said with a smile. I perked up, wondering what he had this time, as he was almost always giving us money or gift cards. "So, what you're going to do, is copy this page right here," he said as he handed me one of two miniature dictionaries from underneath his jacket and pointed to a page he had pre-marked, before turning to Clay and handing one to him as well. He had often assigned Clay pages to copy when Clay was caught using profanity toward or around adults, which seemed like all the time.

"I'll get these from you fellas on Sunday. You both know better than to address adults with those types of words, or use profanity in their presence, even if the adult is your brother. I love you boys," he said as he left.

We both grumbled with the assignments he gave us and tried to keep our lips shut until he left.

9

weekend pep talk

"Why you cussing and shit in front of your teacher? I need to knock you out, bro?"

Weekends were better when Jason was home. Although we regularly talked on the phone, I missed being able to lounge on his bed while he played video games or texted and talk about everything going on.

He had surprised me in my room and was standing over me with his arms crossed looking as though a knock-out was coming.

I threw my headphones down and sat up to greet him.

"Bro chill, when you get here?" I asked after we embraced.

"I just got here. This is only my second stop. My first was in the basement to kick Clay's tail, and you next! So, what's going on? You ready for me to kick yo' ass too?"

I sighed. "We good, bro!"

"Then wassup with this new detention?"

"Come on, bro. What I'm supposed to do when this dude saying he 'bout to use the 'n' word and shit right in front of me?"

"I hear you, but did you have to say that stuff in front of the teacher? It seems like you're doing stuff as though there won't be consequences. You knew she would send you to the principal!"

"I don't have friends at this school and I ain't like the rest of y'all—y'all always have friends on day one. I miss being around black people. I miss knowing what everyone is talking about. These kids drive to school in Maseratis and Range Rovers and shit. They talk about their parents' yachts and beach properties. I've hardly ever been in trouble, but now I feel like I'll be the number one suspect when something goes down. And I know this dude did this stuff to my locker. I hate school right now." I reflected on my words after they left my mouth, realizing that I had never hated school before. In fact, it used to be one of my favorite places.

"Bro, sometimes there's no easy solution. I'm not gon' lie, I didn't know it was gon' be so hard playing basketball for a big school. Some days we have to be in the weight room by 4:45 in the morning! The workouts are brutal. Then I have to go to these early classes. The schedule is no joke, and we're not allowed to really skip classes and stuff. I've already wanted to quit like five times, and the season hasn't even officially started yet. But I know I just can't put in all this hard work just to quit when I'm so close to getting what I wanted.

"You gotta stay calm when this dude at school is trying you. We not really used to that type of thing since we always had each other. And Day and Clay's mouth so loud that nobody ever wanted to step when they were around."

It was true that usually either Daveon or Clay's pre-fight rhetoric took care of most of the fighting. They barked and cussed so loudly that nobody wanted to test their bite, and the few that tested it regretted it quickly. But now my voice boxes were gone, and the cussing and the fighting had been left to me. I had no issues with either one, even though I knew Kemis detested the idea of us starting a fight.

"But look, don't do nothing stupid. Just walk out if you're about to lose your temper. Walk out and then call me, aight?"

I nodded.

"And then tell K the whole story, 'cause you like one more detention from him bussing you in the mouth like he used to do me," he said with a laugh.

I smiled and thought about how much I had missed my brother being home. While there, he introduced us to his roommate Malik, another basketball player on the team. With Kemis spending most of the weekend out with Kory, Malik and Jason told us the truth about what they had been getting into, even showing us pictures and videos from their basketball travels and various parties they had attended.

Since Daveon had mostly been staying out of trouble, Kemis had agreed that he could go to campus soon to spend the weekend, leaving me feeling jealous, and a little regretful that I hadn't stayed out of trouble a little more. I wondered if I could change things around in time for Kemis to change his mind, but figured that would only happen if I changed my responses to Mark Paul's antics, and I wasn't exactly sure if I could.

10

when the ish hits the locker

I had resolved to not let Mark Paul silence me at school, and became more vocal in Civics and Government class, especially after some of the books I had read with the new student group I joined, the Minority Student Union. I did a presentation on government policies and conspiracies to silence black voices such as Dr. Martin Luther King, Congressman John Lewis, Malcolm X, and the Black Panther Party. Mark Paul made it obvious he didn't want to listen, and rolled his eyes throughout my presentation, and at some points tried to disrupt and talk over me despite multiple warnings from our teacher to stop. Growing tired of him, I told him in front of the whole class that he looked smarter when his mouth was shut, prompting the entire class to laugh at him. When it was time for his presentation, I pointed out a few flaws in his reasoning in front of the class, prompting the teacher to start questioning his research methods. I had found out days after that he received a poor grade.

Within one week of that, something humiliating happened, and I knew the two events had to be related. It had been an otherwise good and relatively normal day that was almost over. I was at my locker getting ready for my last class when I was approached by two school security officers and an assistant principal.

"Mr. Lands, some students are reporting that you are selling drugs out of your locker, and we're going to need to search you and your locker."

I knew it was fabricated, and I wasn't completely sure of my rights as a student at a private school. I was mad, but also scared, wondering if the person who had falsely reported me had actually planted something in my locker, and I pictured myself being dragged off to the police station and locked up. I wanted time to call my brother, or call anyone, but my anger prevented me from thinking clearly.

"I don't know where you're getting your information from, but it's not true. And I'm sure you're supposed to notify my parents first." I said, sensing hostility gradually rising up in my chest.

"Actually, pursuant to the school policy which you and your *brother* signed, we are allowed to search at will, whenever reasonable," Mr. Reed, the assistant principal, said in response.

I noticed how he emphasized brother, as if to make sure everyone who was standing around knew I didn't have parents. A crowd of students stood around looking appalled, as if marveling that they had been traversing the halls with an orphaned member of the drug cartel.

"You can search my locker, but you're definitely not touching me," I said with my fists balled up, surprising even myself. I was entirely ready to swing and deal with the consequences later.

With my heart beating ten times faster, I stepped aside and watched one of them shine a flashlight into my locker while the others threw the contents from my locker down to the floor with no regard to whether my things would break, spill, or unravel. Papers, flyers, schoolwork, textbooks, art projects, cards, my water bottle, chess set, bookmarks—my property was strewn about on the floor, and I felt more and more helpless with each item that crashed on top of the others.

Adding to the humiliation was seeing so many faces gathered around to watch it all unfold, with Mark Paul conveniently missing it. They searched endlessly and seemed determined not to stop until they found something worthy of expelling me over. When they failed, they hurriedly walked away, but not before Mr. Reed turned to me with instructions. "Clean up this mess."

With that, they were gone, and the onlookers casually filed away one by one as if nothing had even happened. Paris, the girl from church who was a tenth grader, bent down to the ground alongside me to help me pick everything up.

"You don't have to do this," I said. I didn't want her nearby in case I was unable to prevent an emotional outburst. I tried to suppress my outrage, but my hands shook as I retrieved papers off the floor.

"What they did was shady, and I want to help."

The bell had already rung by the time we were done.

"Are you okay?" she asked. All was quiet, other than the echo of my locker slamming shut once we had placed everything back inside.

I nodded my head in response, having no words to describe my emotional state; I just knew I was enraged, and my thoughts were unintelligible. I felt angry enough to do something terrible, and envisioned myself getting arrested after bashing in a few classroom windows, or the windows to the principal's luxury car, or maybe skipping the property damage and bashing in the principal's dental implants and the partially wrinkled lips that surrounded them.

"Yo, uh, thanks for helping me out," I said, trying to conceal the shaking in my voice.

All I could do after that was walk away, feeling unable to walk to class or face anyone. I walked until I was out of the school, on the sidewalk, and then I began to walk down the street. My feet carried me all the way to the mall, where I finally looked at my phone and realized school was about to let out. I sat and thought before I called Kemis, as it was his day to pick me up.

11

that escalated quickly

Nearly twenty minutes after we had spoken on the phone, Kemis casually walked into the food court and sat across the table from me, rubbing his forehead as though he had a headache, and then looked at me for a few moments as if waiting for me to talk. When I didn't, he started. "Tay, I haven't known you to skip a class since Granny died. Do I need to grab your phone for a few days?"

I looked down at the table and focused my ears on the sounds of people talking and walking around us. I wanted to tell him everything, but I couldn't. I was no longer angry, but fatigued from scrapping around in a battle that I no longer had the strength to fight.

"You used to tell me everything," he told me.

"That's back when you actually listened to what I had to say," I responded, and not with the most respectful tone.

"Bro look, even though you don't like your school, you can't just get up and leave when you feel like it. What the hell is up with you?"

I responded with a shoulder shrug since my mouth was still unmotivated to speak.

He sighed and stood up from the chair. "Let's go!"

We rode from the mall in silence, and I caught him out of the corner of my eye giving me occasional glances as I stared out the window, wishing I had the words to tell him how I was feeling. He didn't drive home, but drove to Uncle D's house, and pulled his truck all the way to the back of the driveway, which wrapped around to the rear of the house.

"I'll be back," he said. He stepped out the truck and used his key to enter their home through the back door.

Within a few minutes, Auntie Robin, Uncle D's wife, opened the passenger door, interrupting the miniature Zen I had created by reclining my seat, closing my eyes, and stuffing my ears inside my headphones to help me drown out any thoughts about school. She had already changed from her work clothes and thrown on her normal t-shirt and sweatpants that she wore around the house. She had pretty brown skin and an inviting smile that she greeted me with, followed with a look of genuine concern. "Tay, why are you sitting in this car when we're inside? Come here for a second."

Her soft fingers clinched my hand within hers after I stepped onto the driveway. "I can tell by the look on your face that something isn't okay right now. You're holding on to something, but you don't need to."

I expected her to say something like that. She was a counselor by profession, and always spoke with us in a different manner than anyone else. For whatever reason, she put her arms around me and gave me a hug. The hug didn't make me feel better. It made me feel broken, and I did my best to hide it. The same humiliation that I felt when I stood in front of my locker and watched it get torn apart had once again revisited.

"Sweetie, why don't you come inside?" she asked me after I broke from her embrace.

I shook my head. "I'm cool, Auntie."

"Come on, boy. I made nachos… Let me make you a plate."

She knew nachos were my favorite, and it made me wonder if the trip was planned. I grabbed my backpack and phone and followed her inside.

Uncle D's home was the most inviting place we regularly visited. It wasn't an extremely large house, but it wasn't nearly as tiny as the space we lived in, where the walls were so thin and floors so frail that I could hear exactly what Jason and Daveon were doing with the girls they snuck in. A formal dining area nested near the foyer at the front door, and on the other side of the foyer was a room with no televisions that had decorative tan couches and chairs and a plush burgundy rug, where they would sit and talk with guests or hang out when they needed a quiet space, something I often longed for at home.

My favorite room was what they called their family room, where there were cushiony couches with oversized pillows that felt like invitations for a long nap, a television, and a fireplace they often used in the colder months to brighten and warm the room. In the back of that room was the door to the garage, and immediately to its right was the kitchen. It was on the kitchen island where Auntie Robin had placed a warm crockpot filled with some of the nacho ingredients that I could smell as soon as we walked in through the kitchen door from the back deck.

Sophie and Caleb often hung out downstairs, as there was a closed off playroom inside the finished basement where they kept all of their books, toys, and games. I always looked at their "kids only" space in amazement, wondering what I would have done if I had such a thing growing up. They both came and hugged me and then ran outside after I arrived in the kitchen.

My mouth watered as I watched Auntie Robin prepare a perfect extra-large plate of nachos topped with melted cheese, grilled chicken, and everything else she knew I liked on my nachos. After she slid the plate in front of me and poured a drink, she sat next to me with her laptop, and the two of us chatted while I ate and she worked on her computer.

After a while, Kemis and Uncle D walked up from the basement, but their chatter ceased once they joined us at the island in the kitchen.

"What he do to get nachos?" Uncle D looked at my plate and then at his wife, jealous that he didn't have any.

"Nothing! I could just tell he needed them, and he looks better already." She looked at me and smiled, and it reminded me of some of the meals Granny would prepare when I was little that seemed to cure any day's worth of pain and sorrow.

"He acted up at school today, though, and he gets nachos? Meanwhile your husband's been on his best behavior and gets nothing," Kemis said.

"Well, I'm sure Tay has an explanation when he's ready to share, and no, my husband has not been behaving," she said with a laugh.

"According to that upgraded ring on your finger, he's been a real good boy!" Kemis said. "And I hope you're right about him being ready to share, because I'm ready to share two chops to his throat!"

"You not gonna be chopping my baby, Kemis!" Auntie Robin said while piling more nachos onto my plate. I was grateful she knew I wanted more without me telling her, and I thanked her quietly.

"Well, your *bay-bee* just got his third detention at school today for the semester, and I'm running out of options," he said as he looked at me and grabbed one of my nachos.

"Ayy," I protested as I placed my hand above my plate to shield it from any more thievery.

"Tay that can't be true. Your third detention?" Auntie Robin asked.

"I didn't know I got detention," I said, since I hadn't formally been made aware.

"But you know you walked your ass—my bad—your tail up out of that school before school was over and skipped out on your last class," Kemis said.

I shook my head and continued chewing, not wanting to discuss any of the day's events.

"What'd you think they were gon' do, give you a reward?" Kemis asked and then took another nacho.

I took a deep breath, and scooted my plate away, no longer wanting to eat with my brother nagging me. My display of disgust didn't stop him from ranting.

"Tay, you seem to think you can just act out every time you get upset, and it's getting out of hand! You can't just straight up leave the school when you have a—"

I felt like I would yell if I had to listen to him utter one more word. I stood up to walk away, but Kemis forcefully snatched my pants and pulled me backwards towards him. "You just gon' be rude and walk away while I'm talking?" he shouted

"Yeah, nigga! Get the fuck off me!" I yelled to his face and jerked away, double-fisting him in the chest to break his grasp of me, causing his body to tumble backwards with more force than I expected.

My push ignited a fury in him I had not seen in years, and a street dude began to burst out of my brother's body. I knew I had taken it too far and was uneasy when he started yelling after me. Uncle D was physically restraining him with his arms wrapped firmly around him and urging him to calm down, while Kemis violently barked after me while jerking his body to wrestle from Uncle D's grasp.

"Bro, I PROMISE I'M READY FOR YOU!" he yelled.

"Tay, go sit in the backyard," Uncle D demanded while struggling to maintain control of Kemis.

"But he—"

"Now!"

I complied, mainly because Uncle D had never spoken to me that sternly before. My brothers all had stories from when he had taken it there with them, and a few times I had even watched him go in on them for acting crazy. He had once popped Clay coming out of a store after Clay, who was around ten years old at the time, had cussed out a grown woman right in front of Uncle D.

I sat outside watching Caleb and Sophie play basketball, and joined in a game of horse when they asked me to. We played until I heard the door from the kitchen open and shut as Uncle D walked out.

"Tay, come over here!"

The same sternness in his voice startled me a little. I tossed the ball back to Caleb and Sophie and wilted over to him.

"Have a seat." He pointed to one of the chairs that sat next to the fire pit in the middle of the yard. I sat down in silence and looked away from him as he reclined in the chair right next to mine.

"Look at me." His tone compelled me to follow his instructions again. "I don't know what happened at school today that has you so upset, but it's time to go ahead and let it out. You're only being destructive by holding on to it, and you're about to make your predicament a lot worse. I told your brother to go home and let you stay here, primarily so he doesn't kill you. Talk to me, son. Tell me what has you so angry."

I sighed and stared off into the tall bushes near the fence line, contemplating how to get out of reliving the story from earlier that day. Replaying it in my head had been torture, and I had no desire to retell it to him.

"Start talking."

I knew by the look on his face that I wasn't leaving until I talked, so I did. I told him what happened at the locker, and how Paris had helped me, and how I left the school. I told him about my presentation and Mark Paul's the week before. I told him about the principal telling me to clean up what they had done. I told him everything, and then stared off in frustration.

"Tay, that's pretty awful. I'm really sorry. You definitely didn't deserve that. Give me your hand."

He said another prayer asking God to give me wisdom, when wisdom was not what I wanted. He then called Kemis and arranged for me to stay with them until after school that Friday, saying we both might benefit from having space and time apart. Auntie Robin took Caleb and me to the mall where she purchased new outfits for me to wear to school for the week, which Uncle D later told her she shouldn't have done because she rewarded my bad behavior.

"Dwayne, he needs clothes for school!" she said at the dinner table that night.

"You didn't have to buy him all those name brands when he was acting up," Uncle D said.

"Are you telling me you would have behaved differently had you faced what he faced?" she asked with her head cocked to the side and her eyebrows raised.

"Did you miss the part where he cussed at and assaulted his brother? And I woulda gotten my behind tore up had I just left the school when I wanted to growing up! The boy knows he's not supposed to walk out of school. I understand he was upset, but these kids gotta learn to channel their anger. This boy gets detention and disrespects and strikes his brother and you done took him on a shopping spree!"

"Tay, next time we'll go to the Goodwill, I guess," she said.

"There definitely better not be a next time with all these detentions. And what's wrong with the Goodwill? That's where I shop!" Uncle D said, making me glad he hadn't been the one to take me shopping.

I settled into a routine that I had adopted on many evenings that I had spent at the Farmer residence. I helped Auntie Robin clean up after dinner since Caleb and Sophie weren't great cleaners, and then I read Sophie nearly one hundred stories. After each book, she kept bringing me another one, until Caleb finally started begging for me to play with him. He asked me to play a video game, but Uncle D wouldn't let me play because of the way I had spoken to Kemis. The three of us played Uno instead until they had to go to bed. At bedtime, the whole family spread out in the family room, read a Bible story together, and took turns praying.

"Aren't you going to pray?" Sophie asked me in a sweet voice.

"Um, sure," I said. I wasn't used to praying in front of an audience, but I felt compelled to say something, and hoped a quick prayer asking God to protect us would satisfy her request.

"You forgot to say, 'in Jesus' name amen!'" she said. She was serious and looked at me like I had committed an abomination. I smiled and corrected the ending of my prayer.

They all left the room, but not before Caleb and Sophie both gave me a hug.

"I hope you stay for two weeks," Caleb said.

I smiled at him and gave him a fist bump before he left. It could be that long before it was safe enough to return to my brother's presence, I thought.

"Tay, is your homework done?" Uncle D asked me after he had tucked them into their beds for the night.

I shook my head. I hadn't been in the mood for homework or any other reminders of school.

"Well, let's get to it. You know you gotta get up early tomorrow."

"Aight," I mumbled as I stood from the couch.

I pretended to do homework when I was actually enjoying the quiet of a room that faced a small cul-de-sac with only a few houses and hardly any noise, unlike the room Clay and I shared at home where it seemed we heard everything from arguments and exhaust pipes to car horns, crying kids, gunfire, and city busses whizzing by. I leaned back into the softness of the bed that I wished could be mine permanently in between texting Daveon, Clay, and Paris late into the night, scrolling on my secret social media page, and intentionally shunning my homework.

The next thing I remembered was Uncle D waking me up to get ready for school. We stopped for an early breakfast before heading to school, where he took the time to question me about my evening activities.

"Do you always stay up on your phone all night? Don't you have a test today?" he asked.

"It wasn't all night," I said. "And besides, I usually don't study outside of just doing my homework, and still get a perfect score, especially in my computer classes."

"I don't know. When I checked on you at three this morning you were asleep with your phone in hand and all your lights on!"

"Unc, why you checking on me at three?"

"Because your lights were on, and you were supposed to complete your homework and go to sleep, and I was up praying. So the real question is, how much homework did you actually complete?"

"You praying at three in the morning?" I asked.

"That's usually what time I pray, but stop changing the subject. Did you finish your schoolwork?"

"Yes, Unc." I was hoping he would stop pressing the issue since I usually took time during lunch to finish anything that wasn't done.

"I would've checked but all those advanced classes you're in, I wouldn't know what I'm looking for. By the way, your brother is going to meet us at the school so he and I can talk to your principal about this locker search. And when you see your brother, I expect you to apologize to him, do you understand?"

I had no plans of apologizing to Kemis. I knew I was wrong for hitting him and getting smart with him, but I blamed him for the entire predicament. Despite him knowing everything that I had experienced at school, he behaved as though he was clueless, and as if I was supposed to carry on as though nothing was happening. The more I thought about school, the more my anger intensified toward Kemis.

"I know you heard me; I want you to answer with your mouth," he said.

"Yes."

I was angry at Kemis when we saw him on the parking lot, and toward every single person affiliated with the school. He and Uncle D stood and talked for a moment while I drifted off to play on my phone, prompting Uncle D to place his arm around me and gently usher me back towards them.

"Tay has something to say to you," he told Kemis, and looked at me with the expectation of filling the awkward silence with my apology.

I looked at Kemis, whose eyes met mine before I uncomfortably shifted my gaze back down to my phone. "Um, I'm about to be late."

I flung my backpack around my shoulder and walked toward the school, afraid to look back, not thinking about either of them again until I was called to the principal's office during lunch.

"Dontay, I wanted to let you know that the decision was made to rescind your detention after speaking with your brother and uncle today. If you ever find yourself in a predicament where something upsets you, I encourage you to go to the guidance counselor's office. You know our school has a policy that you are allowed to go to the counselor's office whenever you need. They will get you excused from class and send a note to your teacher. Does that sound like something you can use?" Principal Calhoun asked me.

I had no desire to talk with any of the guidance counselors. They all seemed like pleasant people and walked around with smiles that seemed surgically secured to their faces. I was sure they were quite knowledgeable about the school and its policies, which they often shared with us when they visited our homeroom classes to talk about yoga and deep-breathing and other ideas that felt like a complete waste of time. But I had my doubts about their ability to relate to one of the few black students in the school.

"I'm not trying to be rude, Mr. Calhoun, but there are no black guidance counselors here. And there's only one black teacher, and she's part-time. I'm really not interested," I said, hoping I was free to head to class.

He remained expressionless in his seat, and I wondered if he was either expecting me to say what I said, or simply did not care.

He sat up in his chair and rolled it closer to his desk. "Dontay, we strive to ensure that all students, regardless of their race or ethnicity, have a positive experience here. We pride ourselves on maintaining a color-blind, family atmosphere that embraces all cultures equally. Do you feel like that's not happening?"

I looked at his hands to see if he had been reading from a brochure, and I was shocked he would even follow up a question that could induce a response that he likely wasn't ready for.

"Not really, but you could start with having more African-American literature in the library. There's hardly anything."

"We just got a brand-new library, and I'm not sure that additional books on top of the ones that we're already expecting are going to make the budget at this time. Maybe you could compile a list for the librarian for next year, and she can submit it to the proper committee," he suggested. He continued on by talking about all the wonderful books he had read by African-American writers but only named one writing by Dr. Martin Luther King, Jr.

"Why would this school hire a librarian that doesn't think black literature is important to everyone? At my old school there were books by black authors or about black leaders that lined the shelves, so I know it's possible. It's not just about the library. Hardly any students in this school know about the Tulsa race massacre, when they burned down black Wall Street. They've never heard of Juneteenth, or the MOVE bombings, or even Emmit Till. This is supposed to be the top school in the state—I ain't buying it. Wherever y'all getting these textbooks from, y'all need a refund. Can I go?"

He sat completely silent in his chair, while I waited for what seemed like an eternity for him to thank me for my time and allow me to leave. The detention being taken back was a win, but it would have felt even better had I left feeling as though the principal actually listened to the things I said.

12

a friend in need

God must've known I was feeling ready to throw hands on that day and sent me Marco Jamison and Tommy Williams, who ended up becoming my two closest friends at school, other than Paris. After leaving the principal's office, I stopped by my locker before heading to class where I encountered Mark Paul and three of his friends, ready to start more drama.

"You know they don't let thugs in our school. They'll give you way worse than detention when they catch you with your drugs," he said with a sly smile.

I was parting my lips to respond when a voice from behind me roared, "Yo, stay the fuck away from my dude!"

I yanked my head around to see a familiar face on a tall body, but I didn't know his name. I knew he was the captain of the basketball team, and he sometimes came to the Minority Student Union meetings. His voice was loud and intimidating, and I could tell he didn't care who heard him cussing. He stood tall enough to tower over everyone else in the hallway, with his hands in front of him as if he was ready to follow his words with actions. Next to him stood another player from the team, who wasn't quite as tall, but was slender and athletic, with the exact same skin tone as mine. They both wore a scowl on their faces.

Mark Paul looked disturbed by their presence, and he and his boys quietly backed away without even looking in my direction.

"You Tay, right?" the tallest one asked me after we were alone.

"Yeah," I told them, likely wearing all of my confusion on my face.

"I'm Marco. I used to hoop with Jason on AAU. He texted me and told me some dude been giving you problems, and I told him I gotchu. A lot of the people at this school ain't used to black dudes—and this is Tommy."

"Yo, don't I know you? Aren't you Clay's brother?" Tommy asked.

"Aw shoot! We used to hoop with you around the corner!" I exclaimed, excited that I recognized a face from my own neighborhood.

"Yeah, and me and Clay hooped in AAU. I've seen you in the hallway, but I wasn't sure it was you," Tommy said.

We all bro-hugged and spoke for a few moments before exchanging numbers and parting ways to head to class. Marco and Tommy were just what I needed that day. I wasn't afraid of Mark Paul and his friends, but I was becoming afraid of myself, and what I would do if my anger continued to stew.

Marco and Tommy told me to text if I needed anything and agreed that we should get together after school sometime. I began feeling empowered, and back to feeling like I had a victorious day.

That feeling changed when Uncle D picked me up, and I learned that defying him would not go unpunished.

"Go ahead and hand me your phone, Dontay," he said after we drove off the school parking lot.

My mouth dropped open, and I turned to him ready to protest.

"Don't even think about talking crazy to me." He was serious, and I was boiling mad. My detention had gotten reversed and my social life was looking better, but now I had to deal with him.

"What I do?" I asked, trying to keep my voice calm enough to keep from being accused of disrespect.

"Didn't I tell you to apologize to your brother this morning? I told you to do something, and you didn't do it. Now it's time to face the consequences. Simple as that." He was stalled in front of a stoplight and giving me full eye contact with his hand held out, ready to receive the only ticket I had to my new friends and a better social life at school.

I reflected on the time Clay threw his phone at Kemis when Kemis was putting him on punishment, and Kemis got up from his seat and tackled Clay. It wasn't pretty at the time, but we laughed about it later. I wanted nothing more than to throw my phone out the window, knowing he couldn't tackle me since he was driving, but I didn't need any drama, especially with him. I pressed the phone in his hand and tried to avoid talking to him for the rest of the day.

13

the best kind of visitor

Finding out that Paris lived within walking distance to Uncle D's house made my night of being punished more tolerable. She texted me that evening after I routed my messages to my iPad. She was a sophomore and had just gotten her driver's license, accompanied with the freedom to leave the house and check in on me.

Paris: Why don't I come by? I'll just tell my parents I'm running to the store.

Me: I would say yes, but I think I'm on punishment.

Paris: lol. By Pastor D? Did he tell you that?

Me: Dude took my phone. I'm pissed!

Paris: well, let's just talk outside on the front porch. Can't stay long anyway

Me: K. when u comin

Paris: OTW

About five minutes later, she texted to notify me that she was outside. I grabbed my jacket and tried to tiptoe toward the front door undetected, when Sophie spotted me.

"Where you going?" she asked.

"Nowhere. Just need some fresh air on the porch."

"Can I go with you?"

"No, Soph. You gotta get ready for bed, and don't tell Mommy I'm on the porch, okay?"

I closed the door behind me, hoping a seven-year-old girl could keep a secret the same way my brothers and I always did when one of us was sneaking somewhere we weren't supposed to.

I greeted Paris with a long hug and felt delighted to see her. We stood around and talked about life with Uncle D and life at school. It suddenly dawned on me how pretty she was, and that she was cool to talk to, and I wondered why I hadn't noticed it before. I wondered if it was because she was laughing at my jokes, or smiling when she talked, or because I finally got to be with her alone without picking books up from the floor.

It didn't take long for me to start flirting with her, saying things I had heard Jason and Daveon tell girls for years. It seemed like it was making her smile, which made me wonder if she liked me. Soon enough, I was holding her and we were kissing, so long that I had forgotten that I had snuck outside to do so, and forgotten that I had a crappy week, and forgotten that my phone was gone.

The kiss turned an unpleasant day into a perfect one, until Uncle D whisked opened the front door and cleared his throat. I had not known he was home, since I thought I had heard him say he had to run to the church. Paris and I jumped apart, and I wiped my lips and tried to act as though nothing happened.

"Paris? What are you doing here?" Uncle D glared suspiciously after he stepped onto the porch with us.

"Oh, uh, hey Pastor D. I was in the neighborhood—"

"And uh I was out here getting some fresh air when she drove by," I said, not wanting her to divulge too much information on how we communicated without my phone.

"Well, you live in the neighborhood. And we live on a cul-de-sac, so nobody really drives by. Does your dad know you're in the neighborhood with a boy?" he asked.

Uncle D was good friends with Paris' dad. They attended men's Bible study and had served together at the church, and I often saw them talking with one another after service. Paris had mentioned a few times during lunch that the two men often visited with each other since they lived only walking distance apart. There were times when she and her sister had walked over to babysit Caleb and Sophie. Some mornings, when Uncle D went on morning walks, he would stop at Paris' home and her dad and Uncle D would have coffee together on their back porch and talk. I knew Uncle D knew her dad well enough to know he wouldn't want her hanging out and kissing me.

Paris looked away, trying to avoid Uncle D's question.

"Y'all come on in here," he said and stepped aside so we could walk through the doorway.

He pursed his lips and glared when I walked by, looking as though he was about to smack me on the arm. The three of us sat and talked in the kitchen, at the spot where Auntie Robin had given me nachos the previous day, and Uncle D stood on the opposite side of the island at the stove preparing a cup of tea.

"So, Paris, are you Tay's guest or mine, because Tay's on punishment." I hardly knew him to ever start a conversation with small talk.

"You never told me I was on punishment!" I said. "Besides, when Caleb and Sophie are on punishment, they not allowed to have fresh air?"

"Oh, you're being smart. I took your phone, didn't I? And it looks like you were getting a lot more than fresh air." Paris and I lowered our heads and smiled in embarrassment. He looked over at Paris. "Paris, do you think you'd be on punishment if you acted crazy with your parents?"

She looked confused. "I guess it would depend on how crazy I acted."

"Well, I won't go into all that," Uncle D said.

"I didn't even act crazy. My brother be overreacting sometimes over some little stuff. All I did was walk away!" I said.

"Boy, you did way more than walk away. Paris," Uncle D continued, "what would your parents do if you tried to walk away while they were talking to you, and then punched them in the chest to do it?"

"Uhhh, I would say they wouldn't react to it too nicely," she said smiling. "Is that what you did, Tay?"

"Unc, it ain't even go down like that, and he's not my parent," I said.

"He's your oldest brother and your legal guardian. But enough about him, I want to know how you two started locking lips on my porch!"

"Unc, you so embarrassing dude!" I pressed my fingers above my eyes in efforts to partially shield my face.

We talked and laughed about church and school and discussed why my week had gone so badly. It was actually fun, even with Uncle D refusing to leave our presence. But after a while he told Paris she needed to go so we could both get our homework done, and she started heading towards the door.

"Be a gentleman and walk the young lady to her car, Tay," he told me, but as I started walking, he grabbed me and pulled me backward towards him. He got close and told me in a low, solemn tone, "And keep your lips off my daughter!"

I couldn't help but to laugh. He always called the kids at the church his sons and daughters, so it didn't surprise me to hear him say it, but I knew right then I wouldn't last as a long-term resident of his household. Although Kemis didn't let us have girls inside without permission, he wouldn't hover the entire time, and I had never seen him interrupt Daveon or Jason while they made out.

"Unc, you be doing too much," I said as I shook my head and walked away.

"I'm serious, Tay!" he called as I trotted out the front door to catch up with Paris.

"Yo, I'm glad you came by," I told Paris once I got outside. "You should come back tomorrow."

"Um, sounds like you're on punishment with Pastor Crazy Strict; we better wait," she said with a chuckle. I was glad she had a sense of humor about my predicament.

"I don't wanna wait too long. Once I get back to the crib we gotta get up. I'll see you tomorrow though," I said as I stood up from leaning over her car door.

"No goodbye kiss?" she asked, looking at me with the prettiest smile I had ever witnessed. I looked up and saw Uncle D watching us with his arms folded from the front porch.

"Listen, I want nothing more than to do that, but that man right there is going to *kill* me if I do. He told me I better not do it when I was walking out."

She turned and looked as I pointed to Uncle D, and she started laughing. "He does the most! Aight, pretend like you're walking away, and when I get close to you put your hands in the air."

"What?"

"Just do it...trust me!" she said.

Jason was right—girls knew how to plot way better than we did. I started walking away like I was going into the house, and she jumped out of her car, ran in front of me, and kissed me, trying to make it look as though it was all her idea so I wouldn't get in trouble. I suddenly loved her, and I wanted to kiss her a thousand more times.

"I said it's time to go, you two!"

We stopped kissing as Uncle D yelled out from the porch, and she waved goodbye as she skipped back over to the driver's seat of her car. I stood in the middle of the street staring at her car as she drove off, secretly hoping she would put the car in reverse and kiss me one more time...or twelve.

"Ahem!" Uncle D stood there obnoxiously clearing his throat, and I hesitantly walked toward him.

"I ain't do anything, Unc!" I said smiling with my hands raised in the air.

"Get your behind in this house boy," he said as he popped me in the head. "That girl's daddy would kill you!"

"I'm not interested in her daddy though!"

"You will be when he's coming after you!" he said before disappearing down into the basement.

I worked on homework for a while, and then read Caleb and Sophie two bedtime stories before they went to bed. Soon thereafter, Uncle D made sure my homework was finished and removed my iPad from my room, stating he didn't want me to get tempted to break my punishment again.

I rolled my eyes as I got up to get ready for bed, knowing I would have to wait until I was at school to tell my brothers about my glorious but rudely interrupted night. For the first time in a while, I looked forward to getting to school the next day, in hopes of making lip locks with Paris a part of my daily routine and telling my new friends and brothers about it.

14

my new school wifey

That Friday morning, Uncle D dropped me off at school early since I had a chess club meeting. I reflected as we drove that I had actually enjoyed my time with the four of them. There was something relaxing about being at their home. They always had good food, and I even enjoyed sitting around and talking, especially at the dinner table. Every day, Auntie Robin had packed snacks in my backpack, attached to a note, like she did with Caleb and Sophie, and insisted on planting a kiss on my cheek before I left for school. Even though I was treated like family, by that morning I was ready to go home and be done with Uncle D's punishment.

"I forgot to ask you, how much money do you need for lunch?" Uncle D asked as he pulled out his wallet after arriving curbside at school.

"We've always had free lunch, Unc. Here it's covered in my scholarship. I don't need any money."

"Oh ok. Have a good day Tay. Don't forget about making good choices! And remember that you're here for an education, not for girls," he said, as he handed my phone over to me. He had already placed my iPad in my backpack. I wondered if he ever left anyone without a reminder of something.

"I'm trying to be here for both, Unc!" I laughed before rushing out the car, happy my phone was back and ready to text my brothers about my new crush.

I had the happiest lunch of my life that day as I sat next to Paris at our table. We talked with our lunch crew, but I kept thinking about the kiss we had the night before. I made her promise to meet me after school for one more, and it was all I focused on during the rest of my classes that day, so much that I wasn't even slightly bothered by the glares of Mark Paul. She sent me a few selfies she took in the bathroom to keep me reminded of what was coming, making me even more excited. She met me outside on the sidewalk after school, and we had just finished a satisfying departure kiss when Uncle D pulled into the pickup lanes.

"You being hard-headed," he said after I got in the car, illuminated with a fresh glow from the joy of kissing Paris.

"What I do?" I asked.

"You think I didn't see what y'all were doing?" he asked.

"C'mon Unc! We were just talking and did one little kiss!"

He sighed and shook his head. "Kissing leads to other things!"

"You think I'ma hit in the middle of a sidewalk in front of school?" I asked smartly.

"Don't make me knock you out. Did you call and apologize for your behavior?"

I wanted badly to lie, but I knew he would just ask Kemis once we got home.

"I promise I'll do it tonight."

He sighed with disappointment in his expression, which made me feel bad.

"Dontay—"

"Unc, for real, you don't have to lecture me. I'ma do it. I was just mad at him," I said.

"Let me get this straight—you walked away from him when he was talking to you, and *you* hit *him* in the chest, and *you* were mad at *him*?"

I put my head down, and then looked over at him. "Aight, Unc. I see what you're saying. I'll apologize when we get home," I said.

"Tay, we really enjoyed having you this week. We would love to have you back under different circumstances. You know my door is always open to you. You can call me whenever you want and I'll pick you up, even if you just feel like you need a break, okay?"

"Thanks, Unc. I actually had a good time too, even though you lowkey strict."

"If holding you accountable is strict, then I'll take that label. I know you had a rough start to your week, but it doesn't excuse your behavior with your brother. And I'm going to suggest you start praying and then finding someone to talk to when things aren't going well at school."

"I do! I talk to Day and Clay! And now Paris," I said with a smile.

"I'm thinking an adult with a fully developed brain," he said.

"All y'all say is lame stuff though."

"Sometimes that lame stuff is what will keep you out of trouble!"

15

best made plans

Daveon was handed a bus ticket by Uncle D so that he could visit Jason at college, but not until Kemis made threats to drive to Kentucky overnight to bring Daveon home if they got too wild. With Daveon headed out of town, I asked Paris if she could meet me at the movies on the Friday night of Daveon's departure. I found out she had a little sister that was Clay's age, but he messed up our chances of a double date. He had still been trying to convince me to do something to get kicked out of school, and nearly got himself kicked out, as his principal had been threatening to send him to the district's alternative school for years.

There were many times I wished my little brother had an off switch. I particularly wished I could've turned his mouth off, which was what usually got him and sometimes the rest of us into the most trouble. I wished I could turn him off when he was in trouble with Kemis. He almost always talked back to Kemis and made his predicaments ten times worse. But I definitely wished I could turn him off at school, just to keep him out of trouble for eight hours until he got home.

That week, Clay's timing was bad, and the off switch would have helped tremendously. To his credit, it was his first suspension for the school year, which, being a few months in, was a huge improvement for him. He had gotten into another fight, which probably, in and of itself wouldn't have been a big deal since he had not started it. But he earned himself an extra day of suspension and a detention when he cussed out the security guard that escorted him to the office, and then left the school grounds with his friend Terrell when he was supposed to be gathering his homework and returning to the principal's office.

Uncle D came over to calm Kemis down after the call came from the school, and he ultimately decided to pack Clay an overnight bag and take him home for the night for an "uncle-nephew talk." Daveon and I both asked him what that meant.

"Just make sure you don't ever get one," was all Uncle D would say before leaving with Clay in tow once Clay finally arrived home.

The house being a little quieter that night provided me with the opportunity to talk to Kemis about my plans with Paris that coming Friday. Daveon, Kemis, and I were joined by Kory for dinner, and we discussed Daveon's plans in Kentucky for that weekend. Kemis talked about how Jason's basketball dorm had strict policies about having female visitors, and that Daveon needed to make sure he abided by all the rules. Since we were discussing girls, I figured I would ask about Paris.

"I got a question, and you gotta hear me out."

"Okay what's up," Kemis said. He was in a much better mood than he had been earlier after talking to Clay's principal.

"So, I was gonna see if you would drop me off at the movies Friday," I said, intentionally holding back on the details.

"Aight, with who?"

"With a friend from school."

By now he was raising an eyebrow. "As in, a girlfriend?"

"Naw, it's not like that. I mean, it is a girl. Actually, she goes to the church."

"Oh you mean Paris?" he asked.

"How'd you know her name?" I asked.

"I've seen you talking to her at church, and I asked Pops why y'all always talking. He told me she goes to your school. I've spoken to her dad a few times too. Y'all like together or something?" he asked candidly.

"That's my luh dude!" Daveon was always celebrating when I talked about a girl, knowing I was usually too shy to approach a girl, let alone kiss one as I had done with Paris.

I rolled my eyes. "No! I mean, I want to be. But she's a sophomore, and I don't think she's feeling me like that." At least, I couldn't fathom that she was since I hadn't had a lot of girls express that they liked me.

"I get older girls all the time! You just gotta talk right to her," Daveon said.

Kemis got annoyed with him. "Please don't take Day's advice on girls so I don't have to buss your head in."

The two of them had some rough clashes over girls, but none bigger than the time that Kemis caught him "giving him nephews" live and in action. He threw a slew of punches and screamed at him for not wearing protection, and Uncle D made Daveon volunteer at the church nursery to watch babies. Soon after that, Kemis caught Jason trying for nephews as well, and after nearly knocking Jason out, made the four of us sit down for an extremely long discussion that he called "Condoms, Cucumbers, and Consent."

"You been kissing this girl?" Kemis asked.

I smiled uncomfortably. "K, come on man."

"I'm trying to figure out where your head is."

"We kissed," I admitted.

He kept at it. "How many times?"

I didn't want to tell him the truth that we had kissed nearly every school day since our very first kiss, because I didn't want him to suspect me of doing anything I wasn't doing.

"Mmm, probably about five or six."

Daveon interjected. "My dawg! Now all you gotta do is—"

"Nothing! He does nothing, Day. You haven't kissed her at church, have you?" Kemis asked, looking concerned.

"Only once." I was honest.

"Bro, please don't kiss that girl in front of her daddy. I don't wanna have to fight that man," he said, laughing. "Man, it's crazy that you're in high school now. I still remember picking you up from the bus stop on your first day of kindergarten. And Granny told me to put you in the tub because you peed on yourself," he teased, causing him and Daveon to start laughing.

"Bro, he tried to sit next to me on the bus!" Daveon said with a frown on his face as if still freshly disgusted by it.

"And you wouldn't let me! So, Jason came and sat with me," I recalled.

"You still got off the bus crying though," Kemis said.

"Awwww," Kory said while making a sad face.

"C'mon Kory, I'm a warrior," I said while they all continued laughing at me.

"Look, I'm cool if you wanna go, as long it's not too late. And you know we gotta have that talk before you go." Kemis said.

"K, you the worst, man!" Daveon said.

"What?" Kemis asked.

Day continued, "He gotta have a sex ed lesson just to go to the show? You always think we bout to do something."

"You and Jason—yes! Look," Kemis responded, "before I got saved, I gotta admit that I saw, and did, some crazy stuff at the movies. It's a dark room, and you're there with a girl you like, and it gives room for temptation to come in. And remember you gotta treat her with respect. Don't put your hands anywhere they shouldn't be on her. And if she doesn't want to kiss you, you need to respect her boundaries."

We talked for a while about my upcoming movie night, and I was excited to text Paris about it. But when I did, she told me there was no way her parents would approve unless we were with others, so I asked Tommy if he wanted to go, and then he invited his girl, Mara. Once Paris could reassure her parents she was going with a group, they approved of our outing. I was excited to be headed on my first official date, and even happier that Daveon was leaving for the weekend so I could borrow something from his closet.

16

playdate prep

Daveon seemed excited when he picked me up the next day after school. I had been in a bad mood after an afternoon of having to hold my tongue during another one of Mark Paul's outbursts, and was thankful Daveon had showed up in time to prevent me from having to spend any extra time on campus.

"Sup bro. K asked me to go pick up Clay from Unc's crib since we out this way, but first I need to go to the store real quick."

"So, what do y'all really have planned?" I asked him of his upcoming trip. I knew he couldn't have been telling the truth to Kemis the night before at the table.

He started laughing as he pulled the car into a convenience store parking lot. "It's not like that bro, for real. Jay said he can't get caught out drunk when they've already started practicing, so he gotta keep it low key. We'll probably do a couple parties. We're going to the football game on Saturday, and prolly go to breakfast Sunday before they take me to the bus station."

"I hope I get to go next time."

"K said we probably all gonna go to Jay's first home game, either that or parents' weekend. Unc coming too."

We walked around the store, where Daveon's only purchase was a box of condoms, making me inquire even further about his weekend plans.

"Dude, is this for Kentucky?" I asked when we walked out.

"Nah, bro, this for you for your lil' playdate tomorrow night!" He looked at me with a mischievous grin.

"Day, you serious? We ain't—I'm not gonna need this at the movies!"

"Bro, I'm just saying, it never hurts to be prepared. I mean, you said she has a car. What if y'all decide to leave the show?" he asked. I had not even considered that a possibility, but Daveon was the type to look for all the possibilities when it came to girls.

"Nah dude. The way she talk about her daddy, he'll probably be conducting surveillance on the parking lot."

"Just always keep two in your wallet. You never know if you'll be in a situation. And here, take this," he said while handing me a twenty-dollar bill.

"Day, she already knows I don't have money like that."

"Bro, yo' money situation don't matter if you make her feel special. Make sure she knows you into her. Tell her how good she looks and act like you can't get enough of her. Let me find out lil' bro out here sneaking girls to the back room at church to kiss." We both started laughing. "Bro, if Unc find out about y'all kissing at church you know he would lose his shit on yo' ass!"

"Dead ass, but he don't need to know about all that," I said.

Uncle D and Auntie Robin greeted us with hugs when we arrived to retrieve Clay after his first day of suspension. Daveon was talking to them in the foyer near the front door while I walked into the kitchen to find Clay seated at the table with his cheeks resting in his fists and a scowl on his face. When we were leaving out, Uncle D handed Clay a dictionary and started giving him instructions, causing Clay to look even more annoyed.

"Now, I highlighted the page numbers you need to copy," he said as he opened it up. Clay, with folded lips and crumpled eyebrows, was surprisingly not saying anything. Uncle D continued. "You're going to give me this on Sunday at church, you understand?"

"Yes," Clay said, looking defeated.

Uncle D turned toward me. "Kemis tells me you're going on a date with Paris tomorrow, huh?"

I hated that they talked so much. I knew they were extremely close, but I didn't always like the amount of information they exchanged.

"We just hanging out at the movies, Unc. It's not a big deal. Y'all overreacting."

He asked, "Who's overreacting? I just asked a question!"

I replied, "I'm just saying, Kemis out here talking about all kinds of stuff and Day over here buying me con—never mind. We just hanging out."

I could tell by that fact that Auntie Robin's mouth was wide open she knew what I was saying before I caught myself. Daveon punched me in my shoulder for not keeping quiet.

"Wayyyyyyminute Day," Uncle D said. His eyes were panicked as he glared at my older brother. "You brought this boy condoms for a trip to the movies with a Christian young lady?"

Uncle D stood in distress, and Daveon was annoyed that I had accidentally outed him.

Daveon tried to reason with him. "Unc it's not like that. I'm just telling him to always be prepared. Some of these girls just be throwing it, and I'm just saying if you being forced to catch something, catch it with your glove on and not your bare hand!"

By now Auntie Robin had put her hands up over her face, with her jaw open even wider. Clay and I were laughing, and Uncle D looked mortified. "We are long overdue for another purity discussion at youth church I see."

Daveon responded, "Unc, you know it's too late for me. I've been impure like my whole life."

Uncle D sighed and looked as though he was about to hold some sort of deliverance service. I just wanted out the door without a sex talk.

"Listen, Tay. I have known Paris for quite some time now. Her parents are really good friends of ours, and they are good people, and—just…don't…just say no. Do *not* listen to Day. Enjoy the movies, enjoy each other's company, not each other's bodies. You don't want to travel down that road before it's time. God desires purity for all of his sons and daughters. And purity is not catching it with a glove. Purity is presenting our bodies as a sacrifice to him, to be pleasing to him…Y'all get out of here and be good. Day, I'm stopping by when you get back, son. We're gonna go to breakfast and talk."

They gave us all hugs as we walked out. Uncle D put his arm around Clay and slowly walked him out as he was telling him something we couldn't hear. Then he told him to remember what they had talked about. Uncle D, Auntie Robin, Caleb, and Sophie all stood outside and waved as we drove off.

"Bro, how was it?" Daveon asked Clay once we pulled away.

"How was what?" Clay asked.

"Your time wit' Unc," Daveon followed.

"It started off kinda rough, and I cussed his ass out!" Clay said from the backseat, while Daveon and I glanced at each other. His mouth was just as wide open as mine.

"Wait, you cussed who out?" Daveon asked, seeking clarification.

"Unc!" Clay said. He sounded as though he didn't want to discuss it, but Daveon and I looked at each other again in complete disbelief and needed more answers.

"Bro, why would you cuss out Unc?" I asked, annoyed at the possibility that he would even go there with someone we considered our family.

"Man, when we got in the car, he started telling me all this stuff he was about to make me do. He said I gotta write a three-page apology letter and do this stupid dictionary shit before he would let me play basketball out back. I was hot, so I started cussing him out in the car," he said.

"Sooooo what did he say?" I asked, somewhat shocked that Uncle D hadn't smacked him.

I couldn't imagine cussing out Uncle D. I had gained a lot of respect for him over the years, and he had done so much to support us.

"Y'all ever had a 'uncle-nephew talk'?" Clay asked.

"Naw bro, he said make sure we don't have one. What he say when y'all talked?" Daveon asked.

"He ain't say shit...'til we got home and he beat my ass," Clay grumbled.

We roared in laughter so hard that Daveon almost wrecked the car. He pulled into the gas station so the three of us could grab a fountain drink before we headed home, and we laughed and cracked jokes on Clay the rest of the ride.

"Bro, I can't wait to tell Jason," Daveon said as he headed into the house. "That's what yo' little bad ass get!"

What Clay didn't tell us until we got home was that Uncle D had also taken him shopping and let him pick out a pair of sneakers, clothes, and a gift card for the video game store. Uncle D put it all in his office and told Clay if he stayed out of trouble for two months, he would get it all. Clay told us he was done getting in trouble, but Daveon had doubts.

"Two months? You'll never see that stuff with yo' mouth. I hope he can get his money back!" Daveon said.

17

back to beginning

"**M**orning." Kemis greeted me with a raspy voice as he pulled himself up from the couch. I hardly looked in his direction when I walked by him toward the kitchen to grab a bowl of cereal. It was our first time speaking after our encounter the night before when he had caught me driving his truck.

"Sup," I said dryly as I walked by.

He got up and followed me into the kitchen, seeming as though he had something he wanted to say, while I wasn't in the mood for talking. He stood with his back against the sink with his arms folded as he stared at the floor, and then back up at me.

"Tay, look...Day told me what happened. He was up a couple of hours ago, and...look. I'm not keeping your phone. Day should have called me and not you, and I'm hot with him. But you know you can't just take my truck like that, especially if you know he's been acting up. And I barely like *him* driving at night in this neighborhood, so it freaked me out to see that you had done it. And you know I get nervous when y'all out late—we just had this discussion a couple weeks ago when you missed curfew going out with Paris. But, when Day told me what happened, I felt bad for coming at you the way I did. I had a rough night last night…I was stressed out, and I took some of that out on you. I'm sorry, aight?"

I poured milk into my cereal bowl after glancing at him while he wiggled his toes with his fingers fumbling around inside his pockets. The apology felt almost as offensive as what he did, since he often acted on his quick temper and followed up with an awkward apology and promise to do better.

"It's all good," I said before stuffing a spoonful of cereal in my mouth. I was still mad at him but had no desire to discuss it any further.

He used the time to tell me about the plans he and Uncle D had made for us to spend the weekend at Uncle D's house after Daveon's basketball game that night. Apparently, Uncle D told him to send us over so he could talk with us about our behavior. The fact that he would have all weekend to lecture me did not stop Uncle D from coming all the way out to pick me up that morning just to drive me to school, which meant I would have to endure a lecture during my morning ride, which normally consisted of me mentally preparing for the school day.

I didn't know a monologue about choices could last for that long, and I was disappointed that he did not run out of content to discuss to allow me at least a few moments of silence. Despite having to endure his talking for over thirty minutes, he reminded me that we would be discussing it more that night after Daveon's game. I knew then it would be an awful weekend.

18

change of plans

Daveon picked me up from school that day in a rush to get home, knowing we had to eat dinner and pack our things before heading to his basketball game. Kemis had already told us that after Kory arrived at the house, they would drop us off at the game where Uncle D would meet us.

But the scene Daveon and I stumbled across when we reached the parking lot in front of our townhouse was completely unexpected. In the grassy area in front of the row of townhouses lay all of our belongings. Everything from the entire townhouse, from each bedroom, bathroom, closet, and even the basement, was strewn about with no order, thrown into random piles of unorganized madness. There were mounds of clothing and shoes underneath and on top of couches, lopsided tables, torn apart lamps, and chairs that had been flipped over with wheels in the air, looked upon by a few neighbors who stood around on their front stoops talking and surveying the scene for clues regarding what would happen next. Clay had beat us home, and we found him texting on his phone while sitting on top of a mattress that was partially rested on the legs of a broken end table.

"Bro, what the fuck happened?" Daveon asked him when we scrambled out of the car, looking around in disbelief.

"Bro, when I got here these dudes was emptying the last of the stuff, and they changed the locks. I had to go pee behind the dumpster! They said they were hired to move the stuff out but that's all they would say," Clay said, seeming just as confused and panicked as Daveon and me.

"Where K at?" Daveon asked, looking frustrated while thumbing through a trash bag filled with kitchen items.

"He ain't answering bro, I don't—there he is!" Clay said. He looked over at Kemis' truck that had just pulled into the parking lot.

The three of us turned to look at him and demanded answers with our body language.

"Look y'all, I know this is jacked up! They told me I had 'til five, and Kory—"

"Wait K, you ain't been paying rent?" Daveon asked, always cutting to the chase.

"It's complicated. But I was going to give them the money. Look, Kory was supposed to be here, and she ain't been answering the phone. Bro, I'ma get this fixed aight? I'm about to go to the leasing office. Day, call Kyle for me while I go talk to them, and please don't call Pops," Kemis begged before storming off into the direction of the leasing office.

Despite his request, I texted Uncle D anyway, feeling less confident than Kemis did in his ability to handle the situation. Uncle D arrived around the same time Kemis returned, and immediately began to ask Kemis all the questions we hadn't gotten a chance to ask.

"Son, when's the last time you paid rent?" Uncle D asked.

"Pops, it's a long story, I—"

"I got nothing but time Kemis. I called one of the members who owns a moving company. He's on his way with his truck and he'll help get this stuff off the ground. But how far behind are you?"

"Pops, um, Kory was gonna pay it for me today—it's about four months behind. I asked them to—"

"Four months? Kemis, why wouldn't you call me? That's insane! I've told you over and over again you can call me!" Uncle D said.

"Pops, I know…" Kemis turned his head for a moment and lowered his voice, seeming ashamed that he had to hash this out in front of all of us. "Look, you just gave me a lot of money last month, and I didn't want to ask for more."

"What happened to the money? That could have covered a few months in rent and gotten you caught up," Uncle D asked.

Kemis sighed again. "I—Kory was putting all this money down for wedding vendors, and I was feeling bad because she was paying for everything, and I couldn't bring myself to tell her how broke I was….so I used the money to put a deposit down for some of the vendors," he admitted.

"Nigga you paid for a wedding over having somewhere for us to live?" Clay asked.

"Clay! language!" Uncle D said with a fierce glare.

"No, Clay. I spent a lot of money the past few months because, well, Jason had a run-in with your dad, and I went ahead and paid him that money so he would leave us alone," Kemis said. He looked frustrated with all the questions coming his way.

Clay's dad had never been a part of our lives, at least I thought he hadn't. I learned otherwise after Clay, Daveon, and Jason were involved in a shooting that left Clay's former friend partially paralyzed. We hadn't known until then that his dad was living above a dumpster where my brothers, and later I, hid the gun that was used during the incident. He was someone that Kemis had refused to even talk about until recently, largely because he chronically abused Ma and Kemis when Kemis was a little kid, usually over missing drug money.

Kemis finally told us that he forced Clay's dad out of Granny's house at gunpoint when Kemis was only ten years old, after growing tired of he and Ma suffering from constant abuse. To his shock, when Clay's dad left, Ma packed her bags and left with him, unexpectedly leaving the rest of us behind with Granny for good, other than her occasional stop-ins. Clay's dad remained bitter, not that he had to leave behind Clay, a newborn at the time, but that he had hidden a sum of cash in the house that he couldn't retrieve, and always accused Kemis of owing him money after that.

"You shouldn'ta gave that nigga shit!" Clay said with a sour tone. He often expressed his bitterness with the man who had managed to cause so much drama in our home without even being present. Clay and Daveon had developed plans to "pay him a visit," but those plans were interrupted when Kemis found out and pounded them both until Jason peeled him off.

"Clay Lands! If I have to say anything else to you about your mouth!" Uncle D said with his voice getting louder. "And Kemis, I told you not to give that man a dime! What could he possibly tell the police?"

"Pops…there's some stuff they finally told me that we haven't told you yet. But we think he might've seen something when Clay's boy…it's a long story…" Kemis said.

"Why—Where were you and Kory last night? The boys told me you were out late. You couldn't have gotten this resolved then?" Uncle D asked.

Kemis sighed a long heavy sigh and took a look down the sidewalk before looking up at Uncle D.

"Last night, I was driving Kory's car—we had left dinner. The police pulled me over and ran my name, and I had an active warrant for this expired plate ticket that I had got—"

"Kemis, you didn't tell me about that either! Son, I know there's a lot on your plate, but this is not a stable environment for any of you, but especially not your younger brothers!" Uncle D said. He seemed to lose more patience each time Kemis spoke, as did Daveon and Clay.

"I know, I know. I got pulled over about six months ago. I hadn't paid the ticket, and then they sent me a court date. I showed up to court and had to pay a fine and court costs…but I never paid it, so they put a warrant out and arrested me on it last night. Kory had to bail me out and pay all my fines. And then I came clean and told her everything last night. She was supposed to meet me at the leasing office at three to get us caught up, but she never came. I went out to run a few errands and came back to this. She hasn't answered my calls or anything. I think last night spooked her and she breaking up with—"

Kemis abruptly looked down at his phone, and subsequently answered a call from Kory's sister, and we could tell something was happening by the way he anxiously paced, and by the portions of the conversation we could decipher.

"Wait...what? What do you mean?...Well, where is she? Oh my God. I told her to never stop there for gas. Okay, where'd they take her. No, I'm on the way!"

He got off the phone with a desperate look in his face, and frantically patted his pockets for his keys.

"K, what's up?" Daveon asked.

"Kory got shot, bro," Kemis said. "She was robbed at the gas station by your school...She's at the hospital!"

My heart and brain went into overdrive with his announcement. I took a seat on the edge of the walkway and threw my head down between my knees.

"Go ahead to Kory," Uncle D instructed Kemis. "We'll get this taken care of and then the boys are coming home with me. Call me when you get there."

We were exhausted by the time we found ourselves on Uncle D's couch hours later, having just finished eating the pizza he had ordered while trying to get in touch with Kemis. Daveon was repeatedly calling Jason and Kyle, Kemis' best friend, to see if either of them had heard anything when Uncle D came into the family room to check on us.

"K not answering any of my phone calls. Have you talked to him, Unc?" Daveon was growing more and more anxious with each unanswered call and text.

Uncle D sighed. "I did talk to him. He's still there with Kory's parents and her sister and Kyle. Pastor James just left. Kory hasn't woken up yet and they said it was too risky to remove the bullet. She's got some swelling in some bad places. That's the only update they have. No one has been allowed to see her and Kemis said he's not leaving."

"Unc, I wanna go to the hospital!" Daveon said.

"I know you do, but I feel like it would stress your brother out more because he would have to worry about you too. Daveon, he's not doing well right now…that's why he didn't text you back. Listen, y'all don't have to go to bed—maybe just go downstairs and lie down on the couches. Take off your coats and shoes—you were already gonna be here the whole weekend, and that's definitely not changing now. And what if I promise that as soon as I hear something I'll come get you, even if I have to wake you up?"

We weren't convinced that going to sleep was a good idea, but found ourselves so exhausted from the day's events that sleep overtook us anyway. But shortly after we had all finally dozed off in the basement, Uncle D and Auntie Robin came down the steps crying to tell us that Kory didn't make it. The words punched me right in my throat, and a sharp pain hit my entire head. I couldn't believe it was happening again.

We knew countless people that had succumbed to gunshot wounds, but the death that impacted us the greatest was Granny's. She was taken away with heart failure, and the sting from her passing had hardly left us. We had returned to full functionality, but only on the outside. On the inside we were still slowly mending and trying to understand how to rebuild our lives. We had accepted Kory as an integral part of that rebuilding. It had just started to feel like we had a sense of direction, with actual goals, and we knew she would help us reach them. I couldn't imagine Kemis being home alone to deal with everything by himself.

Daveon was apparently thinking the same as me. "Where's K?"

"Kyle is taking him back to his place for the night. Don't worry about calling Jason; I'll go ahead and call him."

The three of us struggled to sleep as we tried to process the news, and I used the time awake to convince Daveon not to sneak out. He eventually decided against it, and we spent the night flipping channels in between periodically dozing off and wondering about the well-being of our oldest brother, the rest of Kory's family, and the fact that we had nowhere to live once the weekend was over.

19

at least we're not homeless anymore

What was supposed to be one weekend at Uncle D's house turned into nine days, which found us occupied with school, trips to storage to remove more of our things, and briefly hanging out with Jason, who had come into town for Kory's funeral.

The day before Jason was scheduled to leave, Kemis called another family meeting. We had all been crashing at Uncle D's house except for Kemis, who was only periodically meeting us there. Uncle D and the others had left to go to church, leaving the five of us to meet in the kitchen while they were away. It was our first time since our eviction spending more than a couple of hours with Kemis, other than the day of Kory's funeral.

"Obviously everything has changed since our last family meeting. The church and Pops are helping me through a lot of things, so the last thing I want is for y'all to worry about me.

"But we've been talking, and we think it's best if the three of you live here for a while. So, we're going to request that they have temporary guardianship over the three of you, for at least the next six months, but maybe longer," Kemis announced softly. His low tone and weak voice made it clear he was not feeling like himself.

Although I didn't expect him to come and tell us he had found somewhere for us to stay, I wasn't expecting the news of a changed guardianship either. Neither was Daveon, who immediately became upset and waited not even a millisecond to speak up. "Bro, you are not leaving us in fucking west county wit' Unc!"

"Day, not now," Kemis said.

"What you mean not now? You just dropping on us that you're leaving us here to stay? You our brother—"

"Day I'm still your brother."

"Then why you leaving us here away from school and all my friends! You know Unc strict as hell! You on some bullshit!" Daveon said.

"Right, bro! Plus you said we ain't have to worry about no moves for a while," Clay said.

"Clay, you knew we had to move, bro! We don't have anywhere to live!" I reminded him.

Kemis appeared as though he had not had a decent meal in over a week. His frame was thinner and frail, like he would break a bone if he cried too hard. His fragile appearance made me wish Daveon and Clay had just kept quiet. But I understood that the idea of Kemis dropping us off and Jason heading back to school was unsettling.

"We not some little kids! You being dramatic!" Daveon was practically yelling.

"I *am* being dramatic Day!" Kemis limped up from his seat and started yelling too. He expressed a different sort of anger than we had seen. It was more like despair. His voice cracked and his eyes welled up, and he sniffled in between sentences. It seemed like we were talking to a different person. "The love of my life is gone. The girl who I was going to share my life with and have my kids with and walk down the aisle with and be with forever is gone, bro! I can't have y'all running around that same neighborhood that took her. And, well…"

He turned from us and began to speak a little softer, "Technically we don't live in that neighborhood anymore anyway. The property manager would not give me more time and would not let me sign another lease…Pops met me over there and offered all the back rent in cash, and a check that covered the next six months, and they wouldn't take it. And it's hard to get someone else to rent to you once they know you been kicked out. We pretty much homeless …"

The word homeless blew through the walls of my brain, bouncing around with a loud echo like an indoor racquetball court. Even though I had already known it, it sounded so much worse coming from him.

Kemis seemed to know how badly it sounded too and softened his tone as he continued speaking. "I know you're not little kids, but you've never really had any stability, and you need some! That neighborhood is turning to shit anyway, and I don't wanna see anyone else I love get taken out by it. We lost Granny in that house, we all have friends or know people that got shot in that neighborhood…and now Kory is…." he couldn't finish his sentence and continued sniffling and wiping his tears before continuing. He retook his seat with his head in his hands.

"I can't even keep a place for y'all to live! I'm not fit to parent y'all right now, Day. I can't keep track of where you are or check homework or read emails from teachers or cook or help make sure your car is running. I can't give you anything you need. And Jason already offered to drop out of school and get a job and move back so he could help, but that can't happen—Jay gotta be at school.

"You all gotta focus on school and let me get my shit together. They offered to help, and we need help. They've been paying your insurance and car note and buying your clothes and school supplies for years—I just didn't really tell you the extent of it. Almost everything you guys have needed they have taken care of. Just about every time I was able to buy you guys something, it was because of them. And you know they love all of you."

"This is bullshit, K," Daveon responded dryly. "Yo, why you ain't tell us all this shit! Got us thinking you got enough for rent and bills! I coulda quit basketball and took more hours, bro! You so busy trying to impress her and you ain't even handle business! So now we gotta move in here!"

"Day, chill man," Jason said calmly. "We all make mistakes, bro. Besides, it's just temporary. Let K get back on his feet and then he can find a new spot. And it ain't like y'all getting dropped off in some random spot. This is our family. We've spent hella time here—weeks, weekends, holidays! You can do this, bro…Tay, you straight?" Jason asked.

I looked up from staring at the floor. "Yeah," I mumbled softly. I didn't really feel okay, but I didn't want to do or say anything that added to an already tense atmosphere.

"Clay? You aight?" Jason asked.

"Do it matter?" Clay asked, sounding defeated.

Jason was able to get Daveon and Clay to settle down, and I was thankful that Jason ended up staying an extra day, even though Kemis told him to leave since it was peak basketball season. Jason knew we needed him, and he wanted to help us transition to our new home. He moved more of our things into Uncle D's house while we were at school that Monday, and Uncle D gave him money to buy what we needed to help us feel more at home.

Jason took the three of us out to eat before he left to remind us to be supportive of Kemis and to stay out trouble. He told us after basketball season he could come see us more.

"…And don't act up at Unc's house y'all. He's always been like a dad to us. Make sure y'all listen and be respectful," he said, but he emphatically looked directly at Clay when he said the last part.

"I'ma be good, Jay," Clay said, sounding as though he was annoyed with being accused of bad behavior.

"Day?" Jason looked over at Daveon.

"I'll do my usual!" Daveon said with a smile.

"Your usual might get your head cracked open at Unc's house!"

I felt abandoned with Jason's departure; it stung even more than when he had initially left for college. Meanwhile, Uncle D went from having a family of four to a family of seven and a half, as Kemis still came by occasionally, and infrequently spent the night. While I wasn't sad about our living predicament, I was sad that we had lost Kory, and equally sad that with the loss of Kory, it seemed we had lost Kemis too. He hardly talked or ate when he came around, and often burst into tears unexpectedly. He had become a shell of who he once was, and I sadly agreed that he had made the right choice for us.

20

new roof, new rules

The day after Jason left, Uncle D and Auntie Robin decided we needed to have a discussion about house rules, and I guessed that it was because they knew all the trouble my brothers were capable of getting into. None of us had any rules we wanted to contribute, but they wouldn't accept our silence. The five of us sat at the kitchen table while my brothers and me quietly watched Uncle D with his pen and paper.

"Since you don't want to say anything, tell me what your rules are normally, and we'll see which ones we should adopt," he said. "Put the phone down, Day. She can wait until we're done!"

Daveon plopped his phone on the table and rolled his eyes, just as Clay finally contributed to the discussion.

"Do dumb, boring homework before going to see my friends even though I need a break from school after school and I ain't even got no friends over here but whatever," Clay said.

"Seems like you feel a certain way, but I think that we'll keep that one for now, and revise it as needed since you've had trouble turning in homework. What else?" Uncle D asked.

"No girls inside without permission," I muttered.

Uncle D and Auntie Robin both smiled. "I definitely like that one," Uncle D said as he started writing it down, prompting Daveon to roll his eyes again. "Okay, those are reasonable. Any more?" he asked.

"No sex without a condom," Daveon offered, prompting a snicker from Clay and me.

"Wait, that's one of the rules?" Uncle D asked.

"It is, and I do follow it," Daveon said with a smirk.

"I mean, if we're following number two, I guarantee we're not getting to number three. So, let's just remember I expect you to treat all young ladies like your sisters in Christ. In this house, we'll flee fornication."

"What about in other houses?" Daveon knew he was being smart with his question.

"Glad you asked. Rule number four, I want to know where you are at all times. So, ask before you go to other houses and be prepared to answer questions about who's there," Uncle D said as he continued writing.

Daveon put his forehead in his palm. We hadn't been used to that. When the weather was nice and we hung out at the basketball court or outside on the front porch, a lot of times that was followed up with a walk to one of our friends' houses to hang out or to play video games. We would try to be good about texting Kemis where we were, but not always. And Daveon would check in casually, but usually made multiple stops as he traveled between the destinations where he said he would be.

"Daveon, you seem like you don't like that one," Auntie Robin said, while Uncle D looked up from his writing.

"I'm sixteen, almost seventeen, why y'all gotta treat me like I'm in elementary school?" Daveon asked.

"I don't think that wanting to know where you are is treating you like you're in elementary school," Uncle D said.

"So are all these rules just to keep us from smashing?" Daveon asked.

Uncle D sighed. "Do you know what the Bible says about smashing, Daveon?"

"Oh my God," Daveon groaned.

"Do you know what the Bible says about using the Lord's name in vain?"

"You've told us like a thousand times, Unc," Daveon grumbled.

"Good, then don't make me repeat it again. And I don't want you boys in your rooms on your phones all night. So when it's time to go to bed, I expect the phones to be down. And I don't wanna catch anything crazy on these phones!"

Daveon sighed, growing more impatient with the rules. "So what time is curfew?" he asked.

"Um, do we need to set a curfew for every day? I expect you straight home after school, well, other than practice and games, or if you have to work. Otherwise, you need to come home and do homework. Then, if you want to head out after that, let me know and we'll discuss. On the weekends, if you're going to hang out with your friends, I think nine is a good time to be home." Uncle D said.

Daveon's mouth grew wide. "Clay don't even come home by nine!" Daveon said.

Uncle D looked disturbed. "Clay? Well, Clay, you do not have a nine o'clock curfew, since I generally expect you in this house, unless you've asked permission to go out. Even if it's to the sidewalk to hang out with friends," he said, looking directly at me. "Look, I'm not trying to make you guys feel like you're on probation. I'm open to a ten o'clock curfew. But I do need to know where you are. If you do what you're supposed to do, and be where we agreed you would be, we won't have any problems. I have to know what's going on though. I made a commitment to be responsible for you, and I take it seriously. Which brings me to another rule: Do not lie to me." He looked at all of us when he said it.

"We've all had a good relationship, and I trust the three of you a lot. Don't disappoint me and break that trust. So, if you tell me you're going skating, I don't expect to find you at the bowling alley, and vice versa. Let's agree to be honest."

Uncle D started writing again.

"Okay, I think that's it, other than chores. We emphasize getting our chores done before we're playing on our phones and devices and watching television. And I do take phones," he said.

"We know," I said, rolling my eyes.

He chuckled. "Well, just a reminder. Not that I want to, because I don't. Anything else we should discuss? Oh yeah, two quick things. Let's talk about driving. Dontay Lands…"

"Come on Unc, you don't have to—"

"Naw, I have to. I want it to be unequivocally clear that you are not to drive any vehicles in that garage. Our keys are left out all of the time, and if you ever get behind the wheel, there better be someone needing a ride to the hospital. I can't even believe I have to go over this," Uncle D said.

"You don't!" I said.

"Apparently I do. Do you both understand?" he asked, looking at Clay and me.

"Yes," we uttered in unison.

"Good. And Daveon, I got an email recently about a red light camera ticket you received a few weeks ago. You out here running through traffic signals?"

Daveon's car originally belonged to Granny, but after she died, Jason had driven it and then Daveon. When Kemis couldn't make the payments, Uncle D ended up taking over the note and transferring the title and registration to his name, along with paying the insurance, but still let Jason and Daveon keep it.

"Unc, that wasn't me!" Daveon said.

"So you letting someone else drive?"

"Naw, Unc! I, uh…I don't remember running no red light!"

"Well, there was a picture attached and it was definitely your car and your plate. You will be paying for the ticket with your own money. And if you get another one, we'll be having a talk about your driving privileges. You know I expect you to drive responsibly, especially as a young black man. I don't need you giving police officers a reason to come after you! Hmmm…One last thing, disrespect of adults is not tolerated in this house," Uncle D said while looking directly at Clay.

"Why you looking at me?" Clay asked.

"Well, you've had the most problems in this area. I expect those issues to be left outside of this house, and expect them not to show up at school, church, or here at home. Also fellas, alcohol and drugs are absolutely not allowed. Are we clear?" He looked at all of us but focused in on Daveon, likely due to his night out with his friend Tray weeks before. "And with that, I think we've done enough rules."

"We finally agree," Daveon mumbled.

Daveon's whole hustle was either about to end, intensify, or he was about to be in constant trouble. I highly doubted my brothers would follow the rules, but didn't realize at the time that I would have struggles of my own.

21

everything is fine…ish

The Monday after our rules discussion, Uncle D picked Clay and me up from school early, along with having Daveon come home early in order to meet with a social worker at the house. She said her name was Ms. Dana, and she wanted to talk to us in order to make sure the temporary guardianship was agreeable and to see if she should sign off on the six-month guardianship plan. She was a younger black lady who I enjoyed speaking with.

I sat alone with her in Uncle D's office where she asked questions about school, friends, and my relationships with my brothers and with Uncle D, Auntie Robin, Caleb and Sophie. She asked me if I was happy, and I told her I was happy with everything except for school.

"You go to such a great school, and not a lot of people are able to test into the school and get a full scholarship. Why don't you like it?"

I shared with her a lot of the experiences I had gone through before posing a question. "Since Uncle D technically has custody of us now, can't he take me out of the school if he wants?"

"Actually yes. They have the legal authority to make education, housing, and health-related decisions for you three with the guardianship plan. So, if you are that dissatisfied, ask your uncle. The public school district out here is very good and pretty diverse. I bet you would enjoy it!

Otherwise, it sounds like you and your brothers are thriving here, and they are taking good care of you. Do you have any concerns before I recommend that the judge sign off on the guardianship?"

"No. They're cool. Strict, but cool," I said.

"Well, from what I hear, I believe they truly love all three of you. Plus, the three of you seem to be doing great!"

She was mostly right, other than the fact that Clay's promises to Jason that he would behave himself were empty. He started making bad choices and mimicking behavior patterns he had picked up after Granny died, which was a huge shift considering that he had largely stayed out of trouble since his uncle-nephew talk. Uncle D began to receive reports that Clay was falling asleep in class and using profanity after getting caught, in addition to skipping classes to hang out with his boys and at times refusing to put his cell phone away. After receiving a few bad weekly progress reports, Uncle D had an unpleasant surprise for Clay one morning before school.

"Clay, you're spending the day with me today," he said as Clay was in the kitchen eating breakfast, jolted to excitement about a day out of school.

"Sweet! Where we going? Can we go to lunch at the restaurant by the mall like we did that one time?" Clay asked as though his brain had finally woken up.

"Oh no. They said I can have lunch in the cafeteria today, because I'm coming to school with you! To every single class and lunch. It's going to be a good time!"

Daveon spit out his orange juice and roared in laughter, while Clay froze in the middle of chewing.

"This cap, right?" he asked in a much softer tone.

"If that means I'm joking or something, I'm not playing. I'm in shock of some of the things your teachers say you do at school. I was about to put you on punishment and take your phone, but instead I decided I wanna see it for myself."

I put my head down and cringed, feeling a little bad for Clay. There was no way Clay would carry on as usual in front of Uncle D.

"Man...I ain't doing this," Clay said, leaning back in his seat.

"That's how you want to start your day, by telling me what you aren't gonna do?" The look on Uncle D's face told everyone in the room that Clay needed to backtrack his words, and I almost did it for him. "And you better keep them pants up above your waist...I've already talked to y'all about running around here with your behinds out," Uncle D said.

"Bro, I'm so glad I'm not you today," Daveon said laughing as he gathered his things to leave.

Clay rode with Uncle D to drop me off at school and looked as though he was considering ways to escape as we drove. As I was getting out of the car, Uncle D asked Clay if he wanted to sit up front, but Clay remained in the back, grumbling that he wasn't interested in sitting next to him in the car if he had to sit next to him all day at school.

22

i hate it here

I couldn't stay too amused with Clay's situation, since that same day I found myself involved in my own drama after my Advanced Math teacher told me to stay behind class to review results from a recent test. She asked me a few questions that were on the test, even going so far as writing a problem on the board, making it clear she was testing my knowledge of the subject. Despite accurately answering every single one of her questions and quickly solving the problem on the board, she still behaved as though something was wrong.

"You know Dontay, I find it interesting that you sat in class right next to Jack, and you had the same answers as him. You and him got the same score."

"What are you trying to say?" I asked, knowing exactly what she was trying to say. I was offended that she thought I had cheated off a boy who hadn't had one right answer in class since school had started.

"Well, I don't know how you got into this class—it's for our most advanced students. I'm sure they didn't teach this at your old school, and…well, it just seems like a strange coincidence, that's all. And you hardly pay any attention in class!"

I realized then that she had never taken the time to have a private conversation with me until she accused me of cheating. If she had, she would've known that since I was little, I could calculate most equations in my brain within seconds of seeing them. My old math teacher began sending me to virtual math classes, stating I was too advanced for anything she could offer.

I longed for her while I restrained my tongue from calling my new math teacher a ton of bad names, knowing Uncle D would handle that way worse than Kemis would. I considered cussing her out anyway and accepting my suspension, the way my brothers would have done. I thought about Jason, wondering what he would do; but he would've never been in a predicament like the ones I had found myself in. His teachers always loved him. He was a tall, handsome basketball star that was treated like high school royalty everywhere he went. Even if he had cheated, his teachers probably wouldn't have even cared.

"Pay attention for what? You don't say anything I don't already know! I finished most of the curriculum the first couple weeks of school. This was the easiest math quiz I've ever had," I said, trying to insult her. "If you want to give me another test, I'll take it. I don't need to cheat off the dumbest dude in the class. I'm out."

I grabbed my backpack and stormed into the hallway. It was all I could do to keep from going off and getting in trouble again. I spent the day fuming over the accusations. I asked my next teacher for a pass to the guidance counselor's office, and texted Tommy and Marco and requested they do the same.

"Hey Mr. Phillips. The three of us need mediation, but I think we need to try to work it out ourselves first," I said to one of the counselors after Marco and Tommy arrived. It was a trick I had learned from Paris that only a few knew about as a convenient way to skip class and have privacy without getting into trouble.

"I'm glad the three of you stopped in. You all can use CR room number three," he stated while directing us to the room. "There is a ten-step manual in the room. Once you have gone through the steps, if you feel like you need a neutral party to come and help, just push the button and it will send me an alert, okay boys?" Mr. Phillips asked. I couldn't tell if he knew we were using the space to skip class, but he didn't seem to care.

"Yes, sir. Thank you, Mr. Phillips," Marco said as he closed the door to the room. "Bro, I'm glad you texted. I ain't wanna sit through that boring-ass biology class today."

The three of us settled around a table inside the small room and nestled comfortably into the wide, upholstered chairs just as we heard a quick knock on the door, followed by an older lady cracking it open. She wore a thick wig and glasses, adorned in clothing that looked like she could be married to Mr. Rogers from the old children's shows.

"Before you boys get started, I just wanted to drop in with a refreshments tray! Good luck!" she said as she placed a large, wooden tray of snacks and cold drinks in front of us.

"Damn, bro. We need to start beefing at least once a week!" Tommy joked.

"Facts," I said. "But look, bro. My math teacher thinks I cheated and I didn't."

"Ay, I can call my cousin up here to get her tires," Tommy said.

"No, T! There's a zero-tolerance policy for cheating. It's supposed to be grounds for removal from the school," Marco said.

"They know the gangster nerd ain't cheat on no test. I got accused of cheating once—and I actually cheated. So, that Friday they called me in for a surprise quiz to the principal's office. Something told me they would so I studied real hard and got an A and then they dropped that shit. I think somebody snitched on me. She just think it's you 'cause you black," Tommy said.

"Wait, who's your teacher?" Marco asked.

"Ms. Seiving!" I said.

"Yeah, everybody say she racist for real for real. I heard she once changed a black girl's grade just to make sure she ain't graduate at the top of the class!" Marco said.

"See what I mean? I don't know how y'all can take this place! What should I do?" I asked.

"I'm 'bout to text my cousin," Tommy said.

"Naw, T. You gotta chill. Tay, just ask yo' uncle to let you outta school. You said the social worker said he could do it! Just tell him what happened! If that happened to me my parents would be hot!" Marco said before he snatched open a bag of chips, tilted his head backward, and dispensed the chips directly into his mouth from the bag, crunching so loudly I could barely hear Tommy's response that followed.

"He prolly right. But let's raise our voice a little bit and act like we having trouble so we can skip our next class too," Tommy said. The three of us laughed and hung out until the final bell rang. I was glad we got to hang out and talk, but eager for pickup so that I could approach Uncle D about what Ms. Dana told me and use the suggestions I had received from my friends.

"I need to talk to you," I told him before I was even fully in my seat when he picked me up from school.

"Wow! Hello to you too. Should we go have some coffee? It seems serious," he said.

"I don't need all that. I just want you to listen and not just say Bible stuff."

"I'm listening," he said as he pulled out of the parking lot.

"Ms. Dana said you get to make all the decisions now. And I want you to decide to take me out of this school, Unc. I'm tired of this place!"

He sighed and pulled into a nearby grocery store parking lot before parking and looking at me.

"That's a complicated request, Dontay. I'm a little confused though. You seemed much happier after you started hanging out with Paris and Tommy and Marco. Your grades for the first two quarters were impeccable. You found clubs to get involved with. What's going on?" he asked.

I was already disappointed with his response and felt as though he would treat my inquiry the same way Kemis had.

"Unc, did you have black teachers growing up?" I asked.

"A lot of them…I told you I grew up in the inner city."

"Okay, and I'm used to having a lot of black teachers too. And guidance counselors. They're just…the atmosphere…not necessarily the teachers; it was just different. Will you please just send me back to school with Day? You won't even have to drive me like you do now! On the days he has practice, I'll just go with him and do my homework at the gym. His coach will allow it—we used to go to practice with Jason all the time!"

I gave him the best argument I could without disclosing the day's events, and prayed he would go along with it, or at least give it some serious thought.

"Dontay, you aren't a resident of that school district. The only reason Day and Clay can stay is because we got special permission to let them finish the school year. For now, I told Kemis that you boys are welcome to stay as long as you like—like even until Clay turns eighteen. My door will forever be open to you boys. But, I don't want to make a decision that impacts you permanently when you may only be with me temporarily. If Kemis wishes to extend the guardianship past the six months, I'm definitely open to making that call about school. I will pray and talk it over with your brother, and I'm always open to discuss it more. Okay?"

I sat back in my seat and nodded despite the fact that I wasn't "okay" with his response. I thought it sucked and wanted to tell him that but didn't think I could do so respectfully. I stayed quiet for the remainder of the ride home, pondering the fact that I was trapped in a school with teachers that didn't even think I could solve math problems without cheating.

23

an 'A' and an 'L'

I was summoned to the principal's office the next morning during my first class and found out my math teacher had written only me up for cheating.

The principal asked the teacher to create a new quiz, and he sent for both Jack and me to report to the office where he took us to a private conference room. We sat on opposite sides of a table to take the quiz, while the principal sat in the middle with his laptop open. My anger with the fact that I was there provided me with ample energy to whiz through the test quickly, computing calculations in my brain even more effortlessly than the first time. On the other side of the table, Jack was scratching his head and looking around the room, likely regretting the fact that he hadn't just come clean and confessed to cheating off my test.

With plenty of extra time at the end, I decided to leave a note at the bottom of the first page expressing my thoughts: "Since I know you think I'm a dumb ass black boy that can't math, try not to have a fucking heart attack while you grade my paper."

I handed it to the principal and walked out. I had second thoughts about my note once I entered the hallway, but it was too late to do anything about it. Plus, I had vowed to myself I would no longer keep my feelings to myself, even if it meant I had to set aside my people-pleasing ways and get in more trouble.

My math teacher handed me a note to go see the principal as soon as I walked into her classroom later that day. She barely made any eye contact when she handed it to me, and I clenched my lips together as I turned away from her with a smile.

The principal was waiting for me when I arrived at his office. "You needed to see me, Mr. Reed?" I asked as though I had no clue what I had done.

"I do, Dontay." He reached over and handed me the quiz that I had taken earlier that day. "This is very advanced math, and you earned a perfect score on this quiz, unlike Jack. Your write-up has been rescinded, and you are getting an A for this test. Unfortunately, the note you left is unacceptable. I know you were upset, but that doesn't excuse that language, and you'll be getting detention. I have already notified your uncle. Do you have anything you'd like to say about it?"

"Will I be joined in detention with Jack? Is he getting kicked out? Isn't there a zero-tolerance policy for cheating?" I asked.

"I'm not at liberty to discuss disciplinary actions for other students. But is there anything you would like to say about your own behavior?"

"You mean my behavior of minding my business and getting falsely accused of something this white boy did? I ain't got nothing to say about that. I need my detention slip," I muttered and stood up to leave.

He stared at me with his lips slightly parted, as though he wanted to respond but wasn't sure how, or as though the words I had shared distracted him from his train of thought. He reached over and handed me a detention slip.

"Stay out of trouble, Mr. Lands," he told me as I walked out.

I was completely annoyed with his advice, considering I had done nothing to get into trouble in the first place, but I knew I could have avoided the additional trouble had I skipped out on the note I had written.

Uncle D knew it too, and was undoubtedly unhappy with what I had done, which he expressed thoroughly and tediously in a lecture that afternoon outside next to the firepit in the backyard. I wondered why he enjoyed talking outside so much, when we could have easily sat in his office and been just as comfortable, and likely a little warmer.

"So, you wrote out a note, with profanity on it, *knowing* your teacher and your principal would read it? And yet, you left it *anyway*. I don't understand! Help me understand, Tay. Tell my why you would do that," he said.

I doubted he would consider my answer satisfactory, making me not want to answer at all. I was annoyed with how he focused in on my note and not on my teacher's accusations. I scratched the back of my head and stared at the fire, hoping I could treat his question as rhetorical.

"I asked you a question, Dontay!" he sharply reminded when he realized I wasn't answering.

I sighed, thinking of what I could say to motivate him to end the conversation.

"She pissed me off accusing me of cheating off this dumb dude for an even dumber test! I'm the only one that got wrote up for cheating!"

"You didn't even tell me that she had accused you of cheating. I had to find that out from the principal. And instead of coming to me, you concluded that being disrespectful would be the right answer?"

I shrugged my shoulders, knowing he had posed one of those questions that there was no right answer to.

"Well, you'll have two weeks to think about it, because that's how long you're grounded for. And since you like notes, you'll write your teacher an apology note. Now, hand me your phone."

"Two weeks for a stupid note?"

"I've already told you that disrespecting adults is not tolerated in this house! Hopefully this will teach you not to do it again."

"Come on, Unc! You acting like I *said* it to her! And they the ones coming after me like I caused this mess in the first place!"

"You can lower your voice before I add another week. Writing it is just as bad as saying it. Either way, you knew better. You don't speak to adults in that manner, even if you're upset. Now, you can either go work on your homework first, or your note first, but you need to get them both done. And don't think when you're on punishment you can have guests over because you can't. Hand it over!"

I loudly scoffed before handing him my phone and storming off to Daveon's room to vent, hoping Daveon could help me brainstorm on ways to get kicked out of school without sacrificing my phone. I bolted into the room and slammed the door shut to find Daveon and Clay talking while Daveon was playing video games.

"Damn, you aight?" Clay asked.

"Nah, bro! I'm back on punishment, all because of this dumb, racist-ass teacher!" I said.

"This about your test?" Daveon asked, recalling my vent session from the previous day.

"Bro...I had to take another test. I got an A. This dude that cheated off *my* paper didn't even get written up! He failed the test because he's an idiot and the son of an executive at that huge company downtown and don't know shit because he doesn't have to know shit! So I left a note on the test, basically telling her she's trash, but maybe with a couple of bonus words, and now my phone gone," I said, summarizing the best way I knew how.

"Keep it real, Tay. What your note say?" Daveon asked.

"It had like one f-bomb," I said.

"You lucky Unc ain't smack yo' ass. But I prolly would've done the same thing," Daveon said. That didn't mean much coming from him, a hothead that had cussed out more school officials than all of us.

"Bro, I already told you what to do! Tommy said your school policy says they don't invite you back if you get suspended without some sort of special chairperson approval or something. Getting suspended can't be that daggone hard if you done already had fifty-leven detentions," Clay said.

I reclined onto Daveon's bed, tightly holding a pillow over the crown of my head. I hadn't come up with one solid idea for getting out of the school. I had talked to Kemis, I had talked to Uncle D and Auntie Robin. It seemed that Clay had been right the entire time. And even with trying to do things the good way, I was still in trouble and not getting the results I wanted.

I decided I was no longer interested in being in trouble for doing nothing. I felt compelled to earn my trouble legitimately, go after it on purpose, and maybe with enough trouble, the school would refuse to accept me back the following school year.

24

new school, new you

Not learning anything from having to endure Uncle D follow him at school, or from watching me get my phone snatched away, Clay got in trouble for using profanity with a teacher the very next day, but his was different—he said it out loud, after he and his friend Terrell got caught sneaking out of their fourth period class to smoke weed in a hidden area across from the football field. It hadn't been the first time they had gotten suspended together, and it wasn't the first time they got caught smoking together at school.

He came home with plans to hide his suspension from Uncle D, which he shared with Caleb and me as the three of us shot hoops in the backyard that breezy afternoon. Caleb and I both tried to convince him that his plan wouldn't work.

"Clay, Daddy checks his email all day," Caleb said.

"And your principal already knows to email and call him. If I were you, I would just tell him before he get that email, bro. Besides, what you gon' do in the morning when he drop you off?" I asked.

"I'ma walk inside the school until he drive off, and then roll ova to the train stop," Clay said matter-of-factly.

"Bro you crazy! Did you tell Day?" I asked.

"Naw," he said after landing from a jump shot, "He just gon' call and snitch me out to Jay."

"Just go in there and tell him bro!" I tried one last time, hoping he would listen.

"Tell him that I smoked weed and cussed out another teacher after he already went in on me for it before? You see all that shit he made me do last time. I'ma take my chances," he announced confidently.

But Clay was exposed at the dinner table that night after Auntie Robin asked Uncle D how his day went.

"Well, mine was real good until I found out one of my kids decided he would lie to me about how *his* day went."

"I didn't lie, Unc! I told you Coach made the whole team stay behind!" Daveon said, assuming Uncle D was talking about him for coming home late.

"Oh no, I wasn't talking about you—your Coach sent us a text. But Clay told me he behaved himself today, and the phone call and email I got from the principal earlier told me otherwise. I thought you and I had an understanding that when you get in trouble at school you would be honest," Uncle D said before shooting a vicious glare at Clay.

I looked over at Caleb and then at Clay to see if he would respond.

"I mean, I did behave myself, Unc, I mean, except for—"

"Except for when you decided to skip class and smoke weed and then cuss out another teacher?" Uncle D asked.

I tried to look straight down and keep my eyes focused on my plate, hoping to avoid eye contact with anyone at the table.

"Clay, please tell me that's not true," Auntie Robin said with evident disdain in her voice. There was something about the gentle manner in which she approached everything we did that made us feel extra bad when she was disappointed, and I knew what Clay was feeling in that moment.

"Auntie," Clay said rubbing his head, "it's not like that. I mean, I said like a couple cuss words, but she—"

"That's a couple too many! And then came home and lied to me. It's all good though. We can talk about it downstairs after dinner."

Our attempts at making small talk for the remainder of dinner were futile considering we all knew we were minutes away from Clay's imminent death. Sophie was able to fill the silence with discussion of the second-grade gossip that was on her mind.

Later in the evening, I found Clay sulking in our room with his head underneath his pillow.

"I wanna go back home," he grumbled from under his pillow after I asked if he was okay.

"We don't have one, bro. And K woulda whooped yo' ass too. And Jay gon' kill you!" I reminded him.

He abruptly sat up in his bed and pulled the pillow in front of him. His eyes were red, and he looked as though he had either been crying or was about to. "Unc and Auntie said they pulling me out my school and making me go to school out here! And K agreed with them! I'm fucking pissed!"

I was so surprised that I pulled my headphones down to make sure I heard correctly. "You dead ass?"

"Yes, bro! I hate them right now! First thing I'ma do is get kicked out!"

I sighed, feeling partially jealous that he had gotten a school change without requesting one, but knew he needed to calm down and think more rationally.

"Clay—first off quit talking so loud!"

He didn't heed my advice and kept talking just as loudly. "Watch this school expel me. Then Unc won't have a say!"

I shook my head and messaged Daveon on my computer to come upstairs, hoping he would talk to Clay. Since I had been considering a similar strategy for changing schools, I doubted my ability to be a voice of reason. Daveon arrived and joined Clay on the bed after he saw his head back under the pillows.

"Clay, you better chill before Jay come home!" Daveon said.

"Tell him what you told me you gon' do," I told Clay.

Clay scoffed under his pillow, refusing to answer.

"What he say, he running away or something?" Daveon asked me, realizing that Clay was not going to share voluntarily.

"Bro, you know they told him he changing middle schools, right?" I asked.

"What? Naw, I ain't know that!"

"Yeah, well, he said he gon' get kicked out of the new school."

"Baby bro, you ain't sane! Unc ain't about to be playing with you like that!"

"I don't want to go to no lame-ass school out here!" Clay said from underneath the pillow.

"I mean, I feel you. But it ain't like it's as bad as Tay's school. At least there's black people there. But you better calm down 'cause Unc seem like he'll keep a phone for a decade. I know you pissed about being away from your friends, but you might actually like it!" Daveon said.

"Bro, you hype! K and Unc always hated my friends, and this is their way of making sure I can't see 'em," Clay responded.

"I mean, they've always hated my friends too."

"That's 'cause yo' friends almost got you killed!"

"Yo friends almost got *you* killed! One of them died and the other still ain't walking, and he wasn't shit no way! Besides, you think being thirteen and smoking weed is good for your life?"

"Why you act like you didn't smoke and drink when you were only in elementary school?" Clay challenged.

"Bro, you just mad 'cause he ain't lettin' you get away with the stuff K did!"

"Seriously, bro? From the dude that snuck out all the time to drink and smoke and snuck girls through yo' bedroom window like every week?"

"Nigga, you used our window just—"

Uncle D walked into the room in the middle of their argument, prompting them both to stop talking. The truth was they both had gotten away with way more before we moved in with Uncle D, but I wasn't going to speak about it in Uncle D's presence.

"Clay and Tay, I'm taking your PlayStation out since you're both grounded," Uncle D announced.

"Da hell smoking gotta do with a game?" Clay asked, causing Daveon to palm him in his chest so hard that the smack sound and Clay's subsequent grunt reverberated throughout the room.

Uncle D had been bent down, unplugging the game system from the wall, but stopped and stood up straight to glare at Clay as though he saw green slime protruding from his mouth. He turned his body towards Clay and spoke even more softly than he had when he first entered the room. "Clay, let's go back downstairs and talk."

"Unc, I—aight, my bad. I ain't mean to cuss. I'm just saying, you already taking my phone, my school, my friends! Why you gotta take everything?" Clay asked, trying to retract his previous statement. Video games would be the only way he could stay in touch with his friends, and I knew he was desperate to remain in touch.

"I'll have your phone and your video game for an extra week now for your language."

"He hella extra!" Clay quietly mumbled, but not quietly enough.

"Congratulations, an extra two weeks! Should we make it an extra three?"

Clay finally shut his mouth and threw himself back down on the bed, mumbling again about being ready to go back home. Uncle D quietly returned to unhooking the video game while Daveon and I awkwardly waited for the tension to pass. Once Uncle D was gone, I shook my head, hoping the situation did not have to get worse before it got better, but it did.

Fortunately, Clay had calmed down before his first day at the new school, and actually seemed happy when we arrived to pick him up on the first day. He told us the school had a much nicer gymnasium, and he found some kids playing basketball during the lunch hour that he was able to join in with.

I thought his experience would keep his fire quelled, but the fire reignited when Uncle D refused Clay's request to drop him off at the mall to meet up with his friend Terrell once he was off punishment.

"You want me to drop you off with him at one of the same places you all were stealing from last year? Absolutely not!" Uncle D told him one night at dinner, after Clay told him he was being unfair.

"Unc, the no trespass order is up—it's been a year! And we not even going to steal! We just gon' play video games and watch a movie!" Clay said. "You gon' hold that one thing against me and try to keep me from seeing my friends forever!"

"Clay, if you want to see your friend, tell his grandmother to drop him off at church on Sunday, and I will have him back home by the evening. He can hang out here with us and stay for lunch and dinner. Or stay all night on Saturday."

"Why would I invite him to lame, boring places I don't even wanna be!" he snapped back.

"I'm sorry you feel that way, but that's the only way you will see your friends from your old school for the time being…and you better not even *think* about sneaking out of this house like you did living with your brother!"

Clay immediately scooted from the table and stormed off mumbling under his breath.

"Get back in here, young man!" Uncle D called and quickly stood from his seat, but Clay ignored him and continued to our room.

"Dwayne, sit down and eat. The boy has had a lot of changes, and he's processing it all in his own way. Just let him cool down in his room," Auntie Robin said with her hand on Uncle D's arm. I was concerned there would be carnage, but Uncle D sat back down soon after she said it.

I didn't say it at the table, but I agreed with Uncle D—I had never seen Clay do anything positive when he was with his friends, either at or away from school. His friend Terrell was still doing the things that had gotten them arrested in the seventh grade, and I didn't want Clay to fall back into that pattern.

I had plans to talk sense into Clay later in the week since he spent the week being snappy and sulking around the house, but those plans were thwarted after Uncle D and I had an exchange in his office that Friday night that left me uncomfortable. Our conversation wasn't nearly as warm and inviting as the fireplace next to the couch that was at full blaze.

"Tay," he started hesitantly, "I really don't wanna talk to you about this, but I'm really not sure what to do."

"What you mean, Unc?"

"Well, I had a large sum of money in my drawer in my bedroom. Well, it's actually not my money—it's the money I use from the single mother's fund at church to buy groceries for the single moms. You know Friday nights and Saturday mornings are the days we usually handle that."

"You think I stole your money?" I asked, feeling offended and not masking it. The three of us had been around him for many years and had been to his home on countless occasions. At no point was there ever anything locked up or put away because we were there, and we had never stolen from him before despite the fact that his home was filled with nice things.

"Tay, I definitely don't think you stole from me…I just wanna know if you know anything about it. I brought the money home Tuesday night, and now it's gone. It's not a big deal…I'll just have to use my own money to do the grocery shopping," he added.

My perception of him and Auntie Robin soured in that moment. I was shocked they believed one of us could steal from them, as we had always regarded them like family. While Daveon and Clay had both stolen extensively in the past, I knew they could never steal from Uncle D, and I was angry that he even suggested it.

"I don't know anything, Unc, except I know ain't nobody over here stealing from you!" I said before standing to my feet and leaving the room knowing I couldn't tell my brothers about the conversation. I felt just as out of place and unwanted at home as I did at school and didn't want them to experience the same thing.

25

caught and distraught

"Bro, I need one of y'all to sign Unc or Auntie name on this paper," Clay said. He had come into Daveon's room where Daveon and I were getting ready for a night out with Paris and Candace. I was off punishment and happy to be getting out of the house, and the last thing I needed was something to get me right back on.

"What you mean, bro? You failed your test that Unc told you to study for?" I asked.

"Man, this work hella hard!" Clay said.

"Bro, did you even study?" Daveon asked.

"Studying is lame," Clay said with a scoff, seeming to be growing impatient with the questions we asked.

"Unc don't even hesitate about taking my phone bro. I ain't doing it!" I said.

"Day got a better fake signature than yours anyway," Clay said.

"Yeah, but I ain't never signed Unc name to nothing. I did that shit with K!"

"Don't get weak just 'cause we at Unc house," Clay said.

"Really bro? 'Cause I've hardly heard a cuss word out yo' mouth since that last set of hands you caught," Daveon said, prompting both him and me to laugh at Clay.

"Bump you, nigga! And I ain't seen you sneak not one girl through your window," Clay said.

"Whatever dude! How you gon' flunk out a school you just started? I hope he whoop yo' ass again when he find out your grade," Daveon said.

"Will y'all chill? We gotta go upstairs and talk to Unc before we go. Clay, if I was you, I would ask the teacher to let you take the test again and see what she say. Try to bring your grade up before Unc see it. Otherwise you know he gon' find out eventually…unless you hack into her computer," I said.

Clay looked over at me curiously. "Bro, why don't you do it for me?"

"Naw, bro."

"C'mon, you did it once before for K and—"

"Shhh! Remember we said we never gon' bring that up again. He still don't know he didn't pass that class. You can do this on your own if you would just do your daggone work and study!"

Clay sat down to think about his next move while Daveon and I trekked upstairs to hear our pre-date lecture from Uncle D. He quoted Bible verses and left us with an infinite list of instructions.

"When you pick up young ladies, you don't pull up and text them, especially if they have a family inside. You both go ring the doorbell and show your faces so that everyone in the home sees who their daughter will be with for the night. Make sure you introduce yourself, and tell them everywhere you will be going," he said, which we thought was unnecessary. "And Daveon, get those pants above your behind!"

To avoid receiving a lecture from him, we did as we were told when we arrived at the Johnson residence. I was uneasy standing in the foyer while Mr. Johnson, Paris' dad, stared Daveon and me up and down and asked us one thousand questions while we waited for Paris to find her shoes. Even though I was Paris' date, her dad seemed slightly more suspicious of Daveon than he did me. He studied his every move, listened intently while Daveon spoke, and asked him more questions than he did me. I had already instructed Daveon that he needed to pretend to be "middle class and boujee," but wasn't sure if he could pull it off.

Daveon had grown accustomed to people judging him by his appearance, and he remained calm throughout the interrogation. Kemis and his best friend Kyle joked that Daveon looked like a "Gen Z mumble rapper." He wore his hair in braids at the top like Travis Scott, which had caused some contention at the house since he had told Auntie Robin that Candace was his hairstylist, and he insisted on seeing her regularly in order to get his hair done correctly. He wore ripped baggy skinny jeans nearly everywhere, complete with t-shirts that often bore crazy messages, and a hoodie, which came in handy as Uncle D would often make him cover up the message on his shirt by putting on or zipping up his hoodie.

Auntie Robin had once purchased Daveon a pair of khakis to wear to church, and Daveon refused to wear them. She then purchased a pair of jeans without rips and holes that she thought he would like, and he refused those as well. She eventually gave up the dress code battle, but still banned him from wearing some of his shirts, even just to hang around the house, while Uncle D would have a fit every time he felt Daveon's pants were hanging down too far.

"What kind of plans do you fellas have tonight?" Mr. Johnson asked.

By that point, I didn't want to answer any more of his questions.

"Oh, um, we're just going to play mini golf and laser tag," I answered.

"Daveon, how long have you been driving?" he asked.

"Well, legally, a little over a year," was Daveon's response. Internally, my face was already hidden behind my palm.

"You say legally…"

"Aw yeah, well, we kinda all practiced before we had permits. Tay has already driven a bunch of—"

"He just means that our brother always wanted us to be good drivers, so he's been teaching us for a while," I clarified and shot Daveon a look before he said something that would get us kicked out of the house.

"You know not to drive with a cell phone in your hand?" Mr. Johnson asked.

"Unc put the hands-free stuff in the car. And he told me if I get another ticket for texting while driving, he'll kill me and take my keys for six months!" Daveon said. I could tell he was speaking as properly and cordially as he could muster, but he was still failing miserably.

"Another ticket?"

"Uh, well, that one was actually a long time ago, before I had a license…I mean, well, I had to pick up my brother Jason from something…I learned my lesson though."

"You won't be stopping at anyone's home, will you?" Mr. Johnson asked.

"No, sir, other than picking up Candace. Then laser tag and mini golf!" Daveon answered.

"Either of you ever smoked?" he asked.

"Never!"

"Oh no!" I blurted at the same time as Daveon's exaggerated response, doing my best to sound genuine.

"Drank?"

"No, sir," we uttered in unison.

Mr. Johnson seemed to know we were lying.

"You had any other tickets, Daveon?"

"Not while anyone's daughter was in the car."

Other than the grilling by Mr. Johnson, we enjoyed an eventful evening with our dates. Uncle D wouldn't have approved, mainly since Daveon and Candace could hardly keep their hands off each other. When we got to our location, Daveon handed me the money he was given from Uncle D and instructed Paris and me to go inside and grab a snack since he and his date needed to talk in the car, but we knew they had no intentions of talking while parked in the back corner of the lot.

Paris and I laughed at them half the night, as they still skipped whole sections of mini golf just to make out and do whatever they were doing, causing the people waiting behind us to impatiently scowl.

"O.M.G." Paris said. "Look over there!" she pointed outside of the mini golf area to a nearby neon-lit bowling alley. "Ain't that Mark—"

I quickly threw my hand over her mouth and whispered, "You cannot tell Day that he's here! He will kick his ass and get arrested, and your dad will never let you out with me again."

"Day wouldn't do something to get arrested," she said.

"Uh, yeah, you don't know Day. He's calmed down a lot, but he been arrested more than anyone I know," I said.

"Are you—"

"Bro, why you put your hand over this girl mouth like that?" Daveon said after putting the ball. "You can't be treating no lady like that."

"Bro we just messing around," I said.

"Right! He did it to try to keep me from kissing him," Paris said, right before throwing her lips into mine.

It was the start of us mimicking Daveon and Candace's behavior, which we continued to do on the ride home. The fun ended when we arrived home and were ordered to sit in the kitchen and endure a lecture for missing curfew by thirty minutes, caused by Daveon meeting up with Tray to get weed.

Daveon was still following more rules with Uncle D than he ever had with Kemis. But he was sneakier than ever when he did break the rules, such as the few times he snuck out the house. I found a way to get into the alarm system from my laptop and disable and enable the alarm, preventing it from making the normal beeping noise. I would pray the most sincere prayers, begging God that I wouldn't get caught helping Daveon sneak around.

I also helped him convince Uncle D we were going to the mall one day when we were actually sneaking off to get tattoos. I wrestled with all sorts of guilt when we were deceptive, but my brothers and I had always covered for each other, and I knew I couldn't violate our no-snitch policy.

26

cashing out

Daveon and I couldn't stop laughing as we watched Clay catch Jason's hands when we visited him in Kentucky during spring break. I had never known Jason to beat Clay down the same way Kemis had in the past, but he was beside himself when he found out about Clay's suspension from school and then cussing at home in front of Uncle D and Auntie Robin. It was Clay's only bad night in Kentucky. Otherwise, we had fun living like college students— jam packed into Jason's dorm room, using the money Uncle D gave us for the cafeteria to instead hang out at the dorm and eat pizza throughout our stay. We stayed up late each night and often slept in until lunchtime. We enjoyed seeing Jason in practice and watching him interact as he took us around campus, and it proved a nice mental break from everything that had been going on back home.

The break got even better when Uncle D, Auntie Robin, Caleb, and Sophie picked us up from Kentucky and surprised us with a short vacation at a Florida beach to finish out the break, something we had never done before. Other than wishing Jason and Kemis could have joined us, it was a perfect time, and I understood why so many kids at my new school would talk about their family vacations.

When we returned to town, Kemis stopped by and shared with us that he had been looking for a house near Uncle D's neighborhood and told us we would be staying with Uncle D until he found one, even if it took a year or two. Nervous that they would try to force me into another year of private school hell, I again broached the subject about leaving my school, but was denied by both of them because we only had one quarter remaining of school, which only infuriated me. I knew I had to do everything I could to make sure I was not invited back for the new school year in the fall.

I decided to try out for the spring talent show after learning from Marco that it was a huge deal at school—that one event that made unpopular kids suddenly popular, or unknown kids suddenly visible in the school hallways. It was the event everyone attended and everyone often discussed long after it was over. It made the winner high school famous, as the grand prize included a large sum of cash, a pizza lunch for the winner and nine friends, a GoPro camera, which I desperately wanted, along with instant respect from the student body.

But more than the notoriety and winnings that came with a victory, I had plans to express my discontent with an unwelcoming environment at school by taking advantage of the captive ears of the teachers, principals, and students in the audience. I had a risky but exciting plan to tell the talent show officials I was reciting a monologue by Dr. Martin Luther King, Jr., but on the day of the talent show I would recite an excerpt from one of Malcolm X's controversial speeches called "The Ballot or the Bullet." I knew that Martin Luther King would be deemed safe to them, while Malcolm X would be considered reprehensible, and my overwhelming desire to leave the school had motivated me to put the safe life behind me.

I honed the skills of a Hollywood-level actor when I would perform a speech during talent show rehearsals, but then secretly practice the Malcolm X excerpt at home with my brothers. Marco, Tommy, and Paris came over a couple of times to practice with me in the basement, with Daveon and Clay watching to critique us. We decided that during the speech, the three of them would reenact a police shooting behind me while I spoke. In the middle of the speech, they would rip off their top shirt, revealing shirts that read "Black Lives Matter" in big letters, which Paris and her little sister made for us. We planned to end the speech down on one knee with our fists up, in front of an American flag, paying homage to Colin Kaepernick.

Daveon drove Tommy, Clay, and me to a hair store that we knew sold African-print fabrics and accessories, which we quickly realized was not a good place for us to shop. An older lady who was working surveyed us closely as we browsed and talked.

"Yo, why the fuck you following us?" Clay shouted, startling our in-store stalker.

Her eyes grew wide, and she turned to the side to pretend as though she was rearranging something on a nearby shelf.

"You already know why she following us! Every time I come to a store like this I get followed," Tommy said.

"If you think we don't have money, we do! We ain't gotta steal from yo' ass!" Clay continued. He reached in his pocket and pulled out a thick wad of cash, demonstrating his ability to make a pricey transaction. The lady ended up walking away, but the rest of us stared at Clay and his money, in shock of how much he had.

"Clay, you been stealing again, bro? Jay gon' kick yo' ass again," Daveon said.

"Day, chill! It ain't like that! Don't be calling Jay," Clay said.

"Damn, lil' bro, what you been doing?" Tommy asked Clay in the middle of the aisle. Clay had bent down to pick up a twenty-dollar bill that he had accidently dropped during his rant.

"Ah, nothing T," Clay said smiling. "I just save my allowance."

"If Unc hooking y'all up like that, tell him to adopt me too!" Tommy joked.

We decided to walk next door to the Goodwill, partially because Daveon thought the lady in the store would call the police on Clay, but also because I refused to buy anything in a store where workers stalked us.

It worked out better at the Goodwill since we found a jacket and tie, and a pair of thick, dark glasses like the kind Malcolm X wore. Clay paid for it all, and it dawned on me when we stood at the counter that I knew where his cash had come from. I knew I had to confront him in our room after dinner later that night, and I was shocked to find him sitting on his bed actually doing homework.

"Yo, I gotta holler at you," I said after I crept into the room and locked the door behind me.

"Sup?" he asked, barely looking up.

"Did you take money from Unc?"

"What? Nah bro!"

"Clay, don't lie. Where all that money come from today? Ain't no allowance big enough to save all that. Plus, I know Unc is missing some money!"

"How you know that?" he asked shiftily.

"Because he told me!"

He turned away from me with a furrowed expression, and my heart sank. I felt awful for my defense of him, and for likely making Uncle D feel uncomfortable. But mostly I was angry that Clay would steal from someone special to us.

"Bro, give it back!" I demanded.

"Tay, I can't! I spent half of it. Plus, if I give it to him, he'll never trust me again!"

"He already don't trust us because he know one of us got his money! I'm calling Jay—"

"NO!" He jumped out of bed. "I only took it 'cause he pissed me off about school, and not letting me see my boys and shit. You know I love Unc, man, and I do feel bad about it. I can't erase it though..."

"Unc *and* Jay gon' whoop yo ass, bro—"

"Tay, don't be no snitch, nigga! I'm not gon' do it again, aight? I told you I was pissed! I can't talk to Rel or see him at school, I gotta do dumb-ass homework all the time! I ain't got no basketball court to walk to in this neighborhood…I get my phone snatched every time something stupid happens at school. And I ain't allowed to say what's on my mind!"

"You can say what's on your mind! You just can't cuss them out like you used to do K all the time!"

"Well that's what's on my mind, and I ain't allowed to say it."

"Bro, you out of it! Talk to Rel? Your so-called boy Josh literally put a gun to your face! You coulda got Jay and Day killed or arrested. Fuck your friends, bro!"

"Tay, we done hashed all that out. Rel ain't have nothing to do with that! And Rel my boy and I ain't even had a chance to hang out with him!"

"You gotta figure this shit out, straight up. I don't wanna be no snitch, but you went too far. I never snitched when you stole from anywhere else, but he gives us money all the time! He bought us all this stuff in here! They surprised us with bikes just so we could ride to a basketball court for you. He got the basketball court outside painted for you. They took us on vacation and bought new swim stuff and shirts! Come on dude!" I was even angrier with Clay after I reflected on all the generous things our new family had done for us.

"I'll figure something out. Don't tell Jay though—and don't tell Day either."

I desperately wanted to tell Daveon so I could watch him bash Clay's face in, but I knew Daveon would then tell Jason, who would probably tell Kemis, who already had enough stress to battle. I was so upset that I couldn't stand the thought of sitting in the room with him, even if just to do homework. I gathered the things I needed to go work in Daveon's room.

"I can't stand you sometimes dude. Sometimes you don't think about anyone but you!" I said before leaving.

27

is this good trouble or bad trouble?

It didn't take us long to put our finishing touches on our talent show performance. As Marco was extremely popular, his friends running the sound booth agreed not to cut my microphone off, even if the teachers signaled to do so. Right before the show, they snuck Marco a backup microphone that was connected to a different system.

While we waited backstage, I was shocked when I peeked out into the audience to see Kemis, Uncle D, Auntie Robin, Daveon, Caleb, Sophie, and Clay all seated before my performance, since they hadn't told me they were coming. Seeing them made me feel even more uneasy about what was about to happen.

My heart pounded when I stepped onto the stage, and Paris, Tommy, and Marco joined behind me. Behind the microphone stand I said a brief, quiet prayer for boldness, put on my glasses, and parted my lips to project loudly, the way Malcolm X had in his original speech. I was so focused that I didn't realize they signaled to cut my microphone as soon as I made a reference to "the white man."

I received the occasional clap mid-speech, partially from Clay who was standing in his seat, serving as my "Amen" corner and my personal videographer with his cell phone. A few rows in front of him sat Mark Paul and his crew, whose lips were formed into a hiss while the heat from his eyes could have melted the resolve of a speaker less desperate than myself. He uncomfortably fidgeted around in his seat as though trying to shake off his agitation, in between frantically texting on his phone.

With about thirty seconds left in the speech, my microphone cut out, but Marco quickly handed me another in order to finish, and I spoke loudly enough to still be heard throughout the auditorium, even during the few seconds that passed without amplification. We ended the speech on our knees with fists in the air and looked up to hear the audience roaring. There were cell phone flashes from every direction and loud cheers from the audience that was giving us a standing ovation.

Hearing the applause from the audience gave me the relief I needed to exhale. I had finally been heard and vindicated for everything that had happened to me in what felt like an emotionally unsafe school. I considered that maybe I had more supporters and allies than I had realized.

We all beamed as we stood from our knees and returned backstage, homey hugging one another in celebration of pulling it off. The three of them told me I was "fire," and Paris rewarded me with a lengthy kiss, causing me to forget all the anxiety I had about the performance.

Kemis hugged me after the show was over. "Bro, I had no idea you could speak like that! You've been hiding some stuff from me," he told me with a big smile on his face. I was relieved that he seemed to be referencing my speaking skills as opposed to the speech I had hidden from them all.

He told me he would hang out and order pizza that night to celebrate my performance. Even though my friends and most of my family was happy for me, I still had to face Uncle D, who joined me and Kemis at the table that night. He sat down while I did homework and Kemis worked on his laptop as we waited for the pizza to arrive.

"Tay, let me ask you something."

It was the first thing Uncle D had said to me since we had gotten home, and I suspected he wasn't too happy.

"Uh okay."

"I don't know what you told Kemis, but you told me and Auntie you were performing a speech from Dr. King," he said.

"Wait, that's what you told me too bro!" Kemis said, glaring with a puzzled expression. He scooted his laptop about an inch forward and folded his hands in front of it before turning his eyes back toward me for an answer.

Uncle D continued, "And I'm feeling like that's what you told your school, since I'm pretty sure I saw them trying to cut your mic off, and the kids in the booth pretended not to see it. By the time this lady got to the booth to do it herself, you already had a backup microphone."

I knew I was busted, and I looked down at my shirt and pretended my chest was itching.

"So, what you're saying, by what you're not saying, is that you lied…to us and to the talent show officials."

"Oooh…Gotti!" Kemis chimed in.

I tried to respond: "Unc, I—"

"Wait. Did you lie or not?" Uncle D asked.

I knew I wasn't going to win with them both staring me down and tag-teaming me.

"I didn't! I planned to do MLK initially. The idea to change it up came later, and I just didn't tell them. I wasn't trying to be censored."

I knew I had to lie to keep him from snatching my phone.

"And you broke the rules requiring them to approve your content before performing in the show."

He had a solemn look and tone. I was annoyed that they were grilling me, and I wanted to find refuge in my room. My eye roll didn't go undetected.

"Let's not start rolling eyes just because I'm asking questions. Do you know what the consequences are for doing what you did?" he asked.

"No, but why should that matter? Rosa parks was persecuted for breaking a racist law, and they took her to jail. They locked up Dr. King too. Sometimes we have to get into trouble to make a point. Remember? Good trouble?" I said, sure that they sensed the annoyance in my tone.

Kemis tapped in, "I'm not saying I completely disagree with you Tay. But if you really wanted to make a point, why not tell them your plans up front? If they questioned it, you could have explained why the speech was important to you. They may not have wanted to censor it at all. I think the fact that you caught them off guard; they didn't know what was coming next—I would think that would give them a legitimate reason to cut you off."

Uncle D followed up, "They didn't know if you were going to use profanity or use threatening speech! I will say this, your orating skills were phenomenal. I was extremely impressed. I saw the hand of God on your life. Those examples you name—yes, they all faced backlash. Yet I still don't recall them being deceptive with their message, and I can't help but wonder if the school will have anything to say to you about this tomorrow."

I didn't care what happened at school, but I knew I couldn't say that without a lecture from them both that would likely last the rest of the night, and I had already grown tired of listening to them. I kept it to myself until later on after dinner when Daveon came into the room with Clay and me, where the three of us discussed it freely.

"Man, fuck that school, bro!" Daveon said, loud enough to be heard through the closed door.

"Shhhhhh! Day, chill before Unc hears you!" I warned him and pointed towards the door as Clay chuckled.

"Look man, all I'm saying is they weren't doing nothing to that kid that got your locker raided. And they didn't do nothing—"

Knock. Knock.

"Come in!" I said, as I gave Day an "I told you so" glare.

"So, which one of you should I credit if Caleb or Sophie learned the 'f' word tonight?"

Uncle D stood there with his arms folded, knowing my brothers and I never snitched on each other. We sat in silence looking in different directions, while I thought about how Caleb and Sophie had learned the "f" word long before then. We had heard them repeat it and many other words after Clay multiple times, and Daveon reminded them not to utter them in front of their parents or we would all be dead.

Uncle D continued, "Well, since no one is saying anything, I have three different dictionaries, so you could each use your own to copy pages."

The three of us groaned in unison at his announcement.

"It was me," Daveon confessed, saving Clay and me from a tedious dictionary punishment.

"Thank you for being honest, but you know better. Come see me when you're done in here," Uncle D said before backing out.

"Bro, we should just throw all them dumb-ass dictionaries in that fire pit outside," Clay said, causing Daveon and me to laugh.

The door reopened and Uncle D emerged with his fist balled up in front of his face. "I heard that, boy. You come see me too," he told Clay.

I laughed at Clay getting caught as Uncle D left out of the room. We talked until we were pleasantly interrupted with a Facetime call from Jason. His basketball team had checked into their hotel for their tournament game in Indianapolis, where we were planning to join him later in the week. He congratulated me on my performance, and I intentionally left out the details about being griped at by Uncle D.

"Let me go get this stupid-ass dictionary," Daveon said after we finished talking to Jason. He and Clay headed towards Uncle D's room, while I sat feeling pleased with myself, hoping I had either won the talent show or won a ticket to a new school.

28

uncelebrated

The day after the talent show, my math teacher handed me a note instructing me to go see the principal after class. I looked at her after reading the note, and my gaze was met the sly grin that covered her face. I walked away with my stomach in knots, and I could hardly pay attention during the rest of class. I snuck on my phone to send a group text to Tommy, Marco, and Paris, and then another to Day and Clay to tell them I had been summoned. Day responded with a brown, raised fist emoji, which made me chuckle out loud.

"Mr. Lands, are you on your phone?" my teacher called out.

I quickly slid my phone into my pocket and pretended to be interested in what she was saying, while in actuality I was preparing my defense for the principal.

When I got there, I was ushered into a room where the principal, two assistant principals, along with one of the guidance counselors were seated.

"Mr. Lands, have a seat please," Principal Calhoun said. I tried to gage from his tone how much trouble I was in, but he didn't offer any clues as he sat back in his chair, looking and sounding relaxed. I sat down hoping he would cut to the chase. "We called you in here to discuss your performance yesterday. We delayed announcing the talent show winning performance until we spoke with you. I'll start by admitting that there were parts of your performance that were rather impressive. Obviously, there were some lines and phrases in it I wished weren't there, as it seemed like it promoted violence."

I assumed he was talking about the part where I said "the revolution is bloody," or where I said, "stop singing and start swinging."

"I would even say it bordered hate speech," he said.

"Hate speech? You mean like a noose on my locker?" I asked.

"Well, I mean, a different kind, I suppose. Eh...what I'm saying is that despite some of those questionable statements, your performance actually won the popular vote of the students, but the drama teacher disqualified you, which kept you from winning the grand prize."

My mouth fell open quicker than my ability to remember my plans to show no emotion, but learning that we had actually won the show infuriated me. I would have much rather been in last place than to know we were robbed of money and a GoPro camera.

"She wrote you up because you performed a different speech during the audition and rehearsals than the one you performed for the show, and the students agreed when signing up that their content had to be reviewed and approved of prior to the show.

"We had a meeting this morning, and we have had this happen before, when some students sang a song during the talent show that had some bad language, changing it from their original performance. They were all given two days of suspension for what they did. After meeting, we determined that since your speech did not contain profanity, or language specifically prohibited by the policies of our school, you would only be given one day of detention."

He extended his arm across the wooden table to place a detention slip in front of me and kept his eyes on me in anticipation of my response. I kept my eyes on him as well, pretending to be uninterested in the detention slip, and clenched my fists together to keep from tearing the slip up in their faces.

He continued on, "We'll be notifying your uncle about the disciplinary action. Is there anything you would like us to know?"

I was annoyed by the question, considering they had already adjudicated my punishment before hearing my side of the story, rendering useless any words I may have had. I grabbed the detention slip and my backpack and stood up from the table, feeling slightly gratified by the puzzled look on their faces as I prepared to leave the room. I was bursting with anger, and tried my best to reel it all in. But dwelling on it made me struggle even more, and I knew I needed to leave the room before I said something inexcusable.

"Dr. King was punished for his words too. I'm late for class, and by the way, I hate this fucking school," I told them as I strolled out of the room.

"Wait, Mr. Lands!" I heard one of them call when I reached the hallway, but I kept moving.

29

unheard

"Wait, so you like actually dropped the f-bomb in front of them?" Daveon asked. We were in his room recounting what happened when I was summoned to the principal's office earlier that day.

"I mean, yeah, bro. But it wasn't like that! I ain't even realize I said it 'til I was in the hallway. And the whole reason I left was so I wouldn't go crazy. Bro, I just couldn't believe they took my grand prize away!"

"They definitely on some bull...but you know Unc and Auntie ain't gon' like this news."

"I know...I'm 'bout to roll to go holla at Paris before they get here," I said.

"To do what?"

"Talk...before that dude put me on lock."

I soon found myself pedaling off of our street before anyone else made it home, to a nearby park where Paris was having tennis practice. I watched her while I texted with my friends and brothers and ignored calls from Uncle D.

"I'm shocked you out!" Paris said after her lesson was over. She joined me on a nearby bench while she placed her racket in her bag.

"Why? You think I don't like watching you?" I asked.

She laughed. "Because of what you told me happened at the meeting with the principal," she said.

"I left before Unc got home."

"I told Teela and some of the other MSU officers what happened. They think you should really think about a protest. She was saying we could stage a walk-out during class!"

"Man…I wanna do something…I just don't know what yet. I don't want to get anybody else in trouble. Whatever it is, I need it to be good enough to get the message across, and bad enough to where they won't invite me back to school, but still not so bad that Unc tries to kill me," I said.

"Yeah, as strict as he is, I'm not sure there's anything that would fall into that category," she said.

"Ima just have to take the L from him. But I ain't taking one from the school…not at least until I say what I gotta say."

"I'll brainstorm with the crew tonight. I guess tomorrow I can tell you what we came up with!"

"Aight, guess I better go," I said, standing to embrace her. She gave me a long hug and an even longer kiss, as was becoming our custom. Even though we were alone, there was always a hint of paranoia that somehow Uncle D could still see me.

"Good luck with your L," she said with a faint smile.

"Please say fifteen prayers for me," I joked before hopping on my bike.

I found Uncle D at the back of the house as soon as I went to park my bike. It was as if he knew I was on the way—he was reclined outside next to the firepit with a blaze already going, a cup of tea on a nearby table, feet kicked up in slides with his legs crossed at the ankles, staring off at the sky. I was disturbed by his calm demeanor and wondered if he was just pretending in order to keep me from running off.

I looked around the yard, thinking about how we had rarely sat outside in the backyard at our old house but did it all the time at our new one. I wondered how they knew to trim the backyard so nicely, making it a relaxing spot for all of us to go for fresh air. On the warmer days when my friends visited, we often sat in back to stay out of earshot of everyone inside the house. Clay, Daveon, and I would sit outside and watch Sophie and Caleb play while we talked. The yard was enclosed with trees that were at least twice as high as the houses that grew so thick that during the summer and fall months our view was obstructed of the neighboring rooftops, and there was a tall, wooden fence that helped the trees keep the soccer balls and basketballs in the yard when our shots were off. Auntie Robin would often lie down in one of the lawn chairs and read a book, and Sophie would do the same in the hammock nearby. It felt like a private outdoor resting place, where we could relax to the chirping and chatter of birds, crickets, and cicadas, and the occasional faint sounds of a lawnmower or leaf blower from one of the neighbors; a stark difference from the noises we had become accustomed to at our old home.

"You gonna tell me where you been or you just gonna act like you came home when you're supposed to?" he asked, interrupting my time reflecting on the soothing backyard sounds. He barely moved in his seat. Although his body was lounging, his tone was not nearly as tranquil.

I sighed in response to his question, hoping he would provide time for me to gather my thoughts.

"Let me rephrase…where have you been?"

"C'mon Unc, you acting like I missed curfew or something," I finally said after taking a seat nearby.

"Yes, I am, because you are supposed to come home and stay home until you ask to leave. So where were you?"

I threw my forehead in my hand, realizing he wasn't about to stop. "I just went for a ride."

"You went for a ride on a day that you knew your principal would be calling me?" he asked.

"I just wanted to clear my head!"

"I can relate. I needed to clear my head after I heard what you did today! How long should I ground you for smoking?" he asked.

I looked up at him confused. "Smoking? I ain't smoke anything!" I said, wondering what the principal told him.

"Oh, so you were actually in your right mind when you decided to use profanity in front of a room full of principals? You did that in a full state of consciousness and sobriety? I think that punishment is way worse!"

He had swung his legs over his seat to rest his feet on top of the gravel, while folding his hands and staring directly at me as though I had used profanity in front of him instead of people at school.

"Before I found out what you did today, I was feeling kinda proud of you for at least having a rationale for your talent show performance. It's not how I would have gone about things, but I can't expect you to do things like me. I'm proud of you for taking a stand. I think standing up for yourself is a good thing. But Kemis and I discussed earlier that an important lesson you have to learn is that even if you feel like what you're doing is right, you have to consider the ramifications of your actions before making a decision on what to do. Also, you're not an adult yet, and you're still expected to treat all adults with respect, even if you want to drive a point home. Do you understand what I'm telling you?"

"I feel you," I mumbled.

"Do you really?" he asked.

"Yeah, Unc, but—"

"Good, that means you understand why this needs to be taken from you." He grabbed my phone as he said it. "What you did today was simply rude and disrespectful. Walking out of a room full of adults while they are speaking to you will not be tolerated. And we've already discussed your language. You are grounded for a week. It was gonna be much longer but your Auntie talked me down."

I put my head down and felt my body tense up, from my mouth down to my toes. Without warning, he put his arm around me and started praying, which only frustrated me. I was forced to sit and listen to everything on his mind, as opposed to being able to express my own. I asked him if I could go afterwards, and subsequently walked off to stay in my room.

I was so mad about my punishment from school and my punishment from Uncle D that I was willing and ready to skip dinner even though I was starving, and I could smell the aroma of a delicious Italian concoction coming from the kitchen. Auntie Robin called my name twice to bid me into the dining room to eat with everyone, but I stayed in bed with my headphones on, pretending as though I didn't hear. Within minutes, Daveon appeared in my doorway, and told me in so many words that I needed to make an appearance at the dinner table if I wanted to keep my life and limb intact. I shuffled out of bed and across the house to the table for dinner, and intentionally kept a frown on my face for the entire meal, unwilling to show them how delicious the meal was.

30

the original gangster nerd

When Uncle D dropped me off the next day, he gave me my phone back, only because he wasn't sure if it would be him or Daveon to pick me up from detention that afternoon. I was still upset about being grounded, but I was glad he had given me my phone for the day since I decided the night before I was skipping my after-school detention and would need to communicate with my brothers.

"Bro...you ain't gon' believe this," I told Clay over the phone in between classes.

"Yo what happened?"

"You know how I told you last night this dude trying to actually plant something in my locker?"

"How you find that out?" he asked.

"My boys said he posted something and they sent it to me on my messages."

"Bro if he do, just know I'm coming up there and he done!" Clay said.

"Bro, that ain't even it! They said he the one made a formal complaint with the drama teacher after the talent show. When she ain't do nothing, he had his dad call the school. Apparently his dad gives the school a lot of money, so they do whatever he asks. After he called, that lady disqualified us from winning!"

"Whatchu gon' do?" he asked.

"I wanna beat the shit out him!"

"Then do it! He gotta learn…and then you might go ahead and kicked out and won't have to worry about it anymore!"

For whatever reason, the most irrational person in my world seemed to make more sense than anything else. "I'm 'bout to find this dude," I said.

"Aight, text me lemme know w'sup! I'll go home and get my bike and come over there!"

I went searching for Mark Paul at lunch time in hopes to find him alone, and found him coming out of the bathroom on the second floor near math class. He looked unsettled seeing me without his crew and stopped in his tracks when he saw me approach. We both stood eye to eye in an empty hallway and had our first one-on-one conversation since school had started.

"What you doing after school today? I heard you got some problems with me?" I said as I drew even closer to him. He knew exactly what I was hinting at.

"I'm not gonna fight you on school property. I'm not a thug who wants suspensions on my record like you. How'd that meeting go with the principal after the talent show?"

He smirked at me when he asked. I wanted to stick him right in the smirk, but I knew I had to stand down for the moment.

"Name the spot," I said. "And don't be no punk ass running to the principal or police or calling me a bully. This is one on one, just me and you."

To my surprise, he agreed, and told me about an empty lot about a quarter of a mile from the school, tucked away from the road. I told him I'd be there, and that anyone I brought was just to make sure the fight stayed fair. I knew he wouldn't show up alone, so I texted Tommy and

Marco, and Daveon and Clay, telling them the plan. Clay told Daveon to pick him up in front of his school so he could be there.

Daveon's car swerved into the lot right as Tommy, Marco, and I arrived on foot. Mark Paul was already in place, surrounded by a few friends and an older cousin that also attended the school. The only loose end I hadn't tied up was telling Uncle D I wouldn't be waiting curbside when he arrived at school to pick me up from detention. I concluded that we needed to start and end quickly so I could return without him knowing what I had done.

Daveon announced to everyone that nobody was allowed in the fight to help just before Mark Paul and I met in the middle of the group. I took off my shirt and handed the contents of my pockets to Clay. Before I knew it, Mark Paul threw the first punch and connected to my mouth.

The sting to my jaw was completely unexpected. Daveon, my cheerleader and coach in every task, yelled at me to handle business. I advanced toward my opponent and squared up as he swung again, this time missing my face, but he followed with a punch that landed firmly on my stomach, and caught me in the mouth while I bent down to clutch my stomach. I tasted the blood as it crawled through my lips down to my chin.

I wasn't sure how it happened, but something inside me clicked just as loudly as the punch he landed. My brain and my vision went dark, and I morphed like Bruce Banner into the Hulk. I landed a punch on the side of his face with my right, followed by a solid punch to his neck with my left. I briefly backed up with my fists still raised before shuffling toward him again, swinging at his face until I blacked out. The next thing I remembered was being hunched down with one knee pitted into his stomach, my knuckles taking turns bashing into the sides of his face while he loudly groaned, and his head banging repeatedly into the pavement until blood and sweat splattered through the air with each punch.

The faint sounds of his friends trying to intervene and yell at me to stop were not enough to calm my internal or external ferocity, but after a few moments, Daveon and Marco pried my body off of Mark Paul's and screamed at me that we had to go.

Daveon led me away while the other three sprinted behind us to Daveon's car, and he sped out of the lot to drive Marco and Tommy home. We were yelling and screaming and cussing like we had just won money for knocking out Mike Tyson, and they joyfully congratulated me, with Tommy teasing that I had knocked Mark Paul out like Deebo knocked out Joker in the movie Friday.

"My boy, the gangster nerd came through and shut it down, bruh!" Tommy laughed.

"I ain't think you had it in you!" Marco said.

Caught up in laughing and talking, I had forgotten about my plan to ask Daveon to drop me back off at school so I could meet Uncle D for pickup. I had been too distracted by the celebration, which was cut short a few minutes after Daveon had driven off the lot.

"Shit! They lightin' me up!" Daveon yelled, looking in the rearview mirror. Marco turned around from the front seat to confirm and then started looking straight ahead after mumbling a few profanities.

"Tommy, you gotta give Tay one of your shirts. Tay, just use your shirt to wipe off the blood and then put on Tommy's shirt. Maybe you can sit on top of the bloody shirt!" Marco said.

"Yeah, but if they see them bending over, they gon' think it's sus!" Clay said.

"Just do it fast, and then when they approach everyone put your hands out. I'll start recording on the cell phone. Day, just pull over and put up your hands," Marco said.

"Bro, Unc gon' kill me if I end up in custody," Daveon said.

"Man, if them dudes called the police, it's *me* Unc gonna kill!" I said.

My heart raced as I bent forward to slide on Tommy's shirt, hoping the officer didn't start screaming after seeing me bent forward. But it was nearly five minutes before contact was even made, and we sat silently other than Clay turning around and then announcing that there were two police cars behind us instead of one.

"Whatever y'all do, just tell him I was picking y'all up from school to give you a ride home," Daveon said, making sure nobody mentioned the fight.

"Bro, you straight, right?" I asked Daveon, noticing how nervous he seemed.

"I got something on me. Just pray or something that this shit is over quick!" I knew he meant it when he said to pray, which was exactly what I did under my breath. The last thing we needed was Uncle D finding out Daveon had still been smoking, on top of everything else we would be in trouble for.

"They betta not start talking crazy or I'm going off," Clay said breathing hard. I closed my eyes as soon as he said it, preparing for Daveon to jump into the backseat and strangle him.

"Clay, I promise you, keep yo' lil' bad-ass mouth shut!" Daveon shouted with his eyes still staring out the front windshield.

Within minutes we had officers on both sides of the car. I watched them closely while other motorists slowed down to see what was happening inside our vehicle. Marco reminded us to keep our hands visible, and the only one who wouldn't was Clay.

"License and registration please, young man," the officer who stood by the driver's side window ordered, while the other peered inside the car as though he expected to discover contraband.

"My registration is in the glove compartment," Daveon said. Uncle D checked his glove compartment nearly every two weeks to make sure his paperwork was in place. Daveon was lectured eternally one time when it was missing.

"Do you mind if I open your glove compartment and retrieve it for you?" the officer leaning in the passenger window asked.

"I don't mind," Daveon said. He lowered the window further down so the officer could reach in the glove compartment.

"Do you have any weapons or anything sharp in here I should know about?" the officer asked.

"Why the fuck would he have something sharp? We ain't no crackheads!" Clay yelled from the backseat.

"Bro, shut up!" Tommy told him through clenched teeth.

"I'm sorry for my brother's mouth, officer. His parents were drug addicts, and now he has behavior problems," Daveon said, aggravated with Clay's mouth.

"Really bro? We got the same mama!" Clay said.

The officer silently pulled out paperwork and then glanced over at Marco as though he was studying his face.

"You boys go to Loyola Institute High School? You look like that basketball player!" the officer asked Marco.

"Yes, sir. I'm on the team there," Marco told him nervously. He still was sitting erect with his hands planted over his knees.

The officer looked curiously at Marco and then back at Clay before disappearing to the squad cars behind us. We communicated in only low whispers while we waited for what felt like an eternity for the officer to return with Daveon's license and registration paperwork.

"You boys have a good day, and stay out of trouble," he said as he stepped away.

"Yo what the fuck you pull us over for then?" Clay yelled. He grunted just as loudly as he had yelled when I rammed his rib cage with my elbow. At the same time, Tommy nudged him in the arm from the other side, while Daveon tried his best to talk over Clay and politely thank the officer before pulling off.

"Bro, I'm rolling you out when we get home!" Daveon yelled once we were back on the road.

We mostly rode in silence, no longer feeling able to laugh and joke about the fight after being pulled over. After so much had been happening around the country, every encounter with the police, whether good or bad, was starting to feel like a near-death experience. While I was thankful we hadn't been forced to sit curbside at gunpoint, as had happened to Marco, Tommy, and my brothers before, I couldn't help but wonder what would have happened had the officer not recognized Marco as a star basketball player.

After dropping Tommy off at the train station, we stopped at Marco's house so I could get cleaned up. They all looked at me crazy for requesting a shirt and tie from Marco's closet, but I was convinced Uncle D would kill me if I looked as though I had been fighting as opposed to doing something positive.

"Shoot, this dude been blowing my phone up," I said after checking my phone to discover multiple missed calls from Uncle D. I was mad with myself for forgetting to have Daveon drop me off at detention, and the thought of facing Uncle D was increasing my already heightened anxiety.

"Just tell him you forget he was getting you and you called me." Daveon said.

"By now he knows I skipped detention bro. I'm through. If I lie to him, it's just gon' make it worse. You know how he is," I said.

We sat around for a few more minutes trying to think of excuses we could give Uncle D for my absence from detention. Soon after we left Marco's house, Tommy called and told me that Uncle D had just called him inquiring about our whereabouts.

"What'd you tell him?" I asked.

"Bro, he ain't exactly happy with you! I was just like 'I saw him for a minute after school and then I came home.' You got me out here lying to Unc, and I could tell he ain't believe me! Y'all might wanna turn around and come stay at my crib for the night," Tommy joked.

I wished he had told Uncle D the truth so I wouldn't have to, especially after we arrived home and saw how upset he was.

"He 'bout to kill you bro," Clay said while we peered out the car windows at Uncle D, who was on the porch pacing back and forth with his arms folded.

"I swear I didn't mean to skip detention, but I know he ain't gon' believe me," I said. We mumbled amongst ourselves to decide who should do the talking, and Daveon reminded Clay to keep his mouth shut before we got out of the car and hesitantly crossed the front lawn to head inside.

We walked like the three billy goats who weren't sure they'd be able to cross the bridge guarded by the troll, hoping Uncle D would allow us entry into the house without first eating us alive.

"Clay, why weren't you in your last class at school today?" he inquired loudly when we reached him, and I knew the conversation was about to go south.

Clay conjured up a quick reply. "I had to use the bathroom real bad, like my stomach was like bubbling."

In my mind I was punching Clay in the mouth for saying something so dumb. Daveon turned slightly to the side, probably holding in either a laugh or a cuss word.

"And I suppose that's also why you left your fifth period class early?"

We hadn't thought any of it through, but it didn't stop Clay from continuing his tall tale.

"That's actually when it started was fifth period, and I didn't finish 'til school was almost out," Clay lied convincingly, and had it been a perfect stranger we would have been on the next subject already, but I could tell Uncle D wasn't buying that Clay had a ninety-minute dump that kept him from attending classes.

"And that's what happened to you too, Tay? You missed detention because you were in the restroom?" he turned to me, putting me on the spot.

"Uh, naw Unc. Um, so, um Marco wanted to show me something after school. I thought I could go to his crib real quick and get back in time for detention, but um—"

"You knew exactly where you were supposed to be today! Not only were you not outside for me to pick you up, but they told me you didn't show up to detention at all! And now the three of you just suddenly show up, hours after you were all supposed to be here?" He spoke so loudly that I wondered if any of the neighbors had called the police. "GET IN THIS HOUSE RIGHT NOW!"

"Unc, it's my fault. I—" I tried to get my brothers out of trouble, but he raised his hand up to silence me.

We hadn't even made it to the couch where he had ordered us to sit when the doorbell rang. Uncle D went to open the door, and after a few moments, called me to the door, where one white and one black police officer stood in front of Uncle D on the porch. I assumed the neighbors had called the police, and Uncle D was going to make me explain what had caused him to yell at us outside. Their uniforms were different from the officers that had pulled us over earlier, and I was relieved that it wasn't the same department. I was hoping that my outfit would keep them from labeling me. Still, I was terrified with them being there and felt strongly there was no chance I would avoid handcuffs twice in one day.

The white officer spoke first. "Are you Dontay Lands?"

I looked at Uncle D, trying to decide if I should even acknowledge my identity.

"This is him, officer," Uncle D said.

"Okay, so we're not placing him under arrest just yet, but we do need to detain him. We have another officer out with our victim. Sir, we're told your son attacked Mark Paul Bailey in a parking lot after school."

"Man I ain't attack nobody!" I said, feeling afraid that I was about to get stuffed into the back of their police vehicle.

"Really, 'cause his face was pretty messed up," the black officer replied.

"That's 'cause his weak ass can't fight!" Clay interjected, having come out onto the porch to see what was happening.

"Clay Lands! You will not disrespect these officers by speaking like that!" Uncle D said.

"Officers that I be seeing be talking way worse than that but okay," Clay said.

"Sir, the victim went home pretty bruised and bloody after a fight in a lot near his school, and his mother wanted to file a police report and accused your son of assaulting her son," the black officer continued.

Uncle D's demeanor changed from angry to downright homicidal after the officer discussed the fight.

"Why the hell you calling him a victim when he swung first?" Clay asked.

"Clay, I already told you about that mouth!" Uncle D said, sounding as though he was trying not to yell in front of the officers.

"How do you know he swung first?" the white officer asked Clay.

"I watched him do it. And I got it on video 'cause I know them white boys be lying on us! He been lying on my brother all year!" Clay said.

I knew Clay was trying to keep me out of police custody, but the look Uncle D gave after Clay spoke told me that the three of us might not survive the night.

They asked to see his phone, and Clay played back the fight after Uncle D gave the officers permission to view it. I glanced over at Uncle D, who was either practicing breathing exercises or speaking in tongues. The officers watched the first part of the video but didn't watch it to the end where I pounded Mark Paul's eyes shut. They watched enough to see that he was hitting me as much as I was hitting him.

The officers thanked Clay and thanked Uncle D before leaving and suggested that if I had a conflict with someone at school, I should talk with the guidance counselor instead of resorting to violence.

After being equipped with the entire story, Uncle D ordered us all back to the couch where I knew we'd have hell to pay. We had been his temporary kids long enough to know he wasn't about to give us one of his comforting, pastoral speeches. He remained outside for over five minutes after the officers left while we sat on the couch waiting for the flames of hell to arrive in the family room. Once he finally came back in, Daveon tried to talk, but Uncle D didn't let him get in even one word.

"Daveon Kahari Lands, I'm not trying to hear it. You are the oldest and you should have been talking him out of a fight! Not helping your baby brother skip class to go help your little brother skip detention and fight! What if the police would've come up there while y'all were fighting? Who do you think would've been more likely to get arrested? The crew of black boys or the rich white boys?"

He turned toward me. "It doesn't seem like you've been seeking God about your issues at school! Who came up with this idea that you should fight, Tay?"

I looked down and closed my eyes not wanting to answer, and heard only the sounds of the door to the garage opening, and Auntie Robin, Caleb and Sophie stepping in. While they had been chatting in the garage, their chatter ceased when they realized they had stumbled upon what could soon become a crime scene. Auntie Robin joined us in the family room, but Uncle D didn't stop to acknowledge her presence.

"Answer me!" he rumbled.

"It was my idea," I softly confessed.

"So you decided you would skip detention, which the school is now going to discipline you for. You decided not to call me and tell me that you wouldn't be at pickup and have me worried sick that something was terribly wrong. You decided to have your brothers skip out on their own classes, and you decided to resort to violence to solve your problems? And then you looked me *dead* in my face and lied to me about where you've been, and the police had to come to my house to tell me the truth. How wise have your choices been today, Dontay?"

He was even more intense than he had been when we were outside on the porch. I sighed and looked down to study the dark floral pattern of the rug in front of my feet. I knew I had messed up, but I hated that he was throwing it in my face and making me say it. I knew that any sort of lying or sneaking around really set him off, and I wished I had just answered the phone when he called earlier and told him what I had done.

"I asked you a question, and I'm expecting an answer."

I still didn't want to answer since it seemed like he was doing what every other adult person did, which was focus on what I had done without focusing on why.

Clay piped up, as always. "But Unc, this dude was gon'—"

"I asked Tay a question, Clay." Uncle D said with warning in his tone. But warnings generally didn't stop Clay.

"But he tried to—"

"Clay, let me tell you something…you're in enough trouble of your own for that lie you told me. I'm going to suggest you follow my instructions. You have your nerve—all of you getting here way later than you should be here, after you left school early!"

Uncle D was growing impatient. I was glad Daveon motioned for Clay to sit back and chill. Clay's unrelenting mouth could escalate almost any situation, and we could not afford any additional escalation. Uncle D looked back at me, waiting for an answer.

"It ain't our fault the racist police pulled us o—" Clay suddenly stopped when he realized he had said too much, and I wasn't sure who would explode first between Daveon and Uncle D.

"You got pulled over, Day?" Auntie Robin asked, leaning forward in her seat.

Daveon and I both looked at Clay like he was about to meet his maker as soon as we were alone with him.

"Auntie, it's not a big deal, I promise. I didn't even get a tick—"

"How is it not a big deal that a car full of black boys in West County got pulled over, Daveon? So, another detail you all accidentally left out of your afternoon!" Uncle D turned his attention to Auntie Robin. "I didn't even tell you the part about the police showing up to tell me they were all out fighting. I gotta find out where my kids are through the police because they have told me nothing but lies since they walked in the door. Boy if I wasn't so daggone angry right now…What they pull you over for, Daveon? I've already talked to you about driving recklessly!"

We could tell by the way he asked he expected the worst response. Daveon shook his head. "Nothing!"

"They just pulled you over for no reason at all?"

"Yeah!"

"You know what, you all go to your rooms. I'm so tired of being lied to right now I'm about to lose it!"

"Fine," Daveon said as he stood up, "but ain't nobody even fucking lying to you!"

It was a bad idea for him to go there, and had it been Kemis, there would have already been a shoe tossed at his head.

"I'm guessing you think since you seventeen now you old enough to disrespect me!" Uncle D told Daveon as he stepped directly in front of him and grabbed his arm. "Who exactly do you think you talking to?"

Daveon put his head down, knowing he had gone too far. I cautiously spoke up, in hopes to diffuse the situation and keep Daveon from losing his life.

"They really didn't give us a reason, Unc. Once they saw Marco in the car, they just ran Day's stuff and told us to leave," I said.

Uncle D stepped back, loosed Daveon's arm, and stood with his eyes closed, as though he was in deep meditation. After a moment of silence, he looked as though he had more to say but was too upset to say it.

"You all give me your phones and go to your rooms." He held his hand out waiting for us to comply. I felt bad that I had dragged my brothers into trouble with me, knowing at the same time they would have been mad at me had I done it without them.

"Day, come back here and hand me your keys," Uncle D said. Daveon froze and tossed his head back to glare at the ceiling before he turned around and removed his car keys from his pocket.

"Ah!"

I turned to see Daveon grimacing, while Uncle D was gripping the back of Daveon's arm with a church pinch.

"Let's not speak to me that way ever again, do you understand?"

"Aight, Unc!" Daveon said. He walked away squeezing his injured arm after Uncle D finally released his grip.

I knew Daveon had only cussed out of frustration with the traffic stop and the fact that he was getting yelled at primarily because of me. He generally wasn't the type to express when something was bothering him, but he was burdened with trying to keep Clay and me together in a new environment and making sure we knew he had our back. I, on the other hand, was burdened with wondering how long I would be grounded for, and wondering what would happen at school once word got back about the fight.

31

holy kiss

I wondered what Jason and Kemis would say when they heard what we had done, but we didn't hear from Kemis that night. He had gone to an early morning counseling session and was recommended to check himself into the hospital for twenty-four hours, which he did.

Uncle D explained it to us at dinner that night, which was our first time seeing him after having spent the majority of the afternoon in our rooms. He was much calmer than he had been when we first arrived home, and told us that he had considered punishing us by keeping us home from Indianapolis, where Jason was playing his tournament game later that week, but decided against it since Jason really wanted to see us.

"Is K going?" Clay asked.

"He wants to," Uncle D said, "but I think he needs to stay home and rest once he's released."

"Why he ain't tell us he was going to the hospital?" Daveon asked. He had stopped eating to voice a shared concern we all had about Kemis' well-being.

"I know it sounds bad…and yes, he was in a bad place, but he's much better already," Uncle D said reassuringly. "I talked to him earlier and so did Pastor James. I also talked to one of the nurses tending to him. He's taking some time for himself because one day he wants to be back with you three full-time."

"Can't we go see him before the trip?" Clay asked.

"The staff advised against it Clay. And I think if that's what they advise, we should stand by and pray for him while he focuses on his healing. I'm sure he'll be ready to hang out and talk when we get back to town."

"Daddy, are we going?" Caleb asked him.

"You are. Sophie and mommy are going to stay home this time," he answered.

"That's not fair, daddy! I want to go watch Jason too!" Sophie cried.

"I know sweetie. You and Daddy are going out for ice cream when I get back though, okay?" Uncle D said, prompting Caleb to frown.

"She gets ice cream?" Caleb asked in disbelief. Uncle D shook his head and smiled.

Having no phones forced us to hang out with everyone that night. We played basketball in the back driveway, including a game of horse with Caleb and Sophie. Afterwards, we took the two of them out to roller skate down the sidewalk while we talked about the fight and Uncle D's blow-up, and discussed whether we should try to get in touch with Kemis despite Uncle D's advice.

I was surprised that Paris popped into the backyard just before it was completely dark while we were still out back, telling me she had been calling my phone after hearing what happened.

"Yeah, I guess I'm on a Unc punishment again—me and my brothers," I said, looking around to see if Uncle D could see that I had a visitor.

She laughed, "It's becoming your new normal, isn't it?"

"I don't want it to be. And we ain't get churchy church Unc today. There were no 'God bless yous' or 'I love yous' or nothing!"

She started laughing. "Seriously though, I can't believe you fought that dude! Why didn't you just let it go?" she asked me.

"I just ain't care anymore. You know I want out this school, and Unc ain't gonna let me. Plus, I was pissed about his IG post," I said.

"If I got in a fight over an IG post, my parents would probably take my phone forever!" she said.

"Mine may be gone that long…we'll see."

I hated I wasn't going to see her at school anymore after school was out for the year. I scooted closer to her and slid my arm around her back as we continued to catch up and watch the others play basketball. Within minutes, Uncle D stepped out of the house and joined us on the patio couch, obnoxiously forcing himself between Paris and I and making me slide away from her.

Paris spoke up to fill the uncomfortable silence. "Hey Pastor D, I was just—"

"Naw, I know what you were *just* doing. You were seeing if you could catch him outside since you knew I wasn't going to let him have company."

"No, Pastor D. I mean, everyone needs some encouraging words from time to time. Isn't that the sisterly thing to do when someone had a rough day?" she asked, trying to look innocent.

"Oh, so y'all acting like brother and sister now?" he asked, raising his eyebrows.

We both smiled, and he knew he was embarrassing us but didn't stop. "Paris, where'd you tell your parents you were going?"

"Pastor D, why are you so strict?" she asked.

"I'm just saying, I hadn't parented teenagers full-time until this year, but I realize y'all have this tendency to say y'all will be one place, and actually be somewhere else, which I may knock someone out over soon."

He looked at me as he ended the sentence, and I tried to look away as though his words didn't apply to me.

"I mean, I didn't exactly say I was going here. I might have said I was going to my friend's house, so that's not a lie. I just didn't tell them it was a boy—"

"'Boyfriend?'" he tried to finish her sentence, and we started laughing.

"How about I walk Paris to her car, Unc?" I asked, begging with my eyes that he leave us alone for a few minutes.

"That's a good idea, Tay! We'll walk her together," he said, knowing we wouldn't kiss in front of him. "C'mon, let's go," he stood up and tugged my arm.

I was annoyed by his refusal to leave us in peace. We talked about what Paris was about to get into as we followed the driveway around the house and to the front where she had parked, awkwardly stopping once we reached the end of the driveway.

"Uh, do I have permission to hug my *sister*, Unc?" I asked him sarcastically when we reached her car.

He chuckled. "Y'all can do a holy side hug," he answered and then demonstrated how I was supposed to wrap one arm around her and slightly lean my body toward hers.

"But the Bible says greet each other with a holy kiss!" I told him.

"Amen, preacher!" Paris followed up, laughing.

Uncle D looked surprised that I was quoting a scripture. "I'm about to greet you with a holy kick in the tail. I'm pretty sure what I witnessed between the two of you before was not a holy kiss," he said only semi-jokingly. "Good night, Paris."

"Good night, Pastor D," she said with a sigh. "Good night, Tay." She looked at me and blew a kiss that I extended my hand to catch when Uncle D knocked my hand down and air swatted the kiss away.

"Why you gotta hate?" I turned and laughed at him.

He knocked me in the head playfully before we returned to the backyard.

32

unreasonable alternatives

Jason's team was eliminated from post-season play during the game we watched in Indianapolis. It turned out that the only good thing about us going was when he ended up hanging out with us after the game in the hotel all night talking and laughing. Otherwise, I caught hands from Jason for getting in trouble with Uncle D, and then my punishment got extended when Uncle D saw my tattoo after I came out of the shower. I was moody and exhausted by the time we got back to town that Sunday evening. I was not ready to face the reality that I had to return to school the next day, but Uncle D came in the bedroom with Clay and me as we prepared to turn in for the night to discuss school anyway.

"Well, Tay, your principal emailed. You have to go to detention three times to make up for the one you skipped—otherwise you'll be suspended. They've been made aware of the fight but stated there won't be any discipline for it since it occurred off school property," he told me as he sat down on the bed.

"I ain't trying to do three detentions!"

"So let me make it extremely clear that you don't have a choice. If I have to come to school and walk you to detention myself while holding your hand, I will," he responded. "And if you try to pull something after

I've already told you you're going, I'ma have your phone for another month," he said.

"Unc that's crazy! I—"

"Are you raising your voice at me?" he asked me calmly as he folded his hands.

I leaned back until my head rested against the headboard. "No," I grumbled.

"Good. Clay, I gave Daveon his phone back and I'm going to give you yours too. But let's understand that you are not to leave school without Kemis, myself, or Auntie signing you out. Do you understand?" Uncle D asked him.

Clay nodded.

"You know that's not acceptable."

"Yes," Clay said, trying to curb the annoyance in his voice. He displayed a wide grin after Uncle D handed him back his phone. I stared longingly at Clay and his phone, overcome with envy that they had their phones and I didn't.

"Tay, just a reminder, I expect you to be where you're supposed to be. I don't like being lied to or snuck around on. If you're supposed to be in detention, go to detention, and nowhere else. If you're supposed to be outside waiting for me after detention, I need to see you there and nowhere else. You earned your punishment. You broke the rules, and now you have to deal with the consequences of that. Let's get these detentions served, and then we'll go from there. Do you understand?"

He looked as though he dared me not to answer, but I knew what I needed to say to get him out of my hair, and quickly.

"Yes," I mumbled.

"Goodnight fellas. Y'all know I'm only hard on you because I love you, and I want to see good things for you," he said as he walked out.

"Ay, I gotta go holler at Day real quick," I said to Clay. "I'll be right back."

I left and headed downstairs to talk to Daveon, where I found him in his room on his phone sending celebratory text messages.

"Bro, were you shocked he gave you your phone?" I asked.

"We had a long talk on the drive home when y'all were sleeping. I apologized about the other day, partially because Jay threatened to kill me if I didn't. And Unc said he'd remove my head if it happened again," he said chuckling.

"Bro, real talk, I thought he was gon' remove it that day. But look, why don't you let me keep the burner phone for a while?" I asked him.

Jason had purchased our secret cell phone years before that Daveon was now paying for. Jason bought it when he was in high school in case Kemis or Granny put him on punishment and took his phone. We had all taken turns using it, but Daveon now retained its custody. He said he was glad he kept paying for it, especially after moving in with Uncle D.

"Bro, you sure you wanna risk it? I bet you get your phone back after you handle your detentions."

"He already said I'm getting an extra two weeks for the tat. It's about to be forever, and I gotta text Paris—we making plans for a walk-out."

He got up from the bed and reached into a container that sat in the back of his closet, dug out the phone, and handed it to me.

"If you get caught, don't drop my name, bro!" he said.

33

blackout

"So you still coming to Blackout, right?" Paris asked me. I was sitting in Daveon's room late into the night on the burner phone with Paris, trying to speak in a voice low enough to keep from waking anyone else in the house.

Paris and I, along with the other students in the Minority Student Union club had staged a "Blackout," where we would walk out of our classes to the amphitheater and bonfire pit in the back of the school, in protest of recent events at school. One being the talent show, where everyone concluded that we were only robbed of winnings because of Mark Paul and his rich parents. The other was a recent meeting of school administrators, where they announced they would be banning a number of books from the school library, many of which were written by some of the few black authors that were on the shelves. Paris had heard from other students that the ban idea also started with the talent show, since word had gotten to the principal that multiple students were requesting books on Malcolm X after my talent show performance. It added fuel to an already blazing fire, particularly since we had already complained about the lack of black literature. We had convinced most of the black students to participate in the Blackout, and a large number of white students too.

Paris and I had made secret post-Blackout plans that involved me hanging out at her house since her parents wouldn't be home until late. We had a show picked out to watch on Netflix, and she had made promises to serve popcorn and soda.

I was equally excited about both events for that day, but nervous about how I would keep my plans from Uncle D.

"You know I'm definitely coming! Coming there and coming to see you! You sure yo' parents won't be coming in though, right? I can't have Unc finding out I was at your crib," I said.

"I'm sure. They have a business dinner. They said they're going straight there from the office."

"Aight. I'll see you tomorrow then."

The only other thing complicating my plans was that the next day was supposed to be the final day of my detention, but I had already decided that the Blackout and hanging with Paris would be more important than serving out another unfair punishment from the school.

"So what time you need me to be there?" Daveon asked, seeing that I was finally done talking on the phone. I had told him earlier to tell Uncle D he was picking me up from detention.

"Ah, you not actually picking me up. I just need you to say you are," I said.

"Wait wait, so where we supposed to go? You know I'm picking up Clay tomorrow. We can't come to the house without you. And where you gon' be, bro?"

"Look, just take Clay to eat or to the store or something. Then we'll meet up and come home together. We'll just tell them we made a stop if they ask."

"Bro, you not hearing me; where *you* gon' be?"

"Look, we doing this Blackout tomorrow for most of the afternoon. After that, I'm going with Paris," I said, eager for his reaction since he had previously said I wasn't doing enough to get her to be my girlfriend.

"Wait, so you skipping yo' afternoon classes? And detention? You act like Unc ain't gon' get a text! Where y'all going?"

"To her crib. Their parents coming late. I ain't trippin' off Unc…Once he find out about the Blackout, he'll just think I was at the school. I'll just tell him I skipped 'cause I was pissed off, which I am!"

Daveon looked at me with wide eyes. "Bro, you have officially lost it. He gon' flip his shit! And what you mad about now?"

"Bro, it's just a lot of little stuff adding up. I'm still pissed he didn't listen to me about school. Pissed about this talent show, and about this book ban. Even in detention today, this girl said someone took her new headphones, and the teacher came straight to me and asked to search my backpack. Man, I'm so tired of these people, bro! I ain't even tell Unc about it 'cause I'm done." I had almost forgotten about what had happened that day, but retelling the story made me too angry to care about being in trouble.

"And what you and Paris gon' be doing?"

"Dude, it's not even like that. We just hanging out. She said she'll drop me off when I gotta leave, so I'll call you to meet us."

"If it ain't like that, what you going for?"

"Just hanging out, talking, you know."

"Bruh…ain't no way you just gon' be sitting over there just talking. Her parents gon' be gone…she cute too? Ain't gon' happen."

"Bro, I'm for real. I'm not even trying to go there," I said.

"If you don't hit, don't even call me to come get you, bro. Yo' lame ass can walk home," he laughed.

"Whatever dude," I told him, shaking my head.

"Just make sure you take them gloves, man. We calling you on the burner?"

"Unc always give me my phone before school when I'm on punishment, so I'ma have them both on so I don't miss you. But call the burner anyway. I don't want him to see on my phone later that we were calling each other," I said.

"Bro, you forget Unc went off the last time you skipped detention. You sure you wanna do this?" he asked.

"This will be my only chance to hang with Paris for a while. By the time I'm off lockdown, K and Jay will have moved in, and I won't be able to do nothing," I reasoned, and he agreed.

We both knew we would soon go from having two parents to four, as Jason's semester was almost over, and Kemis said he was moving in with us and leaving Kyle's place soon. I knew there would be consequences for missing classes and detention, but I figured the fun I planned to have would far outweigh the consequences.

34

a trip to paris

In fourteen years on earth, I could recall a handful of events that I knew I would never forget. One was visiting my dad in prison, since I left the correctional center with an eerie feeling that I never wanted to return again. I had been curious to see what he looked like, and what it looked like inside the building, but remembered leaving with expectations that, although probably unreasonable, had gone unmet. And then there was the day that Granny died. I could have been wrong, but I always felt like I was closer to her than my brothers. Even at a young age, she would confide in me things she didn't tell them, and I would keep everything in confidence, even some of the scary things that I was probably too young and immature to know.

There was the day I got saved at church. I remembered the overwhelming feeling that came with walking down the middle aisle of a crowded church to stand in the front of the room to be stared at by the congregation, to have to pray and talk in front of all those people about a faith that felt spectacular and mysterious all at the same time. More recently, it was the day Kory died, which happened to be paired with us getting evicted from the apartment we had lived in with Granny for many years. Both events were difficult to endure, and we were still piecing back together our hearts and our minds from those losses.

But Blackout Day turned into a day that I knew would easily be one of my most memorable. I was holding onto a secret that was even bigger than my talent show experience, and woke up with a zeal I hadn't felt in a long time. I wondered how Harriet Tubman felt on mornings when she knew she would be taking people on a journey to freedom, or how Frederick Douglas felt when he woke up with the knowledge that he would lead another soul to mental freedom in showing them how to read and write. Although I knew my day would not be as significant as days that either of them had, I was excited about finally being able to uniquely express my dissatisfaction with my school, maybe in the same way that Dr. King would have done it.

Everything mostly went as planned that day. Ten minutes into fourth period, at "black o'clock," as we had called it, I stood from my seat and looked around the room to see a few others stand with me, and we all proceeded into the hallways where we were met with other students and confused looks from teachers. We marched and chanted our way through the hallways and outside the rear exit doors to the back of the school and grouped in the small amphitheater, where one of the students already had a fire blazing in the firepit. Our Minority Student Union president stood on the stage, speaking to the crowd with a megaphone, preparing to lead a few chants. Students were recording the events on their phones and going live on social media, and some had invited friends and family from other schools, making the crowd even larger than expected.

We had prepared posters and flyers, which Paris, Tommy, and I were busy passing out to onlookers. A few students shared speeches for the crowd about some of the racist experiences they had at the school, but what I hadn't expected was for Teela, the club president, to ask me to recite my "talent-show-winning speech" in front of the crowd. I was nervous that I had forgotten some of the lines, but once I reached the stage and grabbed the megaphone, everything came back to me as though I had just performed it the day before. The crowd cheered even louder than they had at the talent show, and chanted "Take it back!" when I was finished, expressing that they wanted to take the winning prizes from the group they were awarded to and give us our rightful winnings. Somehow, the enthusiasm motivated me to give the crowd more.

"Yo, I just wanna say something real quick about why we're out here today!" I said into the megaphone. "This school so worried about critical race theory because they're scared for people to know the truth about what this nation has done to black people. They think we're supposed to ignore four hundred years of mistreatment, and act like it doesn't impact us anymore."

The crowd was already cheering and screaming with just those few lines, making me feel as though they would listen if I talked all day.

"The irony is that they are banning books that bring us valuable information, when it's these textbooks with nothing in them that should be banned. This shit is useless if it doesn't teach black history and tell the truth about this nation being built upon the backs of brilliant black people that they stole and turned into slaves.

"You know what needs to be banned? Yo, someone bring my backpack please?" I asked, and watched as Tommy ran it to the stage. I reached in and pulled out the American History textbook, and held it over my head. "This shit needs to be banned!"

Someone in the crowd yelled, "BURN THAT SHIT!" prompting everyone to chant it, including myself, into the megaphone. After a few moments of chanting, I did exactly what we were yelling—I threw the book into the fire, prompting cheers and even louder chants. For some reason, seeing the book land in the flames felt good, and I decided to add more books to it. I took out another book from my backpack and threw it in. Before I knew it, students from all directions were coming up to burn textbooks and library books, prompting the fire to grow stronger. A few handed me their books that I tossed in the fire on their behalf.

Teela retook the stage to share a few more words while the book burning continued, and Paris and I shared a celebratory kiss in front of the fire about how well the turnout had been and how well the speeches had all been received. It was the prequel to what would be an enjoyable afternoon at her house.

We slipped away without telling anyone other than Tommy that we were heading off campus, and stopped only to grab a bite to eat, my first time the entire day consuming a meal. After spending time binging a few shows on the couch, I took Paris up on her offer to tour their lavish home, which was even more impressive past the foyer, which was the furthest I had been on previous visits.

Some of the rooms could have been magazine features. Her dad had a huge room on the main floor that he used as an office, which was way bigger than Uncle D's home office. He also had a plush mancave in the basement, equipped with a huge television, surround-sound speakers, a bar, a pool table, a mini barbershop, a fitness room in the back, a small sauna, and other amenities that made it look like a room from a home remodeling show, making me wonder how much money her family had. In addition to an elaborate living room and fancy dining room, they had a room lined with bookshelves covering the walls, with a baby grand piano in the middle, where we stopped so she could demonstrate the skills she had perfected in her weekly piano lessons.

I was equally impressed with her bedroom, as it was decorated with medals and trophies she had earned from cheerleading and tennis. I started flirting with her because she looked extra cute in her "black students matter" t-shirt and tennis skirt, and I wanted her to finally agree to be my girlfriend, which she did. The next thing I knew, we went from holding hands to hugging, to play fighting, to kissing, and not just any kind of kissing. We were on her bed, kissing in a way I knew we never could with Uncle D in our faces. I could picture him screaming in my ears upon seeing what we were doing, but I tried to block him out and concentrate on her.

I had never kissed any girl the way I had kissed her in that moment, or for that long. I couldn't believe we were kissing in a house without any parents, and I was excited and afraid at the same time. I understood what Daveon meant by saying "you never know what could happen." Things were progressing between us, her hands and my hands were probably roaming more than they should have, and the atmosphere seemed to shift. I asked her if I should grab a condom, and she nodded her head.

My heart raced with fear and excitement as I pulled out my wallet while I watched her stand up to undress. She climbed back in bed while I got ready, and we suddenly heard faint noises from downstairs, followed by the voice of her mother downstairs near the bottom of the steps calling, "Paris sweetie, we're home. I didn't want to startle you! We're going to be working from home for a bit!" We could hear footsteps on the stairwell shortly thereafter, and the two of us jumped out of bed panicking.

"Get… get in the closet!" she shrieked in a high-toned whisper as she forced open the door and pushed me in and threw in my sweatpants, softly closing the door behind me. I was thankful it was a roomy, walk-in closet, leaving me space to slip on some of my clothing. I heard her stuffing her body into a nightdress before she went downstairs to make sure my backpack was hidden and to find out how long her parents were staying.

The two of them ran a company together, and I wondered what would prompt them to come home for the day when Paris had told me they often worked extended hours and had particularly late plans for the day. It was nearly twenty minutes before she returned, stating her dad mentioned something about giving Uncle D a phone and that their dinner had been cancelled but they were leaving soon to do something else.

"Hopefully it won't be long," she whispered through a crack in the closet door. "Oh my God! Pastor D's van is outside. I guess he came *here* to get the phone. I'll be right back!"

The chances of him being there seemed completely impossible, but she only lived a few minutes from Uncle D's house. It became harder to keep my breath low, and I was fighting a whole panic attack at the thought of Uncle D somehow being in the Johnsons' home. I prayed that whatever they were doing wouldn't take long so I could escape with my body intact.

I tried to whisper to her to toss my shirt in the closet, which was lying somewhere around her bed, but she had already left the room. I became mad at myself for becoming trapped in her closet. I wondered if God was making sure I didn't get to home plate, since we had for sure rounded third. I prayed and asked God to get me out with a promise to never come to Paris' bedroom again. I texted Day with the burner phone and told him I was trapped in Paris' closet, but that as soon as the coast was clear I would need him to come pick me up.

I got a text back: "Why weren't you at school? Is this a joke?"

I realized the burner phone had the wrong numbers programmed in it, and the phone number that used to be Day's a long time ago now belonged to Kemis. The sudden urge to vomit took over my body, secondary to my failure to figure out what to text Kemis to persuade him that I was kidding.

I texted him back: "Haha, just seeing what you would say. See you later."

I was hurling expletives under my breath. I called Daveon's actual number and described my circumstances in the lowest whisper I could use that allowed him to still hear me and informed him to pick me up as soon as he could. I moved closer to the closet door to try and hear if everyone had left the house. I heard footsteps and was relieved Paris was finally coming to give me an update.

The door opened, and I peeked my head out from under her clothes.

"Yo, P! Throw me my shirt!" I whispered.

"Boy! GET YOUR BEHIND OUT HERE!" were not the words I expected to hear, or the voice I wanted to hear them from.

Uncle D yelled at me and tugged the waistband of my jogging pants while he yanked my arm with his other hand, practically dragging me out the closet. Mr. Johnson stood in the doorway to Paris' room with his arms folded, and had fire in his eyes when he saw my shirtless body get hauled out of the closet.

"Unreal! This is unreal!" Mr. Johnson yelled as he turned and stormed into the hallway with his fists clenched above his head.

"The Lord always reveals, Dontay," Uncle D said as he pulled a large, wooden brush from his pocket and started painfully paddling my backside with it after grabbing onto me.

"Wait! Ah! Unc! It ain't like that! We ain't—we ain't do nothing!" I protested, as I found myself stumbling and scrambling to get out of his reach.

I thought I could wrestle my way out of his grasp like I used to do when I was getting hit by Granny, but his grip was firm, and by the way he swung I could tell he was uninterested in the fact that I hadn't made it to home plate with Paris. I squirmed and dodged as best I could to get out of the spontaneous uncle-nephew talk and was finally able to dive across Paris' bed to the other side of the room after about the fifth or sixth strike.

"Get up!" he ordered, but I was reluctant to do so.

"Unc, I—"

"I SAID GET UP!"

Scared that round two could pop off at any moment, I stood to my feet while attempting to maintain an arm's length distance and keep an eye on his hand and brush. My backing away didn't stop him from getting up close.

"This is your sister in the Lord, and you got her lying and sneaking around behind her parents? And you're in here without clothing on? You can hide from everyone but God, Tay. He always knows what you're doing. You have lied to me one too many times, and you're about to face some music! And you decided to skip class and make a viral video with profanity in it today, huh?" he asked.

"Naw, Unc! I—"

Apparently it was the wrong answer, evidenced by the fact that he picked up where he left off with the brush. I again dove toward the floor to break away from him, but he dove right after me, striking me until I apologized and begged for mercy.

"Where is your shirt?" he asked when I was finally able to return to my feet.

I sheepishly pointed in the direction of the pillows on top of the bed, where my shirt was balled up hanging off to the side of one of them, right next to my boxer shorts. I stared at them, wishing they had been on me during his brush attack. He froze when he saw them and looked back at me with wide eyes.

"Whose are these?" he asked.

I opened my mouth as though I was going to answer, but wasn't sure if I should answer with a lie or confess to the truth. I looked at his brush and then at his threatening glance before a sound escaped my mouth that did not contain any words, deciding my safety was more important than my honesty.

He shook his head and sighed, shoved his brush back into his pocket, to my relief, retrieved my things from Paris' bed, and tossed them in my direction. I put on my shirt and stuffed my underwear in my pocket, hoping Paris' dad hadn't seen them.

"Go get your things and get your behind outside to the car," he ordered stiffly.

I reluctantly strode into the hallway, afraid to see Paris or Mr. Johnson, who was standing with his back against the wall near the top of the steps. While I didn't want to make eye contact with him, the possibility of him giving me a hard left hook was at the forefront of my mind and seemed to be at the forefront of his, and Kemis had always trained us to never take our eyes off an opponent before, during, or after a fight.

I looked his way and was met with the angriest glower I had ever seen on a grown man. I felt his eyes piercing through my back until I arrived at the bottom of the steps, where I grabbed my backpack, which had been set by the front door, and my cell phone which was resting on top of it. I was cursing modern technology in my brain as I opened the door to go sit in the van and wait for death to arrive to the driver's seat.

"Bro, just go home," I called and told Daveon before Uncle D got to the car. "Unc caught me."

"What? Bro, this cap, right?" he asked me in a fearful tone.

"He coming bro, I'll tell you when I—"

Uncle D ripped the phone out of my grasp before I could finish my sentence.

"Daveon Kahari Lands, we got a *lot* to talk about. I'll see you when you get home," Uncle D said before ending the call.

All I could do was put my head down and try not to make any sudden movements. I knew Daveon was cursing the fact that he had gone along with my plans since it seemed like I was getting caught every time I tried something. It was harder to sneak around at Uncle D's house than it had been at home. It felt unfair, especially knowing my older brothers had spent years sneaking in and out of girls' rooms with no repercussions.

Uncle D ordered me to sit downstairs in his office once we arrived home. I usually liked hanging out in the comfort of his office; it was nice and warm, and I enjoyed looking at the books he had on his shelves and the pictures on his walls. He had added pictures of me and each of my brothers to his picture collection, right next to his pictures of Caleb and Sophie on his desk. The office was complete with a large television across from his desk, and a long, comfortable couch that nested in front of a gas fireplace, which he would sometimes turn on in the winter when we would sit and talk.

This particular time in the office wasn't as comfortable as normal. I could hear Uncle D in Daveon's room, loudly lecturing him about lying again. I overheard him tell Daveon not to ask when he was getting his keys back before closing his door. I rested my head in my hands, battling extreme guilt for turning into the brother that had been causing all the trouble.

Uncle D stormed back into the office after about twenty minutes. "I just got off the phone with Kemis. Hand me the other phone!"

In my brain I was cussing up a storm. I knew Daveon was going to kill me for having our years-long secret confiscated. I wished I could just slide it across the floor to him or somehow have it transported through any available magical medium—any alternative to walking it over to him and placing it in his hand would have sufficed.

"How long have you been using this while you've been on punishment?"

While I was thankful I didn't catch a hand when I gave it to him, I hadn't had time to rehearse any answers about the phone and felt completely unprepared. And with the web of lies I knew I was already caught up in, I didn't want to risk getting caught in another one. I shrugged my shoulders, reflecting on how I had hidden in the closet for what seemed like forever just to get caught and get the phone caught too. I had no desire to explain the phone's history.

"That's alright, we'll get to the bottom of this later. Go put on some underpants and some shoes and meet me in the garage. We're going back to the Johnsons' house," he told me, to my dismay.

After he walked up the steps, I ran over to Daveon's room.

"Bro, you gotta talk to Unc. He making me go back to her house!" I was panic-stricken and desperate for Daveon to intervene.

"Bro, you know I would normally try to help you, but I ain't exactly in a good spot with him right now. Just play it cool and tell them you're sorry," he advised with a defeated expression.

"Bro, her daddy saw me without no shirt on. My underwear was on her bed! Unc is pissed! What am I supposed to say? 'Sorry for trying to smash your daughter'?" I asked, causing him to laugh. "Day, it's not funny!"

"Dontay Jamal Lands! Let's go!" Uncle D yelled from upstairs.

"I think you better hurry up, dude," Daveon told me. I could tell by Uncle D's tone and usage of my full government name that Daveon was right. Still, I wished there was somewhere I could just run and hide for a few hours.

I sat down on Daveon's bed, contemplating my next move. "I can't do this bro."

"So, you actually trying to die tonight," he said.

"I'ma die from embarrassment for going back to the house he just beat my ass in!"

Daveon rolled over on his bed and covered his face.

"It's not funny, Day. Shit hurt like hell! And her dad looked like he wanted to crack my jaw!" I said, impatient with his laughter when I was being serious.

"I guarantee he does! You tried to smash his daughter! Bro, you don't want Unc to come down here. Just go upstairs, tell him you're sorry for lying and skipping school and detention and try to talk him out of it."

He had given me his best advice, and I supposed it was better than making a run for it, which was all I had come up with. I trudged up the steps hoping the suggestion would work and dreading the outcome if it didn't.

"Unc, I promise I'll never lie to you again, but please don't make me do this. It will be embarrassing enough seeing them at church!" I told him when I got upstairs.

"We are definitely doing this. You two are in the same youth group, and we're going to be seeing them a lot, especially if you all end up living in the same neighborhood on a permanent basis. We're going to get this done now," he said without any change in his expression.

I continued to beg after we pulled away in his van. Every time we met a stop sign, I considered trying my odds at jumping out of the car in hopes that I could injure myself enough for a hospital trip.

35

another trip to paris

Her parents greeted us at the door when we arrived and invited us in, but I stood stiffly with my feet glued to the porch and my fists balled up in the pockets of my jogging pants. Uncle D, having entered and realizing I wasn't behind him, came back out and tugged my arm, pulling me inside the house and giving me a look to pull it together. We walked through the house and joined her parents at the kitchen table, where I would have given anything to be beamed out to any other place on earth. Their kitchen in that moment seemed way worse than the fiery furnace Uncle D talked about from the Bible.

"So, let's start with a quick word of prayer, if you guys don't mind," Uncle D said, but I minded, because Mr. Johnson grabbed my hand to pray and squeezed it hard enough for my blood vessels to burst.

After Uncle D prayed, he told them that I had something I wanted to say, which was a lie, but I knew I couldn't say that. I wasn't exactly sure what to say, but I tried to take Daveon's advice.

"Um, I'm sorry for coming over without your permission. It was a bad idea, and um, it won't happen again," I told them, making as little eye contact as I could get away with.

Her mom fixed her mouth to speak, but Mr. Johnson cut her off and spoke up. I could tell he was using all of his strength to remain cordial.

"What were you doing in my daughter's room by yourselves? And please don't lie to me," he said.

I internally cringed, as I had less than one second to decide whether to say I was just looking at her trophies, or admit that I was his worst nightmare, all without the privilege of knowing exactly what she had told them. I knew the entire truth would not be an option.

I looked at Uncle D in hopes that he would save me from answering, but he was looking back at me just as curiously as the other two. I took a deep breath and unsuccessfully tried not to stammer.

"I mean, I was, um, mostly just looking at her trophies and things. But um, we, uh, we did kiss a little." My voice faded as I offered a partial truth, and I hoped it would be enough.

"And what's a little?" he followed up.

I wondered how far Uncle D would chase me if I ran out the door. I wondered why God hadn't blessed me with the same speed he had given Clay, who could have easily rocketed back home.

"Um, not that long," I told him, really hoping Uncle D would interject.

"Did your hand go under her shirt?"

I nearly choked on my own breath, wondering if there were cameras in the room, and how many more follow-up questions there would be. He had no idea what he was asking, and I knew he wouldn't be able to handle any truths regarding what had actually transpired.

"No!" I exclaimed in a tone three octaves higher.

He frowned like he didn't believe me, and I couldn't blame him. My brothers were right that I was a horrible liar. They used to get mad at me when they would have me lie for them to Kemis or Granny, who always knew when I wasn't being truthful. Usually by the end of it we would all be dodging hits from Granny, thanks to me and my lifelong inability to lie on the spot.

"I mean, maybe, on accident! I, I don't remember! We didn't have sex." I blurted out. It was the only thing I thought I could answer honestly without him standing up and giving me my second beat down for the day. But my answers seemed to piss him off more. "Mr. Johnson, I wasn't trying to disrespect you. I mean, I like Paris. I like when we're together, but I have fun just being around her." I was being mostly honest, and maybe trying to change the subject.

"You think I haven't been a teenage boy before, Dontay? My daughter told us she liked you a long time ago, and it made me very uncomfortable. There had been rumors at church that your older brothers had slept with all the young ladies in the church, and I honestly didn't want her around you. I didn't really want her out on a date with you and your brother, because I was nervous she wouldn't make good choices. This made me wish I had never let her go out with you. I called you some ungodly names tonight."

I had never let anyone utter an unkind word about my brothers without at least a threat of retaliation, but I couldn't exactly refute any of the rumors. I wondered if Kemis was included in his presumptions about my brothers, but I had firsthand knowledge that he was right about Jason and Daveon.

"I'm gonna be honest, Dontay—I'm not happy with you right now. But before I took Paris' phone tonight, she texted me the video of you speaking at school in front of everyone. It made me realize I shouldn't judge you based on what I thought I knew, or based on one mistake. I'm not opposed to you coming to my house, Dontay, as long as it's okay with Pastor D, and I'm talking wayyy in the future, when my daughter will be allowed to speak your name again in my house. My only rules are that one of her parents are here, that you remain downstairs at all times, and that you ask permission first.

"I have two beautiful daughters, and I'm not happy that we've reached this phase of their lives, but I knew it would come eventually, and now it's here. And here I am talking to that knucklehead boy I always said I'd have my shotgun ready for. And you're actually not a knucklehead at all. She told me you got an academic scholarship to school, and she told me a little about your upbringing. And Dwayne has told me about how bright you are, and how you've been in gifted programs your whole life. Other than the fact that you were in my daughter's bedroom today and the fact that she really likes you, I'd probably be kind of impressed with you."

His words weren't making me angry anymore, but it made me feel terrible about what I had done. I was feeling ashamed about sneaking around, and I wished I could erase the whole day.

"Do you think we have a deal, that you can visit my daughter, but only under my terms and conditions?" he asked me and held out his hand for a shake. I nodded my head and shook his hand.

"Patrick, why don't you go ahead and have Paris join us for a moment," Uncle D requested.

I looked at him like he was speaking another language. Just when I thought the encounter couldn't be any worse, Mr. Johnson got up to retrieve Paris from upstairs.

"I gotta use the bathroom," I said standing up, but Uncle D grabbed my pants and yanked me down until my backside banged into the seat.

"We won't be long. You can handle that when we get home," he said. He looked over my head as Paris joined us in the kitchen. "Paris, have a seat, young lady."

She looked just as mortified as I felt when she pulled out a seat to join us at the table.

"I want to tell both of you something. If you have to sneak around us to do something, it probably means God wouldn't want you doing it either. Dontay is not allowed to have young ladies over without advanced permission, and you are not supposed to have any young men over. There's a reason we put these boundaries in place, and I'm confident based on what I saw today that you both know what that reason is.

"I'm going to encourage you both to make sure you pray, read your Bibles, and study what God says he wants us to do with our bodies. One day when you are grown, you'll be able to decide if you're going to follow him. But for now, while you live with your parents, you are obligated to follow our rules. Do you both understand that?"

I couldn't tell if Paris was nodding or not since I was too busy staring at my shoes under the table. Uncle D lectured for a few more minutes before he dismissed us, her to her room and me back outside to the car. I caught her before she headed up the steps to engage in a brief discussion out of earshot of the parents.

"I'm sorry, P," I whispered.

"Don't worry about it. Today was lit! Besides, they can't keep us grounded forever," she said.

"You sure?"

"Well, no. Either way, you know you gotta come back one day. They'll be watching closely for a while, but they'll stop eventually. I'll see you tomorrow," she whispered, before leaning in and giving me a peck on the lips.

I smiled at her. "Yo' pops already look like he tryna kill me. How about a hug instead." My suggestion was a bad idea, but she had somehow entranced me once again with a kiss, and I was momentarily unable to make any rational decisions.

She chuckled and reached her arms around my neck, while I tightly wrapped my arms around her waist and held her close to me, resting my face on the top of her head and taking in the fresh scent of her hair, suddenly wishing I could rewind time to earlier in the day when I kissed her without restrictions.

"NOPE!" Her dad's voice echoed in the hallway.

Mr. and Mrs. Johnson, along with Uncle D, rounded the corner to the foyer where Paris and I quickly unlatched from each other.

"Didn't I tell you to go to the car, Dontay?" Uncle D asked, pulling me further away from Paris.

"Unc, I was! I just was saying bye! I'm not allowed to say bye?"

"Not like that," Uncle D said. "Go on outside. Good night, Paris. I'll see you Sunday."

36

grounded [2]

Back in our room, I was filling in Clay on my two trips to the Johnson residence for the day as we worked on homework, but we were interrupted when Caleb stormed in with his arms crossed.

"Bro, what's wrong with you?" I asked as he sat on my bed and put up his feet, all while his arms remained folded.

"You!" he said.

"What I do?" I sat up and looked at him.

"You were already on punishment and Daddy said you got in trouble again and he not letting you play PlayStation for at least a few more weeks! So now you can't play on the game with me this weekend. Why you get in trouble again?"

He looked at me with a sad expression. I felt bad knowing I had promised him we would play soon. Back at the old house, it was always Clay on punishment, forcing me to find someone else to play with. I wasn't used to being the one on punishment and banned from video games.

"Yo, aight, C. I messed up. I was kinda bad today."

"What'd you do?" he asked me, causing Clay to laugh.

"Shut up Clay! Look, I um, skipped some classes, and said some stuff that ended up on social media, and got caught lying, and I went and hung out with my girl!"

"You on punishment for a dumb girl?" he asked.

"You'll get it in a few years. But I won't do it again, aight? When I'm off punishment, I'll let you pick the game for us to play."

It seemed to make him a little happy, and he stuck around to hear more details about what got me into trouble. Uncle D came in after a few minutes, and Caleb committed to getting answers.

"Daddy, when is Tay getting off punishment?" he asked Uncle D.

"I guess Tay and I will have to have a talk about that," Uncle D said. "Speaking of which, Tay, come join me."

I reluctantly got up and followed him outside, where he had started a fire in the firepit. It wasn't completely dark yet, but it had gotten colder out. Despite the peaceful scene and warm fire, it was the last place I wanted to be, knowing he would probably talk to me until it was time to go to bed, and I would have much rather been left to myself to do homework.

"Unc, I know you mad at me," I told him after we had taken our seats.

"I'm not mad. I was earlier, but I'm not anymore. I'm very disappointed in you though. Both of your brothers have actually improved their behavior these past few months, and yours has gotten worse. I never expected you to lie to me this much. I feel like I've been fair to you."

His words pierced me. I considered our relationship to be close, even before we moved in with him. He had always been someone I could confide in, even when I wasn't making the best choices. But it was much easier to be honest with him when he wasn't the primary one giving consequences.

"So, what happened?" he asked me.

"You mean, with Paris? I told you we didn't do anything!" I said.

"That's the lie you told in front of her daddy. But I saw what I saw, and I know you did more than kiss."

Suddenly, there were images I was fighting to get out of my brain so I could finish the conversation. I didn't think I would be able to ignore them enough to put out a lie.

"That's mostly what we did. I mean, I, uh, pulled out a condom, but we didn't actually use it," I said, and I could tell he didn't expect that answer.

"You said you pulled out a condom, or did you say you put *on* a condom?" he asked for clarification.

I had no desire to clarify and was saved by the sound of the kitchen door opening, and we turned to see Clay come out with his basketball, not realizing we were there.

"Didn't I ground you to your room?" Uncle D asked loudly, startling Clay as he walked toward the hoop.

"Unc! Hey! Um, I didn't do nothing though! You grounded me for *him* smashing?" Clay asked, looking confused.

"I didn't smash," I clarified.

"Bro, if you hid in a closet and caught a beatdown from Unc, you should have smashed. And that's on Mary, Martha, and they brother! That's even worse—How I'm grounded and he ain't even smash?" Clay asked.

He held the ball while looking at Uncle D as though waiting for an explanation. I couldn't help but laugh that Clay was technically right; for maybe the first time, he was uninvolved in the plot, and was only riding along.

"So, you just thought, since I unjustly punished you, you would give yourself a pardon and let yourself out?" Uncle D asked.

"It's not like that! I was going to ask you, but you seemed too focused on going to yell at him some more, so I just figured I'd talk to you about it later," Clay said.

"I have not been yelling at him!" Uncle D said. "Go ahead and shoot. I may have moved too fast taking your phone away. When you done, you can grab it from on top of my dresser."

Clay amused us both by making up a celebratory dance with the news of his phone returning.

Uncle D turned to me and spoke softly, "You know I love you, Tay, like my own son. I was shocked when I got that video of you today. And I was disappointed to see you in that closet. I second-guessed myself a little, wondering if I reacted too quickly. Maybe I hit you out of anger...I'm not exactly sure. I had to self-examine to see if I owed you an apology. I kinda wished I at least talked to you and let you give your side of the story first, even though I caught you in a lie. To that end, I'm sorry. Is there anything you want to tell me about what happened today?"

I was shocked he had just apologized to me, especially when I was feeling so horribly about what I had done. The fact that I had lied to him had really eaten at me the most. I figured I had lost his trust forever.

"I'm sorry for lying...and skipping class...and detention...and being bad...and everything," I told him and leaned forward, looking down wishing he would send me back to my room. But instead, he threw his arm around me, and told me he forgave me.

"You're a good kid, Tay. I would never call you bad. I wanna ask you something—who gave you the sex talk?" he asked.

"You think I need a sex talk when I got four brothers and the internet, and an uncle that basically has banned sex from our lives?" I asked.

He softly chuckled. "Nobody has banned anything. And I wouldn't trust all of your sources at this point, when I know that at least three of your brothers, and the internet, have a corrupted view of sex. My only goal is to help you follow God's will so that when you're an adult you can enjoy a healthy sex life. When you give in to the flesh and all of its desires, when you allow yourself to become sexually active, when you give in to a lot of smoking and drinking and hanging with the wrong people, you are strengthening your flesh and distancing yourself from hearing from God and from being in his perfect will.

"And on a practical level, this is one of those areas where once you start it's really hard to stop. It's much better that you don't start until it's time. And not starting becomes difficult if you find yourselves in a lot of situations where you haven't established strong boundaries."

His words made me curious, and I thought about asking about what he had said but didn't out of fear he'd pull out the Bible and start preaching.

"Tay, part of me is really proud of you for today. I remember being too afraid in school to speak up about some of the things that were going on. I was proud of you for helping organize what started as a peaceful protest. When I was watching, I wished that you had told me about it so that I could come support you," he said.

"For real? But you seemed mad about it earlier," I said.

"I was mad that I found out you skipped classes and detention when you were already in a lot of trouble. And I definitely wasn't happy when I found out there's a viral video of you using profanity and destroying school property."

"That part wasn't really planned, Unc. Well, none of it was. I just was kind of in the moment...and I hate this school," I said, knowing I no longer had credibility with him to try and persuade him to do what I wanted.

"I know you do...unfortunately, you have to be punished for what you did today. But first I have to hand you something. I didn't want to give this to you at the same time I tell you your punishment, but I can't exactly keep it from you either. Kemis brought this by today; he said it came in the mail."

He handed me a white envelope, and I knew exactly what it was. I could tell by the prison address on the envelope that my biological father had finally taken time to write, after nearly a year of not hearing from him. I held it for a moment and then looked over at Uncle D.

"Not really interested in what that nig—that dude has to say right now," I said and laid the envelope under my seat, although I considered tossing into the fire.

He looked up to the sky for a moment and then over at me. "Tay, you're probably the only one of your brothers that has even the potential to have a relationship with your father—one day he'll be out of prison. Mine reached out to me once, and I was too angry at the time to allow him in. By the time I let the Lord heal those emotional scars, my father had already died. I regret that I never at least sat down with him and told him how angry I was.

"I'm sure you're upset that your father doesn't reach out to you like he should. And it's definitely his loss to miss out on the life of such a phenomenal young man. But maybe you could work on a letter where you tell him that. Maybe send it to him for Father's Day, that way you have plenty of time to work on it."

It was too late to reverse the actions that got my father into prison. But he still had the power to communicate, and the periodic letters were nothing but offensive coming from someone who had nothing but time and copious amounts of paper and ink.

"Your school suspended you today…and I was more upset with you than I had ever been before—with you or any of your brothers. But I spoke with your principal, and I begged him not to do it. We talked about how bright you are. And I told them everything that you didn't want them to know. I told them about your father, your mother, how you lost your Granny, your brother's fiancé, how you all were evicted from your home and practically homeless. I said that you were one of the smartest kids I've ever known, and yet too stupid to realize that you don't want a suspension on your record. So instead, they're giving you two weeks of afterschool detention."

I hung my head and let out a soft growl. I would take a suspension any day over being forced to stay after school for two weeks.

"And I had to promise them full restitution for destroyed books. Today I wrote a check for nearly four thousand dollars—it may turn into more once they finish taking inventory."

I didn't think I could feel more awful, but knowing he had paid all that money when he was already spending so much just to house us, feed us, and give us money for grades, birthdays, and everything else, not to mention the fact that Clay had already stolen from him. I went from feeling bad to wanting to run away from him and forever hide my face in shame.

"Don't beat yourself up, because you'll pay me back in labor…Dontay Jamal Lands, do I need to walk you to detention for two weeks in a row?" he asked.

"No, Unc," I responded, annoyed at the possibility of him doing so anyway.

"If I find out you are even one minute late to one detention, I'm coming up there every single day for the rest of them—are we clear?"

I sighed in defeat, wishing more than ever that I could be living a different life.

"Clay, go tell Day to come here, please," Uncle D called over to the basketball court. Clay walked inside to bring out Daveon, while Uncle D checked his phone.

"You wanted to see me?" Daveon came outside a few minutes later with his arms folded.

"Have a seat, please. I wanted both of you here for this. Daveon Lands, you are seventeen years old, nearing adulthood, heading into your senior year of high school. You have a car and car keys that you have access to, which you could use to take you anywhere in this city. You can drive to doctor's appointments, or you could drive to drug deals. There's a lot of good opportunities that come with having a car, and there's bad opportunities that could come as well. I have to be able to know that you are responsible enough to handle it. If you lied to your boss at work about something that happened on the job, what do you think he would do?"

"I mean, I guess it would depend on the lie, but I could get fired."

"You could get fired. If you lied to your girlfriend about being out with another girl over the weekend, what would happen?"

"She'd break up with me," Day said

"She would and she should. Lying has consequences. All sin has consequences. We've talked repetitively about you being where you're supposed to be, and you let me down. So, I bought you something. Here's a two-week bus pass. The closest bus stop is a two-mile walk. I found out you need about three buses to get to school, so that's what you'll be doing. Your car is staying here with me. And you better get there on time. I'll be waking you up in the morning at four thirty-five a.m. to make sure you don't miss your buses. I promise you Day, let me find out you weren't in every single class tomorrow. Here you go," he said as he handed him the bus pass.

Daveon looked as though he was actually biting down on his tongue and forcing his lips shut. His right leg was lightly bouncing up and down, and he turned his head to avoid eye contact with Uncle D. A vein in his forehead protruded out of his skin while he impatiently waited for Uncle D to finish talking.

I put my own head down feeling bad and felt like I should say something. "Unc, this is my fault though."

"I don't disagree with you, Tay. But what he's going to learn is that there are consequences for him too, since he lied to me again, even if it was for you. You both lied, but he and I just had this conversation about lying to me after I found out about the fight, and the tattoos and the skipping school!"

Not only did Daveon's tattoo get discovered, but on report card day, Uncle D also found out that Daveon had skipped a few days of school. Daveon tried to lie and say the school messed up his attendance, but Uncle D verified the attendance records with all of his teachers.

"This house doesn't operate like that, where you all lie to me, and I don't do anything about it. So, if I have to keep your phones and car keys until summer, I promise you I will. I don't want to, but I will.

"And speaking of phones, Tay, here's your phone for the next two months. There's no big screen or touch screen or internet or anything else. Here you go."

He had reached in his pocket and handed me a phone that looked older than him. Part of me knew I had earned the most severe punishment ever, but I still wanted to hurl the phone over the fence as soon as I laid eyes on it. I glared at him in disbelief as the phone rested in my hand. The phone he was handing me was the reason I had gotten caught that day. After all the notifications he had received for the classes I had missed, he arranged to purchase the phone from Mr. Johnson, which is why he had been there when he caught me. He was extra suspicious since my location was turned off and called my phone and heard it buzzing while he stood in the Johnsons' living room.

"Can I go?" I asked, wanting to be away from him.

"Not yet. I know you two are mad at me. I don't like it, but I know I have to do this. So, let's say a quick prayer," he said before grabbing our hands and praying.

I moped away when the prayer was over, with Daveon right behind me. I told him I was sorry before he sulked down the steps to sulk some more in his room. I was slightly angry at Uncle D for what felt like a harsh punishment, but I was more mad at myself since my nonchalance regarding the rules had completely backfired. Not only did I not get taken out of school, but I had no access to my girlfriend or friends outside of school, and I would be stuck in the house for the foreseeable future with an antiquated phone that I probably wouldn't be able to hack into to make it do what I needed. The best day ever had quickly turned into the worst day ever, and there was no one to blame except myself.

37

tko

We hadn't seen Mark Paul at school in the days following the fight, and Marco and Tommy were convinced he was too embarrassed to show his face. Clay had forwarded the video of the fight to Marco and Tommy, who had forwarded it to some other kids at school. There was rumor that someone had even posted it on YouTube.

Mark Paul was back at school the week after my Paris incident and didn't even make eye contact with me. Tommy got detention late in that week, and Marco and I got written up for bullying, all because Mark Paul walked by the three of us when Tommy yelled that he got knocked out, causing everyone in the hallway to explode in laughter, including myself.

Tommy, Marco, and I were sent to the principal's office by a hall monitor, and we joked and laughed all the way there, with Tommy telling people my name was Deebo as we passed them in the hallways. The three of us were lectured about the video of the fight circulating around and were told it was "bullying and poor taste" to engage in such activities and then record and share it with the world. We were then lectured about how laughing at a comment in the hallway was just as bad as saying it, and it was also considered bullying.

"Tay been bullied all year just for being intelligent and black and not keeping quiet!" Marco said.

I was shocked to hear him speak up for me, but he was in a good place to do it. He was a graduating senior and already had a basketball scholarship in hand. Like Jason, he was popular, and held in high esteem with everyone at the school since he generated income and notoriety for the school through the basketball program.

"I was not informed of any of you being bullied. If at any point you feel you are targeted or treated differently because of your race, you should notify us immediately," Principal Calhoun said.

Had I not been in so much trouble at home, I would have channeled my inner Clay and cussed him all the way out. My next thought was to get up and leave, but I remembered how that had gotten me in trouble too.

"Are we getting a detention slip, 'cause otherwise I need to go," I said.

"Tommy, you will be getting detention for your language in the hallway. This is a warning for the two of you to be mindful of your activities. If we find that any of you posted this video to the internet, you will be subject to discipline pursuant to our policies. You boys are free to leave. Stay out of trouble!" he called as we started walking away.

We shook our heads once we entered the hallway and started discussing our weekend plans.

"Tay, you and your brothers should come over on Friday night, bruh. Some of us gonna hang out at my crib on GTA and then walk to Tara's pool party. You know they have an indoor and an outdoor pool that's heated, and all the cheerleaders are coming," Marco said.

"Bruh, I'm on lock lock," I emphasized.

"Yo' trip to Paris must not have worked out too well," he laughed, causing Tommy and me to laugh too.

"Not well at all, bruh! Unc caught me hiding in her closet with my shirt off and lost it."

"And his draws on her bed! You already know Unc brought the fire," Tommy said.

"Oh, snap! I know he wasn't even having that!" Marco said. "Didn't he lose it when he caught y'all kissing?"

"Yeah, man. He so extra!"

"I know he 'bout had a heart attack, bruh. Next time we kick it, you gotta come out to my crib!" Tommy said. He enjoyed much more freedom at his house. He lived with his mother, grandmother, and brothers, and sometimes an aunt and older cousin, all of whom seemed to always be gone.

"Unc gon' make sure yo' body count stay low," Marco said.

We talked for a while and then went our separate ways to class. Uncle D called me before my last class, which I later found out was to tell me he would be running late, but I was giving him the silent treatment and ignored his call. I didn't hear the end of it during the ride home, especially after I told him I didn't know how to work old phones.

"You expect me to believe that someone who knows how to code, build, and reprogram a computer from scratch and answer every single question I have ever had about every single electronic device in the house can't work a cell phone with barely any buttons? Tay, don't make me cast out a lying devil," he said. He went in on me non-stop the whole ride home. I couldn't tell him I was too embarrassed to pull the phone out in front of my friends.

Uncle D gave Daveon his phone back before dinner that night, as the two of them, along with Kemis, Clay, and me sat at the table talking.

"I discovered some things on both of your phones that shocked me," Uncle D started.

"Unc, at what age do we get privacy on our phones in your house?" Daveon asked without hiding the annoyance in his voice.

"Eighteen. Any other questions?" he asked, prompting a fierce eye roll from the three of us. "Watch that. Anyway, I learned that the calculator app on your phone is more than a calculator."

We all tried to keep straight faces and pretend as though we didn't know what he was talking about, knowing we had used secret apps for messaging and to hide pictures for a long time.

"Don't worry, I deleted all of it, and the apps. I'm gonna suggest you have a discussion with your young lady friends about the pictures they are sending you," he said.

"Unc, why you tripping like that? I have discussions all the time!" Daveon told him after growling.

"And what are you telling them?"

"To send more!" Daveon said, causing Clay and me to crack up. Uncle D looked as though he was about to snatch Daveon's phone right back, or knock him out, or both.

"Unc, come on, I'm just playing. It's not like I ask for these pics!" Daveon told him.

"What are you sending in return?" Uncle D asked.

Daveon smiled. "Heart emojis."

"You better not be sending any crazy pictures on there. What about you, Tay?" he turned to me.

"Um, if I missed a pic, can I see it?" I asked.

"No, I'm not going to show you. But I might show Paris' mother!" he said

"Can you just turn my phone off, please?" I asked.

"Unc, don't block, man, that's not cool," Clay told him.

Uncle D turned to Clay and glared at him with his eyes partially squinted. "Let me see your phone, Clay."

"I don't got it!" Clay exclaimed.

"I'll go get it for him," Kemis said, getting up from his seat.

"Hell no! I'll get it!" Clay said, jumping up and sprinting away.

He bolted toward our room with Kemis behind him, but Clay was too fast. He got in and locked the door before Kemis reached him. Daveon and I laughed, knowing Clay was deleting pictures and messages from his phone, while Uncle D groaned and shook his head.

"I tried, Pops," Kemis said as he returned to the table, disappointed he didn't catch Clay.

"Clay! Get your behind out here right now!" Uncle D yelled.

"Coming!" we heard him call from the room, but he didn't come out.

"I'm about to knock this boy out," Uncle D said.

After a few minutes, Clay casually strolled back and got popped in the head after placing his phone on the table.

"Ah! What was that for?" Clay asked, holding his head while the rest of us laughed at him.

"You know what that was for. I might replace all three of your phones," Uncle D said.

"Unc, you lame, but please don't go next level lame on us," Daveon said shaking his head.

"Too late," I chimed in.

"Oooh the disrespect," Kemis said

"How is that disrespectful when all I did was express my opinion?" I asked.

"Tay, you need to be expressing why you got written up today," Uncle D said.

"Oh my God," I groaned.

"Don't use the Lord's name in vain in this house, boy. I guess I really have to ground you until summer since you don't want to act right! I told you to leave that Mark boy alone!"

"Unc, I ain't say nothing to that dude. He was walking down the hall and someone made a joke. That's it!" I said. He seemed content with my response until we found ourselves unintentionally getting introduced to Mark Paul's father.

I had finally completed my detentions when Uncle D picked me up from school a few days later. Mark Paul's dad was picking him up in a decked-out, shiny, bright red luxury SUV, idling directly behind Uncle D's old blue minivan. His dad suddenly exited his car and knocked on Uncle D's window while we waited to exit the lot, asking him if he could pull out of the carpool line and into the adjacent parking lot to talk. Uncle D agreed and asked questions as he followed Mr. Bailey's vehicle to the back of the lot.

"Did you and him get into again? Didn't I tell you to stay away from that boy?" Uncle D asked with an accusatory tone.

"Unc, I haven't said two words to this dude, I swear to—"

"Don't do that!" he said while he pulled two spots over from Mr. Bailey's vehicle. We both got out of the van to face a short, angry man wearing scrubs standing next to Mark Paul, whose face was nearly as red as the fancy car he stood near while waiting for the encounter to be over.

"I'm Doctor Bailey, Mark Paul's father, and who are you?" he asked Uncle D.

"My name is Dwayne. It's good to meet you," Uncle D said.

"Well, is this your kid? My son said he doesn't have parents. I'm wondering who it is we need to sue if he attacks my kid and keeps bullying him at school!"

"Bullying him? You need to talk to your son about his own activities!"

I guess you guys aren't from around here, but we pay a lot of money for this school, and I don't send my son here to get assaulted and bullied by a bunch of black kids. If you're here on some sort of basketball or football scholarship, it probably doesn't bother you as much, but we are serious about getting a good education!"

"Oooh…fix it Jesus," Uncle D clasped his hands together, took a step backward, and briefly closed his eyes before addressing Dr. Bailey. "Let's get something straight! This is my son, and he's a brilliant kid. I guarantee he's much brighter than any kid of yours that thought he could outwit or outfight him. He doesn't need a football scholarship to be here!"

"I bet they're giving him all kinds of help just to keep him off academic probation so they can say it's a diverse student body!"

"What? He is thriving in this school without the privilege of having a father that can bribe school officials for his admission and throw his money around to control the school!"

"You don't know shit about how we got into this school, and your kid is nothing but a thug that knows how to cheat on tests! I heard he's had more detentions than can be counted. They only let him in because he's bla—"

"Who you think you're calling a thug?" Uncle D got into his face and grabbed his shirt as though he was about to use one of Kemis' martial arts tactics.

"He attacked my son and deserves to be called something much worse!" Mr. Bailey said while attempting to back away.

"Call him something worse in my presence and watch me give you the same face your little snobby son had!" Uncle D said. His voice had softened in a way that I knew meant he was actually getting angrier. He followed after Mr. Bailey the same way he did to me on the day he caught me in Paris' closet.

Mr. Bailey broke free of Uncle D's grip and stepped backward. "It's a free country! If you can't handle it I guess I'll have to call the police to help you calm down!" Mr. Bailey threatened while reaching in his pocket for his phone.

"Unc, it's cool man!" I interjected, fearful that the police would be called. By this point Uncle D's face was close enough to Mr. Bailey's to bite his nose, with his body squared up in a manner that suggested he had channeled his inner Muhammad Ali. I pressed my chest against his and grabbed his arm, terrified he was about to do something that would land him in handcuffs. "Let's just go, Unc. Don't let this punk-ass dude get to you!"

Uncle D slowly backed away and told me to get in the car, and I knew he was in a zone when he didn't correct me for my language. Seconds later he turned out of the lot and pushed the button to turn on his gospel playlist. We rode in silence for a moment, until I turned to look at him and the two of us simultaneously burst into laughter.

"Unc, were you about to fight?" I asked, still processing what I had just witnessed.

"Tay…I was. And I remembered I used to be the chaplain for the police department here. It would have been pretty bad to explain to them why I was fighting, and even worse to call Pastor James and tell him I spent the night in jail. I can't handle someone talking like that about you. I shouldn't have done that. I went in heavy on you after you fought his son, and I almost turned around and did the same thing I told you not to do. I understand why you wanted to fight that boy if he's anything like his father," he said.

We laughed and joked about the altercation for the entire ride home, and I wondered if he would tell Auntie Robin, as I had every intention of telling my brothers. I felt something in that moment that I had never felt from anyone other than my brothers—a sense of belonging and protection. I felt that this man actually truly loved me the way he had been telling me for so long. I had never seen anyone besides my older brothers confront someone on my behalf. While it was nice to have four brothers that I knew would always have my back, it felt different, and for some strange reason, made me feel bigger. There seemed to be hardly any limits on what Uncle D would do for me, and I wished I had made better efforts to be just as good to him.

38

new friends

I had assumed that my first break-up with a girl would involve a fancy dinner, and a teary-eyed girl telling me that I was too focused on studies and didn't spend enough time with her for us to continue in a relationship. It turned out that Paris thought a text to Clay's phone with instructions to deliver it to me would suffice.

"I think we should be friends. You still my peeps though," was the entirety of the message Clay showed me on a Friday night where I had nothing better to do than wish my phone wasn't stupid and my girlfriend wasn't stupider. I typed no less than fifty messages to respond, all of which I erased, unable to type the right words that would convey my feelings without sounding desperate. After giving up trying to win her back over with words in a text, I watched television on the couch with Caleb and Sophie and otherwise moped around the house, thinking of what to tell her that Sunday morning when I would corner her at youth church and demand an explanation.

After rehearsing in my brain what I would say, I caught her in the hallway right before youth service and asked her to walk outside with me. After first looking around to ensure no one saw us, we walked out to the side of the church where people usually didn't come and sat down on the curb, finally able to catch up, but our catch up was interrupted after about sixty seconds when Daveon ran up on us from the back door of the church, out of breath.

"Bro, Unc is out on the other side of the church looking for both of y'all!"

"Shoot!" I exclaimed.

We all sprinted to get back toward the building and into the youth room, and I found my seat as Uncle D walked back into the room glaring at me. I could tell by his expression I was getting another lecture that night, but I was distracted by the fact that I had failed to salvage my new relationship. Daveon had always told me it wouldn't last since I was a freshman and she was a sophomore and almost two years older than me, but I had never accepted those words.

"You aight?" Daveon whispered to me as we sat in the back while Uncle D taught.

"I was cool 'til she broke up with me," I whispered back, hoping he could provide me with some of his wisdom on girls.

"Don't sweat that. There's plenty of girls that want you, bro. Some of them are in this room. You can rizz one up! Besides, with nobody to do stupid stuff for, this will probably keep you from getting any more uncle-nephew talks," he whispered, causing us to chuckle.

"There's not one girl that has ever tried to talk to me like that, bro. And she's cute, cool to talk to, likes watching basketball, and she's a good kisser!"

"Dude, how you know she a good kisser when you hardly kissed anybody?" he challenged me.

"Yes, I have! Remember old girl I used to meet at the library?"

"Bro, that was middle school. When you off lockdown, well, when we both off lockdown, we going out again. I'ma have Candace bring one of her friends so you can really know what a good kisser is. Shoot, we could go to Candace crib late and just miss curfew—I guarantee she'd be worth it," he said.

"Bro, I don't know about any more double dates with you, dude," I said.

"Why not? Last time was fire!" he said.

"Bro, you spent half the night—"

"Who was he referring to in this passage, Daveon Kahari Lands?" Uncle D posed a question to Daveon using his full name in front of the whole group, indicating that he knew we weren't paying attention to his lesson. He had already lectured us about paying attention in youth church and making sure we weren't on our phones or talking excessively.

"Just say Jesus," I whispered to Daveon, figuring that it could never be the wrong answer in church.

Daveon took my advice. "Uh, Jesus?"

The whole room erupted with snickering and face hiding, and we knew we had just solidified a second lecture for when we returned home.

39

worst. day. ever

Even though we weren't together, I was sad that I had hardly been able to talk to Paris since Uncle D was still holding my phone hostage. He would take my punishment phone away after school each day and was taking my other devices after I completed my homework in the evenings. I was occasionally able to use Clay's phone to text or call Gia, Paris' sister, who would put Paris on the phone. But it seemed after a while that Paris lost interest in talking other than when we could sneak in a chat at church or school, and more and more Gia would tell me that Paris couldn't talk.

On the Monday of the last full week of school, I was looking forward to seeing her after a weekend of not being able to talk. I took a stroll with the intention of surprising her at her locker in between homeroom and first period. I had even written a poem for her that Sophie helped me fold and seal with a heart sticker for delivery.

I drew closer to her locker only to find her arms reached up and around the neck of another guy, and the two of them were kissing just as heavily as she had kissed me in her bedroom. I gawked at them with the eyes of a creepy stalker, standing frozen in the crowded hallway, staring at them kiss as though I was enthralled by a movie scene. I didn't want to watch it, but couldn't manage to peel my eyes away.

The reactions of others around me only added to my frustration. Mark Paul and his friends walked in between them and me and made sure to greet me with a sneer while pointing in Paris' direction, obnoxiously celebrating his last laugh in my face. Tommy walked up with wide eyes as they were finally bringing their tongue-tasting to an end, and seemed disappointed at the sight of me staring them both down.

"You can't go out like this, bruh. C'mon before she see you," he said as he tugged on my arm to pull me from the middle of the hallway.

"Naw, I gotta say something! She was just about to smash not that long ago!" I said.

"Dude, I can't let you embarrass yourself like that. Let's just roll. I heard he *been* hitting."

"Hitting who? Her?"

"Yeah, bruh."

"Well why you ain't tell me?"

"Because, you acted like you so in love and shit! That girl ain't no virgin, bruh. She lied to you. Even Mara said it. C'mon dude," he nudged again.

"Hold up, man. I'm saying something," I insisted. I retrieved my arm from Tommy's grasp and walked towards Paris' locker to confront her about what I saw and heard.

The hallway was crowded with students shuffling to and from classes, while others loitered and chatted nearby at their lockers, enough noise to drown out the sounds of me embarrassing myself even more. Paris was startled to see me approach the two of them, and the guy she was kissing frowned at me as though my breath stank when I spoke.

"P, who is this?" I asked her, demanding an answer.

"Tay! Um, this—"

"I'm Jarvis. This must be the little freshman friend you told me about," he said smirking while his scaled my entire frame from top to bottom.

"Nigga do I look like a little freshman friend to you?" I asked loudly as I squared up and inched toward his face.

"Ay you need to back up!" he yelled, causing me to get even closer.

"How bout *you* back me up and see what happens," I threatened.

Tommy quickly stepped in between us and pulled me away.

"Whoa, whoa, bro. You done already had one fight this year bro. Let's go before yo' uncle kill you for getting suspended," he said as he continued to edge me away.

"Call her when you ain't a virgin no more, young buck," Jarvis called out, as Tommy continued to pull me down the hall.

"Yo, I'll drop yo' ass in this—"

"Shhh! Bro chill before one of these teachers write you up again! She ain't worth it, dude," Tommy said in a low tone while he continued to back me away and down the hall.

All I could think about the rest of the day was how badly I wanted to swing on Jarvis. I could hardly concentrate in my classes, and I avoided the lunchroom altogether at lunchtime. I instead joined Tommy in the gym, where he often went during lunch to practice free throws or shoot around with some of his other teammates when the season was over.

I couldn't believe what I had seen and heard about Paris and didn't want to be at school. It was humiliating to think that I had probably told half the school that she was my girlfriend, even though she wasn't. If I didn't tell them with my words, I made sure they knew with my body language any time she was around. I made sure my arm was around her and made sure everyone that would watch saw my affection toward her. It was humiliating to think I had done all that, and she could have been kissing with Jarvis behind my back the entire time.

I stared at the ceiling when I got home that day, reflecting on all of my failed plans. Not only had none of my efforts gotten me kicked out of school, but I had also failed to secure a relationship with the girl I loved, which meant I would have to face her and all her boyfriends every day the following school year. I sat wondering what Jarvis had that I didn't have, wondering if she liked him because he was older, or because he had a car, or because his family probably had money, or if she thought he was better-looking than me. I wondered if he was better at sneaking to her home, or did he have parents that let her come over and provide them privacy to do whatever they wanted.

Daveon told me he thought I had been acting strange when he came to our bedroom that afternoon, and I filled him and Clay in on everything that happened.

"Bro, you think she told him I'm a virgin," I asked, still reeling over the fact that Jarvis seemed to know more about me than I knew about him.

"She probably did!" Daveon said. "He probably asked her why she be around you so much and she probably said something like, 'Don't worry about him, he just a freshman and a virgin.'"

"That shit jacked up if she did," Clay said. "Day right though—you need to leave her alone. Get wit' that girl you showed me a picture of from the track team!"

"Bro, I can't get with nobody right now without no phone. I'm so tired a being on punishment!"

"Just be hopeful that by this time next year, you might be out this house and able to live your best life again."

"Bro," Clay said looking down at his phone. "Paris wanna talk to you."

"How you know?" I asked.

"Gia texting. She said meet Paris outside in five minutes."

"Make sure you go out the front," Daveon instructed. "Unc and K in the backyard."

I slipped on my shoes and stared out the window until I saw Paris' car and then tiptoed out the front door like I had the first time she had ever come to see me. She parked directly in front of the house, and I opened the passenger door and sat inside, looking straight ahead without greeting her.

"Tay, c'mon, don't be like that. We not even together, and all I did was kiss that dude!"

"Okay, but I heard you been letting him smash for a minute, and you never told me that. And we just broke up! You already kissing other dudes, and we just broke up?"

"It was just a kiss. You seriously didn't have to act like that today. And me and you are friends, which means you can kiss other people too!"

I didn't want to kiss other people, but I wasn't sure if I could tell her that without feeling overly exposed and weak.

"Ride with me real quick," she said, turning the keys in the ignition.

"Whoa!" I said. I turned her keys the opposite direction to turn the car back off. "I'm on lock…and I can't be sneaking around anymore on Unc."

"Alright…I guess I'll go then," she said, turning the keys and restarting the car. I was upset that she was leaving, as I didn't feel like I had completely expressed myself, but readied myself to go inside unsatisfied, right when I noticed she had suddenly put the car in drive to move us forward. "It'll be quick. You'll be back before they know anything."

"P, come on man. I'm in enough trouble—"

"All I need is five minutes. I promise," she said with a sly smile.

40

real love

"Bro, have you lost it? You were supposed to be sitting on the front porch!" Daveon stopped pacing to grill me as I stepped out of Paris' car after our return. "I lied and said you were in the bathroom, and then down the sidewalk, and everything else. That man 'bout to kill us both! Where you been?"

"Bye, Tay!" Paris called through the window as she drove off, reminding me that I was back in love with her.

"Yeah, uh, bye!" I called after her. I looked at Daveon, who was demanding an explanation of my whereabouts, and then at the front door of the house, where Uncle D walked through and stood on the porch with his arms and lips folded, watching Paris' car drive away.

I whispered to Daveon, "Damn. Just be cool. She made it up to me, but I'll tell you later. Just tell him we sat in the car talking."

"He know that ain't true because he was just out here since I told him you were walking down the sidewalk, nigga!" he whispered back.

"Dontay Jamal Lands, get in this house!"

I sighed and looked down at the ground, knowing things were about to get ugly.

"Just take yo' beatdown like a man, bro," Daveon cracked.

"Bump you, dude," I told him, as I walked across the yard, mumbling profanities and prayers under my breath as I inched toward Uncle D.

He closed the door behind me once we got into the foyer, but made it clear he wasn't letting me move even an inch further.

"What does punishment mean to you?" he barked.

I lowered my head, knowing his talk wasn't going to be pleasant, but he grabbed my chin and forced my eyes up to meet his.

"I asked you a question, and I expect an answer," he said. He had lowered his voice, but still had a sharpness in his tone.

I was already feeling like a small child that had been sent home with a naughty behavior note from the teacher and felt even smaller that I had to answer his question while he cradled my chin in his hand. "Unc, we— we was just talking—"

"Let me stop you there before you start lying to me and make your predicament a lot worse. Get downstairs!"

I nervously headed down the steps and into his office, and watched him close and lock the door behind us as we entered in.

"So I have to teach you what a punishment is, huh? You think it's okay to just go out with your friends after I've specifically told you that you're not allowed to do so? We've gone over what punishment means. So you either don't understand, or you're being defiant! You better have a good reason for disobeying me, or you're about to have a couple of problems. And the only acceptable reason is that there was an emergency!"

"Unc, aight, I know I'm on punishment! She just broke up with me, and then was kissing this dude at school today, and I thought we were on something else, and then she knew I was mad at her and she just wanted to talk to me."

"So where were you?"

"We rode around talking," I lied hoping I was convincing.

"Even though you're on punishment."

"Okay, I know you don't believe me, but I told her I was on lock and I couldn't go nowhere with her. I thought we were just going to sit in the car in front of the house and talk it out for a second. I didn't even take anything with me. Next thing I know, she starts the car and drives off! I told her I couldn't, and she kept driving, saying it would be quick. I promise I didn't intend on leaving!"

"Okay Dontay, even if that is true, you were not even supposed to be outside. YOU ARE ON PUNISHMENT!"

I stared at the floor, wishing he wasn't raising his voice at me, but knowing there was nothing I could say to justify what I had done.

"Sit down," he ordered.

I sat and looked at the floor, and then at him, who joined me on the other end of the couch.

"You forgetting that I used to be a teenager, Dontay."

"You were a teenager, and you didn't ride around and talk to girls?"

"Sometimes I did. And sometimes, I did things with my body that I knew wasn't pleasing to the Lord."

I tried to look straight ahead without giving any indication that what he was saying may have applied to me. Sometimes it seemed like he knew exactly what was going on in my brain, but I still tried to pretend like he had no clue what he was talking about. I immediately recalled the guilty feeling that consumed me when I was about to get into Paris' backseat and wished that I had made better choices.

He continued. "One of the most exciting days of my life was the day I watched you give your life to Christ. I was rejoicing that you made such a great decision at thirteen. And once you did that, the Holy Spirit came to live inside of you. God is with you everywhere, and our bodies are supposed to be a living sacrifice to him. Our bodies are no longer our own. They are his temple. So, when we do things with our bodies that don't honor him, our actions are grieving him."

My heart was burdened with guilt over what he had said, but I didn't want him to speculate about what I had done. "We didn't, like, have sex, Unc."

He looked down, and then back up at me. "Why not?"

I shrugged my shoulders, not wanting to divulge the details of what we did. I wanted to run upstairs and hide in my room.

"I did something bad," I blurted out while fixing my eyes on the bottom bookshelf across the room. The guilt from everything was beating me up inside, and I nearly offered a detailed confession. "You think God mad at me?"

He blew out a heavy breath and turned from me as though he was still deciding whether or not to thrash me.

"You know what I hate about what your parents have done to you?"

His question confused me, and I wondered why he even brought it up when I had largely put them both out of my mind and had just admitted that I had misbehaved.

He continued without a response. "They didn't give you a point of reference. I always ask Caleb and Sophie if they know how much I love them, and they tell me they know. And I follow that by telling them that God loves them even more than mommy and daddy. We changed all their diapers, provided all their meals, kept a roof over their heads, and we buy everything they need. We make sure they are well taken care of, make sure they get all the hugs and all the kisses, and do everything to show our love, and yet, our love is still not as vast as God's. So even on days when they don't feel sure or certain about God's love, they have a comparison.

"Your parents took that from you, maybe not intentionally, but they made choices that have kept them from ever parenting you. So let me ask you this, which of your brothers are you closest to?"

It was a hard question, and I wasn't sure how to answer. I had a special bond with each of my brothers. I was probably the least close to Kemis, but only because he had been physically and emotionally absent for the last several months. Clay and I had always done everything together, and Daveon and I trusted each other limitlessly, in a manner so deep we didn't need to discuss it because it was understood. When Jason was home, I probably confided in him just as much as Daveon and Clay.

"I'm not sure," I told him.

"Okay, I'll ask you this, who are you able to share your true self with the most?"

"Probably Jason," I admitted.

"Why Jason?" he asked.

"Because Jason always has good advice. He accepts me for me. And even if I do something wrong, I still feel like I can tell him even though I know he'll have something to say."

"And do you believe Jason loves you?"

"Yeah!"

"Jason definitely loves you. And he wants what's best for you. Just know that God loves you even more than Jason does and wants what's best for you even more than Jason. God's way is holy, Tay. But he knew we would fall short sometimes, and he gave us instructions for those times. If you confess your sins, he is faithful to forgive you and cleanse you. He is faithful. And that's the gospel and his grace. All you have to do is confess, Tay.

"I shared with you before that I made mistakes as a teenager. I wished I had saved myself for marriage. I won't sit here and pretend like it's super easy. But if you desire to live for him, he will give you grace," he said sighing.

He leaned back and looked up at the ceiling. He seemed to be carrying a heavy weight, and I felt like I was burdening him.

"You know you're my son, right?" he asked.

I nodded my head and looked at him.

"You know I love you, right?" he asked.

"You making me nervous, but yeah, Unc," I chuckled.

"I just want to be sure you know because you know I'm extending your punishment, right?"

I clenched my eyes shut and lowered my head, realizing the possibility of remaining on punishment until summer was looking more and more like reality.

"What's interesting is, God loves us, and gives us all this grace, and we don't deserve it. But the Bible also says 'whom the Lord loves he chastens,' which means disciplines. And I'm disappointed because I don't like being a disciplinarian, but you keep doing things you know better than doing…I learned a new phrase hanging around you guys."

"What's that?"

"Catching hands…you know what that means?" He looked at me like he dared me to say the wrong thing.

"I do," I hesitantly told him.

"Good, 'cause that's gon' be you if you leave this house again while you on punishment. We clear?"

"Yes, Unc."

"You can go, as in go to your room and not to the back porch or anywhere besides your room. And I better not catch you outside your room unless you're using the restroom."

"It's like that?" I asked.

"It's beyond like that," he said

I stood up to head upstairs.

"I know you think I'm old, but you can always come talk to me…even when you disobey. I may be able to help you more than you think," he said.

While I enjoyed talking to him, I knew if I shared too much it would only cause him to monitor my activities more closely.

"I love you Tay."

I looked over at him and nodded my head, not wanting to leave yet. I wanted to respond to him but was hesitant to do so.

"Unc, can I say something without getting in trouble?" I asked, unsure if I should even engage.

"Are you going to be disrespectful?"

"It wouldn't be on purpose if I was."

"Go ahead, have a seat."

I sat down, wondering if I should be honest about my feelings. I sighed and proceeded. "Unc, I love you, but sometimes I hate you though."

"Wow!"

"Was that disrespectful?"

"I'm...actually not sure, but I would love to unpack those feelings. Tell me more—is this because of the money situation? I feel awful about that and I shouldn't have accused—"

"NO!" I abruptly cut him off, but my thoughts froze as I was unsure how to respond and stumbled over my words. I attempted to proceed without sounding too awkward. "Um, I'm, uh, not mad about that...you know my brothers love you too," was all I could muster.

"So, I guess they also hate me too."

"No. I mean, maybe when they're on punishment. Like, you say you want us to be honest, but when we break the rules you take our phones, so what's the incentive for being honest? So, sometimes I can't stand you for that. But I feel bad saying it because none of us have ever had a real dad, um, except for you. And when we not in trouble, you actually okay to talk to and hang out with. Caleb and Sophie are lucky...And I thought about what you said about my bio-dad. And I really hate him, like for real, and I will never write him a letter. I'll save that energy. And I decided to write you one instead, but then I ripped it up because I was cussing at you in it...like, a lot."

He turned his head and started chuckling, and I was somewhat relieved that he was humored.

"Why?"

"You gon' say it's stupid...but I was mad about my phone. And I'm not saying I didn't deserve to be on punishment, but I was still mad."

"I understand all of your feelings. You and your brothers puzzle me sometimes, especially when you don't come to me even though you know you are caught. Your words are hard to hear. At no point do I want you to hate me, but I know I have to hold you accountable for your behavior. I can't let you openly defy the rules and not let you earn the consequences. So, if you think of ways that I can become more approachable, without letting you get away with murder, I'm open for suggestions. You can always tell me if I can improve, as long as it's respectful. But I'd probably be much more open to your ideas if you were doing your part and being respectful of the rules.

"Parents are not perfect, Tay, and sometimes we miss the mark. I feel like I've made a lot of mistakes, particularly with you. But I promise you that we are trying our best and will continue to do so..." He looked at me intently, and his expression looked slightly saddened. "Will you pray with me?"

I nodded, and he moved close to me, grabbed my hand, and bent forward.

"Father, I love you, and I know you love us, and I'm coming to you because my son here needs love, discipline, affection, and guidance, and I wish I could provide all of those things perfectly and I don't. Lord, his earthly father has failed him, and at points I have failed him as well. I have raised my voice when I shouldn't have and been impatient when I should have been patient, and sometimes I talked or lectured when I should have listened to him talk instead. I pray that you provide him with everything we couldn't, but also that you give me the wisdom to be for him what he needs. Help him to know my heart. Help him to know that I truly, truly love him so much, and that I only want what's best for him.

"Help us to seek you and follow you and put you first and to display the fruit of the spirit, even when we are upset. Especially help us to walk in love and patience with one another. And please help my son to make good choices with young ladies, Father. And please forgive him when he falls short of your will and repents. It's hard for these young men, but we know you can protect and preserve him Lord, and help him to guard his heart. In Jesus' name I pray, Amen."

41

going back

"**D**ontay, come over here with me," Uncle D said after the doorbell rang. I hesitantly followed him toward the door, confused about who was coming to see us so early on a Saturday Morning. He opened the door and let someone in that I didn't expect to see. "Principal Calhoun, so glad you could make it!"

Principal Calhoun soon turned to Auntie Robin to greet her, and lastly to me, with a smile on his face and his hand held out to shake mine.

"Thank you all for having me over. Hello Dontay! How have you been?"

"I'm okay," I said, still wondering why he was there.

"Good! Your summer going okay?" he asked with a faint smile.

It was a question I was hesitant to answer, primarily because I was still suspicious of his reasons for stopping by. I had been enjoying spending a little more time with Jason. Uncle D was driving me to and from a summer college prep program, and had signed me up for other classes. Clay and Daveon actually didn't have to attend summer school, and spent the summer primarily playing basketball with their traveling teams, while Daveon continued working and generally staying out of trouble.

"Um, it's okay," I said.

227

"Well, you're probably wondering why I'm here," Principal Calhoun stated after Uncle D offered him a seat. "The truth is, we hadn't received your Intent to Return Letter back. I called your uncle about it, and he told me you weren't returning to our school in the fall."

I looked over at Uncle D in disbelief, wondering if what the principal was saying was true. He only offered a brief, mischievous smile before darting his eyes back toward the principal.

"I told him that we really want you back on campus, and he told me I'd have to come over here and win you back...otherwise he had already enrolled you somewhere else. Dontay, I know that you didn't have the most enjoyable experience with us, but I want to change that. Our school got some bad press this spring, and we realized some things need to change. We decided to hold off on the book ban, and I also instructed the librarian to make sure we have more diverse options in the library. But mostly, we are building up a diversity, equity, and inclusion board, and want you to be one of the student representatives on that board. Dontay, I think we can learn a lot from a student like you, and I would hate to see your talent go to a different school.

"I heard that you have aspirations of going to law school one day. We have had a large number of students that ended up at law school, many of whom were given full scholarships.

"We are ready to not only guarantee your tuition for the next three years, but we also want to offer you a partial scholarship to the college of your choice after you graduate. We will also extend basketball scholarships to both of your brothers until they graduate. Also, we are ready to wipe your student record completely clean.

"Lastly, we are willing to write a check to any school you would like, in order to help them build or update the school library. That way you could still feel like you are having a positive impact on the school district you came from, if you choose. What do you say, Dontay?"

I looked over to Auntie Robin, who was seated across the table from me. Kemis, Jason, Clay, and Daveon had filed in while Principal Calhoun spoke.

"It's your decision, sweetie," she said.

"Wait, if y'all told him I wasn't returning, what were you planning?" I asked.

"We went to the high school in the Parkwood district and registered all three of you for fall. They have a program for gifted students like you and a lot of clubs we think you'll like. And they have a pretty popular basketball program for your brothers," she said. "We were going to surprise you with the news last night, but you were hanging out with Jason."

"Dontay, Parkwood is a good school district, and admittedly much more diverse than our student body. But I would like to point out that our school averages higher test scores, college acceptance rates, and college scholarship rates, not to mention your scholarship will cover test preparation classes for you at no extra cost."

"Well listen, Principal Calhoun, thank you so much for coming by. I think Dontay might need a few days to make his decision. But now he has all of the information, so I think he's all set. Any questions, Tay?" Uncle D asked.

"No, Unc. I'm good," I said, feeling unsure of what was expected of me.

"Well, thank you folks. Dontay, I really hope we'll be seeing you in the fall. Your uncle has my phone number and my email if you want to reach out with additional questions," Principal Calhoun said before Uncle D escorted him to the door.

"Auntie, you really letting me decide this whole thing?" I asked.

She smiled at me. "Yes! For you, that is. Now if you decide to go, Daveon and Clay can decide if they want to join you, but I think it's only fair after the experience you've had to make the call and decide what's right for yourself," she said.

I quickly pursed my lips and jerked my gaze toward Kemis to sneer, gloating that I was finally receiving the validation I had been looking for.

"Don't do that to your brother," Uncle D said. "He didn't know it would get this crazy...and frankly I didn't either."

"Okay, but even after I told y'all it was bad, y'all wouldn't listen. All you both did was put me on punishment all school year!" I said.

"That's 'cause you was acting bad as hell!" Jason said.

"Jason Lands! We're not doing that!" Uncle D said.

Jason shrugged his shoulders. "Sorry, but I didn't lie!" Jason said.

"Not about that, anyway," Clay said, causing Daveon and me to laugh and Jason to glare at Clay.

"I know you ain't snitching bro!" Jason said.

"For the first time ever, Clay hardly got any dirt, bro. He might go ahead and turn into a rat," Daveon joked.

"Dirt? Y'all been up to something I should know about?" Uncle D asked.

"They would never tell you if they had been," Jason said.

"I'll tell you what…since we are starting a new season, y'all can tell me anything you want. If you did something that you want to get off your chest without consequences, go ahead," Uncle D said. We looked at one another with our eyebrows raised, silently daring the others to test it out.

"I mean, we already found out that you boys were doing something in that bedroom window in the last house…I'm just wondering, were any windows used here? You can tell me the truth," he emphasized.

"Wait, what you mean…about the window?" Jason hesitantly asked as if he had no idea that he and Daveon used to regularly sneak girls into our apartment through their upstairs bedroom window.

"When Kemis went back to the apartment complex to see one of his friends, one of the neighbors told him he saw a lot of activity around that window. Anybody want to tell us what was going on?"

"Don't say shit," Daveon whispered.

"What you say, Daveon?" Uncle D asked.

"Uh, nothing Unc," Daveon replied.

"Anything you wanna tell me about your time here? Did you lie to me?"

"I didn't lie to you, Unc. Well, I did, but you caught me already."

"So, there's nothing else?"

"Unc, you technically still our legal guardian for another month," Daveon reminded him.

"This is true. And for the next month, and for the rest of your lives, I will still wring every one of your necks if you act up. That being said, this is consequence-free. I have been close with all of you for a long time. I think we became closer this season, but I want you to know you all can still come talk to me about anything… Anything you wanna tell me, Day?" he asked.

"Nothing," Daveon said looking away. "But I will say that I'm sorry for the times I acted up with you. You've done a lot for me and I don't always, like, act like I'm grateful I guess," Daveon said. I was shocked to hear him say it, even though he didn't fess up to his dirt.

"I really appreciate that, Daveon. What about you Jason?" Uncle D asked Jason, seemingly dissatisfied with Daveon's response.

"I wasn't here!" Jason said.

"What about before you left for school? Or even after you've been in school…have you told me any lies?"

Jason started chuckling. "I feel like it's a trick question."

"Not at all…just an opportunity to clear your conscious if you so desire."

"You remember how I told you I stopped bringing girls to my dorm room?" Jason asked.

"I do remember that," Uncle D said.

"Aight, that was a lie," Jason confessed, prompting us all to laugh.

"Nigga we knew *that*!" Clay said.

"Clay Lands, what did I tell you about that word!"

"My bad Unc, I confess I've been using it even though you told me not to," Clay said, causing the rest of us to laugh.

"Anything else you need to confess?"

"Remember that time you couldn't find your keys during youth church, and I told you I had to go to the bathroom?" Clay asked. I was shocked he was about to share the secret, but it was minor compared to what he could have shared.

"I do remember that," Uncle D cautiously acknowledged.

"Oh my," Auntie Robin whispered while throwing her hand onto her forehead.

"It ain't that bad. I, um, opened up the van, and entertained a guest," Clay said with a smile, while everyone else's mouth, other than mine, flew wide open.

"As in, a female guest?" Uncle D asked like he was afraid to hear the answer.

"Yeah…one that lives real close to here," Clay said, continuing his confession.

"As in a thirteen-year-old middle school guest that helps babysit sometimes?" Auntie Robin asked, seeming distraught.

"Yeah, Auntie. I'm sorry. She fine fine though. And she fourteen now," Clay said.

Uncle D looked as though he was trying to hide how disturbed he was. "Okay…well… thank you for your honesty, Clay. Um…thank you…yes. And, how about we make better choices in the future, son. Um, when you say you entertained—"

"Trust me, you don't wanna know, Unc," Clay said, likely causing Uncle D and Auntie Robin to imagine something slightly worse than it actually was.

Uncle D quietly cleared his throat before drawing in a deep breath. "I'll move on. Dontay, what about you?"

He looked at me intently, as though studying my countenance for clues. I couldn't imagine what he could have been trying to get at. I had pretty much kept it low-key after the Paris incidents. Clay and Daveon were the only ones with major secrets, but they had already declined their respective opportunities to confess.

"Unc, you already caught me. There's nothing else!" I told him.

"You sure?" he asked with partially squinted eyes.

"Unc, yeah! I ain't do anything!"

"Did you sneak out, or sneak anyone in?" he asked.

"Unc, I swear to G—"

"You better not! A yes or no will be acceptable."

"Unc, I ain't do nothing!" I reassured him.

"According to the alarm company, there were a few times since the three of you were here where the alarm was disabled from a computer in the middle of the night. For some reason they weren't able to trace the IP address of the computer used. I'm just curious if you remember doing anything like that."

"That…uh…naw, that wasn't me," I told him, trying to keep my poker face. I knew helping Daveon would eventually catch up with me, but I wondered exactly how much damage was about to be done. I kept my eyes glued to the table, hoping Daveon could read my energy and speak up before I went down alone like I had before.

While I definitely wasn't going to confess to helping Daveon, I had been feeling guilty since finding out they had enrolled me in a different school. "I might have something to tell you, Unc."

Daveon skirted his eyes at me, looking nervous that I was about to disclose his secrets.

"What is it, Tay?" Uncle D asked.

"I might have acted up a few times, hoping maybe the school wouldn't invite me back for the fall, or that you would change your mind and take me out," I said.

"You might have, or you did?" Uncle D asked.

"I'ma kick yo' tail, lil' bro," Jason announced.

"Jay, you always threatening somebody!" Clay said.

"I cash all my checks!" Jason said.

"Tay, why couldn't you just take my advice when we talked about it? Remember I told you to start praying…did you actually do it?" Uncle D asked.

I sighed knowing my answer wasn't acceptable in his eyes or God's. "Unc, I know I should have! I was just pissed 'cause K wouldn't listen, and then you wouldn't either!"

"He was listening. Maybe you were just impatient," Kemis said. "He called the school about transferring you in the middle of the year, but they wouldn't have been able to get all your classes to transfer, and they said it would be easiest if you stayed through the end of the year."

"And unlike you, I have been praying," Uncle D added. "The night before that incident with Mark Paul's father, I asked the Lord to give me a sign, and I guess that was what I needed. But I am extremely disappointed in you for trying to take matters into your own hands, especially when some of the times you didn't even want to tell us when things were happening."

I once again felt bad for the way I had been behaving, silly for actually considering Clay's advice, and a little unworthy that I was being given an opportunity to leave when I hadn't even done what I was supposed to.

"Tay, I appreciate you coming clean. I think next time we should probably both communicate a little better. I could have done better with letting you know what I was doing. But I forgive you. I know you had a challenging year," Uncle D said before turning to Kemis. "But listen, we have more to discuss."

"Wait!" Clay yelled, startling all of us. "Um I gotta say something else."

My heart hit the bottom of my stomach as I peered at him in disbelief that he was going to confess what I thought he was.

"I um, I stole some money," Clay said. I immediately took a deep breath, bracing for my brothers to lose it.

"From where? You still out here acting crazy at these stores?" Jason asked.

"NO! I mean, aight, only like once. And it was just a little. And after that I stopped 'cause I ain't want Unc to catch me. But that's not what I'm talking 'bout," Clay uttered with a lowered head and a lowered voice. While he looked as though he wanted it off of his chest, I could tell he didn't want to share it with Jason there.

"Then where you stealing from?" Daveon asked.

Clay looked as though he regretted starting a confession. He cringed before tucking his face into his forearms, reluctant to quell the silence that had invaded the room.

"Baby bro, you crying?" Kemis asked.

"NO!" Clay exclaimed, but we could hear in his voice that he was lying.

"Then what's up! What happened?" Kemis asked.

"I stole from Unc," Clay said after a long pause.

"You did what?" Jason yelled, slamming his phone down on the tablecloth.

"Stop, Jason, let him talk," Uncle D said. "Clay, tell me what you mean."

"I stole money…out your room…when we first started living here," Clay said.

"Bro, are you serious right now?" Jason was livid. I was certain he was about to reach across the table to strangle Clay, but he instead stood to make his way towards him. "You stealing from Unc after all the shit he's done for us, and taken us in his home? Bro, I'm 'bout to—"

"Jason, take a seat!" Uncle D demanded, as he stood to grab Jason. "I got this. Sit down! Clay, how much money did you take?"

Clay sighed and slightly lifted his head, and uttered what was nearly a whisper. "It was like four."

"Four what!" Jason yelled from his seat while Uncle D's arm was rested across his chest in efforts to keep him in place. "I know you don't mean four hundred. Bro, you catching—"

"Stop Jason! Clay, why did you steal from me?" The look and sounds of heartbreak echoed in Uncle D's eyes and in his voice, and he looked as though tears could fall at any moment. I knew Clay already felt bad about what he had done, but I was sure in that moment he felt ten times worse. "I've given you more than all of your brothers, Clay. It wasn't intentional—you just kinda needed more, and we wanted to make sure you had everything you needed. We've given you an allowance when you stayed out of trouble and completed your chores. We paid you for your good grades when your behavior improved. I let you pick out more shoes and video games. Auntie bought you something nearly every time she stopped at the mall, including the new Lebron jerseys you and Caleb wanted. You had everything; why would you take more?"

Other than when grieving, I had never seen Clay cry without a belt being involved. He sniffled and wiped away tears, sinking his head so low that his twists on the top of his head were nearly touching the table. I knew he felt terrible, and wanted to speak up on his behalf.

"Unc, he—"

"No, Dontay. He needs to tell me this. Clay, come here, and Jason keep your hands off of him. Come here, Clay."

Uncle D bid Clay to join him on the other end of the table, and Clay reluctantly obeyed. He sat down, still attempting to keep his head down. There were some moments and emotions Uncle D never let us escape, and Clay was basking in his own shame. Uncle D grabbed Clay's chin and turned his face toward his own, forcing teary, uncomfortable eye contact.

"Why did you steal from me? And it wasn't actually me, it was for four single mothers at church. It was the church's money that people donated so that kids who are growing up like you all have had enough food and toiletries in their homes. That same fund was how we used to bring you all groceries when your Granny was alive, and we would use that fund to purchase school supplies for you that Kemis and your grandmother couldn't afford. But there are other families in our congregation that still rely on the money and food we bring."

"Dis nigga done robbed God for real," Daveon whispered, prompting a vicious glare from Uncle D. Jason and Kemis attempted to hide their snickering by ducking their heads down.

Clay's face and the top of his t-shirt were flooded. He shrugged his shoulders in response to Uncle D, unwilling to talk and cry simultaneously.

"No, I want an answer. A truthful one."

"I was mad," Clay whispered.

"Mad about what?" Uncle D asked. He was calmer and cooler than Jason wanted him to be.

"School, punishment, not getting to hang out wit' my boy…"

Uncle D sat back and took a deep breath before continuing. He closed his eyes the way he did when he was in prayer. He turned to Clay upon opening them and continued speaking softly. "Clay, the only regret I have with you as that I did not reach out to your friend's grandmother and have him over. I don't regret not allowing you to go to the mall with them. But I should have gotten them here for you to hang out. You had a lot of changes this year, and I shouldn't have isolated you so suddenly— and I admit your Auntie told me that and I didn't listen. I'm sorry for doing that to you. The school and the punishments, I don't regret because you earned them with your bad behavior, and I believe the change of schools has helped you. Now, what do *you* have to say?"

"I'm sorry," Clay mumbled. It was probably the only heartfelt apology I had ever seen him give.

"You are forgiven, Clay. I prayed that the Lord would lead you to confess, and my prayer was answered. I'm very happy that you told the truth, and I'm super proud of you. I told you this would be consequence-free, and I will keep my word. However, I hope you will volunteer when we go to some of the homes of the single mothers for yard work and cleaning. But I tell all of you, when you mess up, just come tell me. Do you understand?"

"Yeah, Unc."

"You will always be my son, Clay. And that goes for all of you. I'm always here for you boys, and I don't want you to ever feel like you can't tell me something. Kemis, that still includes you," Uncle D added.

"You think I haven't told you something?" Kemis asked.

"I don't think you've been honest with me about how you've coped with your loss. But we'll discuss that later in private. For now, I think I need to confess something as well," Uncle D said. "Tay, I did some things wrong with you too. One of them we've already talked about. I remember being kind of sad that you didn't tell me about the Blackout.

But it dawned on me that maybe I didn't create an atmosphere that made you feel like you can come talk to me about things. So that's my commitment going forward. And, Auntie and I bought you something."

He handed me a box that was wrapped in shiny blue wrapping paper with green ribbon around it, with a note on the top:

"My son, I feel like I didn't tell you enough that I am very proud of you. I know I was hard on you last semester, but it was only because you have crazy potential. I regret not supporting you a little more. To that end, I have no doubt you and your friends were the rightful winners of the talent show. God blessed you with amazing creativity, and you have used it in very impressive ways. I agree with you that the school only punished you because of the content of your speech. Even though you broke the rules, I believe you deserve this. I pray you enjoy it half as much as I enjoy you."

I put the note down to open the box, which contained a brand-new GoPro Camera and a wad of cash underneath it. All that time, I thought Uncle D was upset with me about the way I handled the talent show, and I was utterly surprised with the gifts and the note. I knew I needed to make another attempt at the letter I wanted to write to him, expressing what he meant to me.

"Unc...this is dope! I definitely didn't expect this!" I said.

"Bro, you been wanting one of them forever," Daveon said.

"I know...thanks, Unc and Auntie. Does this mean I'm off punishment?" I asked, prompting everyone to laugh.

"After what I found out, I should probably extend your punishment...yours and someone else's," Uncle D said.

"Whatchu mean, Unc? You said our confession time was consequence-free!" I said, already wishing I had kept my mouth shut.

"There's one thing none of y'all confessed about." Uncle D turned around to a wooden cabinet behind him and opened up a drawer. He pulled out the burner phone and placed it on the dining room table, along with a few papers next to it.

Daveon leaned back in his seat while Jason leaned forward, both attempting to keep blank expressions on their faces.

"Jason Lamar Lands and Daveon Kahari Lands. These phone bills go back many years, and I don't know how y'all managed to get bills in your names before you were eighteen, but I'ma need an explanation about how this started, who all has been using it, and how it ended up with Tay," Uncle D said.

"Wait wait wait...you saying y'all been having an extra phone for all these years when we've been taking y'all phones?" Kemis asked.

"Unc, remember how you said we should start telling you more, and that you gon' be more approachable? 'Cause this ain't feeling like that," Daveon said.

"Guess what, Day," Kemis said, slowly rising from his chair and cracking his knuckles.

"Wait K! Who you mad at?" Daveon asked, discerning that Kemis was about to pound one of us.

"Can y'all do me a favor?" Kemis turned to Uncle D and Auntie Robin.

"What is it, Kemis?" Auntie Robin asked.

"Can y'all just close your eyes and ears, and gimme custody of my brothers for four minutes? That's one minute each," Kemis said.

"Yeah, I'm out!" Jason said, rushing out of the room, prompting the rest of us to follow.

Seeing that Kemis chased the older two first, Clay and I sprinted outside and a few blocks over, where we were surprised with a sight much more pleasant than Kemis' fists could offer.

"Hey guys? What y'all doing here?" Paris asked. She was with her sister Gia, walking what appeared to be a new puppy.

Clay and I glanced at each other after stopping to catch our breath. His eyes were still red from his confession time a few minutes before, but his somber countenance suddenly transformed when his eyes traveled up and down to take in all of Gia in her tightly-fitted pink workout pants and matching shirt. "We had prayed and asked God for a jog with the most beautiful scenery ever, and he answered our prayer," Clay answered.

They both rolled their eyes and laughed, knowing Clay was the most obnoxious flirt that existed.

"You jog with slides on?" Gia asked him with her eyebrows raised.

"If it means I get to see you," he responded.

"Well, we would ask you to walk with us, but ain't you still on lock? You think Pastor D would mind?" Paris asked.

He would definitely mind, I thought to myself. I had made him countless promises to stop the sneaking around, and told him that he would know about my dealings with Paris beforehand. But the girl had a way of looking exceptionally cute at the most inconvenient times, and I didn't want to cut our encounter short just to return home to a beatdown from Kemis. Clay seemed to think the same, and urged me to continue on a walk with the girls.

I grabbed Clay's arm to keep him from walking away. "We can't. But when I'm off punishment, y'all should let us treat you to—"

"A romantic double date at that steakhouse in midtown!" Clay said, finishing my sentence the way he thought it should go.

"Uh, something like that," I said, wondering how we would get money for Clay's plans, especially since I had planned on convincing him to come up with ways to repay Uncle D. "We'll hit y'all up later."

Made in the USA
Monee, IL
08 March 2023

29436217R00143